What the critics are saying...

~ A Fine Work Of Art ~

"I didn't want *A FINE WORK OF ART* to end, and I couldn't put Elizabeth and Boone's story down." ~ *Hunter McKenna, Sensual Romance*

"Reed's thought-provoking characters offer an eye-opening look into how love can bloom in the most unlikely of places…" ~ *Suzie Housley, Romantic Times*

"This is Ms. Reed's first romantica tale, I beg her not let it be her last! I devoured this book quickly and non-stop, it's simply delicious and one that I know I will read many more times...Did I mention [hero] Boone McCrea? He is *A FINE WORK OF ART* indeed!" ~ *Tracey West The Road to Romance*

"Ms. Reed's obvious talent shines through in this first erotic offering. The hero, Boone, is incredibly tempting in every way; how can any woman resist him? Elizabeth's life is one many women can identify with, making her all the more likable. Readers will cheer her on as the sexy younger man makes his own desires known." ~ *Miriam Love Romances*

~ *Zeke's Hands* ~

"*Zeke's Hands* by Madison Hayes is highly recommended. The author has penned a story with characters that are vividly alive within the pages. Zeke and Sara are memorable and very passionate about life and each other. The world of engineers was interesting and fascinating." ~ *Tracey West, The Road to Romance*

"Madison Hayes writes consistently fabulous stories and *Zeke's Hands* is no exception. Right away I liked Sara with her brash attitude and her fantasies about Zeke. I laughed out loud at some of the metaphors she used while thinking about all the things she wanted to do to Zeke." ~ *Miaka, ECataRomance Reviews*

"Eloquently written with vivid descriptions and steamy scenarios, *Zeke's Hands* by Madison Hayes had me fanning myself within the first 10 pages…I felt this story was erotic romance at its best and I'll be looking for more from Ms. Hayes." ~ *Jacqueline, The Romance Studio*

Shelby Reed
Madison Hayes

Love a Younger Man

An Ellora's Cave Romantica Publication

www.ellorascave.com

Love a Younger Man

ISBN # 1419953222

Edited by Mary Moran
Cover art by Syneca

Trade paperback Publication January 2006

Warning:

The following material contains graphic sexual content meant for mature readers. *Love a Younger Man* has been rated *E-rotic* by a minimum of three independent reviewers.

Ellora's Cave Publishing offers three levels of Romantica™ reading entertainment: S (S-ensuous), E (E-rotic), and X (X-treme).

S-*ensuous* love scenes are explicit and leave nothing to the imagination.

E-*rotic* love scenes are explicit, leave nothing to the imagination, and are high in volume per the overall word count. In addition, some E-rated titles might contain fantasy material that some readers find objectionable, such as bondage, submission, same sex encounters, forced seductions, etc. E-rated titles are the most graphic titles we carry; it is common, for instance, for an author to use words such as "fucking", "cock", "pussy", etc., within their work of literature.

X-*treme* titles differ from E-rated titles only in plot premise and storyline execution. Unlike E-rated titles, stories designated with the letter X tend to contain controversial subject matter not for the faint of heart.

~ Contents ~

A Fine Work of Art

Shelby Reed

ꙮ

Chapter One

Who would think a single red hair could end a marriage?

Elizabeth rubbed a hand against the throbbing pain behind her left temple and tried to force her attention back to the half-graded term paper in front of her, but it was no use.

The culprit had been an auburn hair, actually, glinting in the sun that streamed through the door behind Stuart as he'd set his briefcase and overcoat on the kitchen counter and leaned to offer Elizabeth's cheek a perfunctory kiss. That was when she saw it on his lapel, the red, silky remnant of his infidelity.

She closed her eyes and fought down a wave of nausea born of grief and exhaustion. Somewhere out there, Stuart was frolicking with Cecilia Aldorf like a sex-crazed teenager instead of the highly accomplished, forty-five-year-old neurosurgeon he was.

The hair was unquestionably Cecilia's. No one had tresses, long and wavy and clingy, quite like Stuart's surgical assistant. Elizabeth's own hair, cut in a conservative, shoulder-length style, was unarguably brown. Naturally so. Apparently Stuart's taste ran the gamut of artificial, because the redhead's breasts were round and perky and as utterly questionable in their authenticity as her hair color.

Months ago Stuart had sworn to end the affair. Anything to save the marriage, he'd said. Elizabeth meant everything to him, he'd said.

Liar. Last night he'd even smelled like his lover—floral and cloying and sexy-sweet. Elizabeth had nearly choked on the scent, half-blinded by the flash of setting sun on the evidence of Stuart's guilt. A single hair. And he hadn't bothered to deny her shriek of accusation.

The urge to laugh now bubbled in her throat, followed by an unexpected sob that rose so fiercely, she clapped her hands over her mouth and sat back in the chair, her welling eyes fixed on the beige, concrete-block wall above her desk.

A mere twenty-four hours had passed since the denouement of her ten-year marriage, and in that time she'd managed to give two art history lectures, counsel three freshmen on the upcoming semester schedules and grade an impressive stack of term papers, all without shedding a single tear. She couldn't keep a husband's attention, but she made one hell of a college professor.

"Dr. Gilstrom?" The male voice, followed by a soft rap at the door, drew her attention from the concrete wall.

Immediately Elizabeth straightened at the sight of the young man standing at her office threshold. He was a student in the graduate art history class she taught three times a week. Although they'd never formally spoken, she knew his face intimately. Too intimately. For the first weeks of the fall semester, even in the midst of slide shows and lectures, her gaze had strayed to him of its own accord. He was, quite simply, one of the most attractive men she'd ever seen. A work of art that stirred something within her most creative—and feminine—core.

And right now she couldn't remember his name.

"I know you're probably trying to get out of here for the night," he said, a smile curving his full, sensuous mouth, "but could you spare a moment?"

The castors on her desk chair squeaked as she pushed back and turned toward him, motioning to the folding metal chair a foot away. "Of course. Have a seat…"

"Boone," he offered, and sat, filling the six-by-eight office with the scent of autumn, faded shampoo and healthy, warm male. "Boone McCrea. I'm in your 506 Art History class."

"Yes, I know." Elizabeth could think of nothing clever to say. She certainly wasn't a flirt, and had always worn her marital status as protective armor against temptation. Now, stripped of it, she found herself the object of the young man's intense contemplation, and she felt…naked.

He was too young to look at her with such solemn fascination. Perhaps twenty-three or twenty-four, with sculpted features, a golden complexion and wonderful, expressive lips. A face from a dream.

She studied the wave of rich, dark hair that fell across his brow and experienced a fleeting sting of satisfaction. She'd actually managed to forget about Stuart for all of two minutes, thanks to Boone McCrea's extraordinary beauty.

"I need to ask you about tomorrow's field trip to the Binoche Gallery," he said finally. "I know you gave the pertinent information yesterday in class, but I had to leave early."

She squelched the indignant urge to demand *why* he'd left her class in the middle of lecture, and lifted the pile of papers on her desk to withdraw a photocopy of the trip's itinerary. "Did you get one of these?"

"No. Thank you." He took it from her, folded it and slipped it into the pocket of his navy windbreaker. He had strong-looking fingers. Paint-stained. The hands of an artist. Elizabeth felt her own fingers tremble slightly and crossed her arms over her breasts to hide the reaction.

"We're meeting in Georgetown, in front of the gallery," she said, forcing her attention back to his face. "But some of the class is gathering at the Tenley Metro station around three o'clock to ride together."

His dark lashes lifted and he met her gaze with clear, clover green eyes. "What about you? How are you getting there?"

She hesitated, surprised at the question. "I hadn't thought about it. I suppose I'll drive."

"Does your husband like art?"

Again, she was struck by his directness and the wayward direction in which their conversation seemed headed. "I…yes." She noticed his gaze linger on her naked ring finger, where the pale circle of skin spoke of her wedding band's recent removal. Its absence hadn't felt so obvious before now. Hurriedly she tucked her hand beneath her other arm and added, "But he doesn't have time to attend galleries often."

"That's too bad," he said softly. "He's missing out."

Silence crashed between them, and all Elizabeth could hear was the inexplicable thunder of her heartbeat. She had to think of something to say, because Boone McCrea gave her the feeling he'd sit across from her all evening, perusing her every feature if she allowed it. Maybe she'd given him the wrong idea. Had he noticed her attention lingering on him in class?

That's what you get for playing with fire, Professor.

Straightening her spine, she swiveled back toward her desk and said in a cool, clipped tone, "I have work to do, Mr. McCrea. Is there anything else?"

"Nothing." The rustle of his jacket as he stood to leave told her he'd gotten the message. "I'll see you tomorrow at the gallery. I'm looking forward to hearing what you have to say about the Fielding exhibit."

"I have plenty to say about the exhibit," she said, and used her red pen to vehemently circle an abysmal misspelling of Michelangelo's name on the term paper in front of her.

"But not so much about the artist?" The smile in his voice brought her gaze back to his face. "People say he's a real piece of work."

That was putting it mildly. Ferber Fielding was a brash, disagreeable old man who had a way of showing up in Elizabeth's world whenever she turned around, armed with a sarcastic barb or a disheartening scowl. Even a simple greeting stuck in her throat when they came face-to-face, whether at a gallery opening or the nearby Seven-Eleven. But Fielding had more talent than any artist Elizabeth had encountered since moving to Washington, D.C. a decade before, and despite his surly demeanor, she held a grudging respect for him. At least enough to haul thirty art history students to view his work.

"He's scheduled to lecture here before Christmas," she told Boone. "I'll make it a point to introduce you to him."

"That should be interesting." He studied her a moment, his humor fading to just a slight, curious tug on the corners of his mouth. "I'm sorry to interrupt your work."

She shook her head. "You didn't interrupt my work. I was daydreaming."

"About something sad."

Elizabeth blinked at him. How could he know that about her? Her own husband hadn't been able to read her emotions in a decade of marriage. Hell, until this moment, *she* hadn't even known that her sadness was as great as her rage over Stuart's betrayal. Maybe Boone was young, but his perception probably ran circles around most of the men she knew.

She heaved a sigh and glanced back at her work. "Yes. Something sad."

He paused in the doorway. "It'll fade, you know," he said, in a voice that made her feel oddly comforted. "Nothing lasts forever, Dr. Gilstrom."

Not love, nor marriage. Not even life in general, she thought, staring at the empty space he left behind as his footsteps disappeared down the hall. *No promise was truly kept.*

For the first time since realizing her marriage to Stuart was over, Elizabeth put her head down on her desk and cried.

*****

It looked like bloody handprints smeared on canvas.

Thirty-one pairs of eyes fixed on the chaotic abstract mounted on the gallery wall while disconcerted silence stole the soft, good-natured chatter.

"How awful," muttered one female student.

Elizabeth glanced back at her pupils and smiled. "Just the reaction I'm sure Mr. Fielding would relish."

"So much of his work seems to be about death and violence," the girl continued, sidling through the spectators to take a closer look over her Coke-bottle eyeglasses. "Is there something wrong with him?"

"I'd say there's something right," a familiar male voice spoke behind them, and Elizabeth turned to find Boone McCrea at her side, his hands clasped behind his back as he studied the painting.

She was surprised to see him. He hadn't shown up at the Metro station when the group convened to ride to the gallery together, and Elizabeth had tried not to feel disappointed. In her shadow-swathed existence of the previous few hours, he was a tiny, guilty pleasure, a pinpoint of light. Their brief encounter in her office last night had piqued her interest further. Earlier at the subway station, she'd been so busy staring up the escalator for a sign of him, she'd nearly missed the train's arrival. A silly, broken woman, in love with youth, with the past, searching for…for what? She couldn't explain her odd preoccupation with the young graduate student. It was too ridiculous.

When he hadn't appeared at the Metro, she'd assumed he would miss the field trip, and silently, firmly, she closed him out of her thoughts…leaving only the bitter remnants of Stuart, and the sharp return of depression.

Now Boone McCrea had materialized before her like a sweet, silky breeze across her skin, and she shivered with misplaced delight. His dark hair was windblown and curly, his lean cheeks ruddy from the autumn afternoon. The maroon shirt he wore beneath his denim jacket set off the crystal clarity of his gaze, like red velvet behind emeralds in a jeweler's showcase. He was…how could one adequately describe such balanced, sensual features? Or do justice to the shine of intelligence and humor in his green eyes?

Elizabeth stifled the urge to laugh. He was a distraction, a means of frivolous relief sent from heaven to offset the pain of her pending divorce. There was no other explanation.

Abruptly she realized she was staring and quickly regained her composure. "What do you think the artist intended with this particular piece, Mr. McCrea?"

He lowered his gaze to hers and smiled, an odd, secretive smile, before turning to address the chubby student who found the painting so disconcerting. "Manipulation of the masses. He knows how to flip the switch on the public's emotions. Most people who look at this painting will automatically see violence."

"And yet the painting is entitled 'The Chocolatier's Hands'." Elizabeth's own mouth curved into an ironic smile. "It's not blood that makes the handprints. It's chocolate."

Wry laughter and murmurs floated through the group as they shuffled on to the next canvas.

While they examined the smaller, more traditional landscape, she glanced back to locate Boone. He still lingered at "The Chocolatier's Hands", but his attention wasn't on the painting. He was quietly chatting with another student, a blonde, his dark head inclined toward her as they spoke. His gaze focused on her as though she were the only other soul on earth. Either he found her honey-skinned beauty totally entrancing, or Boone McCrea was a damned good listener.

Elizabeth tried to look away, but found herself mesmerized. Despite the unseasonably cool weather, the girl wore a cropped T-shirt and low-slung, bell-bottom jeans that bared her flat tummy. Her silver navel ring caught the light and glistened like a droplet of water ready to drizzle into the waistband of her Levi's. But Boone wasn't gobbling her up with a hungry, sweeping gaze, the way Elizabeth had seen a thousand other men his age regard such a beautiful girl. His eyes were locked on the blonde's as she gestured to the painting. He was listening, with what appeared to be genuine interest, to what she had to say.

Elizabeth swallowed her resentment, returned her attention to the smaller painting before her, and flipped through her notes to find information on the landscape. "This is one of Fielding's earlier works. Note the tighter brushstrokes, the realistic color and rather unimaginative subject matter. It's amazing how twenty years of living can change an artist's style."

* * * * *

It's amazing how ten years of living in a loveless marriage can change a woman's sense of self.

The screech of the Metro's brakes and the train's accompanying lurch brought Elizabeth out of her maudlin reverie. She gathered her briefcase, tugged the lapels of her trench coat across her breasts, and stepped out onto the platform to bid her students goodnight. Boone McCrea wasn't among them. Suspiciously enough, neither was the blonde with the navel ring, whose name Elizabeth couldn't remember. They'd simultaneously disappeared as the students filed out of the gallery, and she wasn't exactly surprised. Resigned was more like it.

"If you come up with any further questions about the exhibit at the Binoche, bring them to class with you on Monday," Elizabeth told the remaining students as they rode the escalator to the darkened city street above.

Her gray Mercedes sedan sat in the deserted Kiss-and-Ride Metro lot near the college campus. Juggling her briefcase and purse, she activated the keyless entry, slid inside the chilled leather interior, and drew the seatbelt across her lap. God, it was cold for a late September night. But it was the thought of returning to a silent, empty house that chilled her to the bone.

She slipped the key into the ignition, turned it, and…nothing. Frowning, she tried again. Only a single click. The battery light came on.

"Damn…" She let her forehead thud against the steering wheel. "Damn!"

The five-minute walk across campus to her office left her trembling with cold beneath the thin trench coat. To make matters worse, it had begun to rain, a soft, misting drizzle that made the grass glisten in the streetlights like a field of diamonds.

"Forty-five minutes," the tow company told her when she called from her office in the eerily silent art building. "Stay at your car, miss."

"By myself, for almost an hour in a deserted parking lot?" Astonishment curdled her tone, and she immediately clenched her jaw and breathed patience. "I'm sorry—cancel the tow. I'll think of something."

Setting down the phone, Elizabeth rubbed her hands over her face and squelched the urge to cry. A dead battery. Big deal. A dead marriage, a dead life.

"Damn," she whispered again, and with a slow, deep inhalation, banished the self-pity that circled her soul like hawks over carrion. Then she called a cab.

Outside, the crystalline mist had turned to a steady rain. Bracing herself against the cold night, she tucked her chin into the collar of her coat, stepped out of the art building...and abruptly collided with a warm, hard body.

"Whoa." Two strong hands encircled her arms and steadied her. "Dr. Gilstrom, this is a surprise."

Elizabeth looked up, faltered, sputtered.

And found herself smiling into clear, green eyes.

Chapter Two

Where the smile came from, Elizabeth didn't know. Five seconds before colliding with Boone McCrea, her mood had felt like a wasteland where pleasure would never bloom again. Now she had to search for the cause of the fast-fading misery.

Oh, yes. Her car. The cold night. Her divorce. Being miserable was a massive, piteous waste of time.

"You're here late," Boone said, his warm grasp slipping from her arms. His breath rushed in even clouds between them. Rain clung to his dark lashes, beaded on the bridge of his nose.

"I was on my way out." The rain began to pound the sidewalk around them, and she stepped back beneath the shelter of the art building's entry. "What's your excuse, Mr. McCrea?"

He followed and shook the moisture from his dark hair. "Basically I live here. Until my latest painting is finished, anyway."

"But the studio is locked at seven on weekdays."

"Not since I bribed the custodian with a six-pack of beer." He paused to examine her face. "You're shivering."

The sympathetic observation made Elizabeth feel vulnerable, self-conscious. She shoved her hands in her pockets. "It's cold out here. And my car battery seems to be dead."

"You need a lift home?"

She shook her head. "Thanks, but a taxi's on its way."

"Where's your car?"

"At the Kiss-and-Ride."

Boone was silent for a moment, unreadable shadows shifting behind his eyes. Then he caught her elbow and swung open the glass door to usher her back into the warm building. "Come with me."

"Where are we going?" Elizabeth was too surprised to argue.

"To cancel your taxi. I can give you a jumpstart. I've got the cables in my Jeep."

"What if it doesn't work?" she asked as they rounded the corner and paused at her office. "What if the motor still won't start?"

"Then I'll give you a ride home, and you'll call a tow truck in the morning."

"But I live in Alexandria," Elizabeth said weakly, stunned and flattered by his concern. "Thirty minutes from here. You'd have to drive all the way past Old Town."

Boone nodded. "All the better. There's a little bar in Old Town that makes great coffee. It'll take the shivers right out of you." He stooped to recover her keys when she dropped them with a noisy clank. "I'll buy if you accept."

She took the keys from him and jammed the right one in the office lock, started to open it, then turned to stare at him again. How had the conversation evolved to this unexpected place? In the decade that she'd taught college students, none had ever asked her out. So why now? Why Boone, so hard to turn down with his incredibly earthy, verdant-green eyes?

For crying out loud. It wasn't a marriage proposal. What rule would she break by having a single cup of coffee with him? And then only if his jumper cables didn't revive her battery. The chances were slim. Still...

Thoughts of what could transpire with a man as attractive —as *young*—as Boone were forbidden, mortifying...and merely wispy musings. Actions, or the lack thereof, were the important thing, and nowhere was it written that a cup of coffee equaled a torrid sexual foray. Besides, the blatant admiration in his gaze coated her raw wounds with a refreshing dose of flattery. It was nice to imagine he had a crush on her. She was a slightly older

"Twenty-four." His regard was steady on her face. "And you, Professor? How old are you?"

"Thirty-six, Mr. McCrea." Her eyes darted from the menus to the salt-and-pepper shakers, to the flickering glow of the oil lamp between them. Anything to avoid looking at him.

"Then despite what you seem to think, that makes you young enough for us to be on a first-name basis." His hand crossed into her field of vision and slid the menus aside, followed by the condiments. Breaking down her merciful distractions. Clearing the field between them. "My name is Boone. Not Mr. McCrea."

She finally met his gaze. "Elizabeth."

"Elizabeth." His brows lowered. "Such a solemn name. Is that what people call you?"

"My friends and co-workers, yes."

"Your family?"

"Beth. But my parents are gone now. I was an only child."

"I see." He pushed the oil lamp aside and let his fingers stray back to the center of the table, where her hand rested. So close she could feel the heat from his skin, but not quite touching. "What about your husband, Elizabeth? What does he call you?"

The sudden huskiness in his voice brought her startled attention back to his face. "I…he…" She cleared her throat, tried again. "He used to call me Liz. But since we've separated, he doesn't call me anything." A smile crossed her lips. "'Hey you' is about the extent of it these days."

His fingers nudged her sleeve and lingered there. "How about a little whiskey in your coffee?"

"You read my mind," she said with a rueful laugh.

The waitress stopped at their table and took their drink orders. She didn't ask for Boone's ID when he ordered a beer, and she didn't slide a suspicious, knowing look at Elizabeth as though to say, *Robbing the cradle?* Still, Elizabeth released a pent-up breath when the girl was gone.

Boone's hand still rested by her wrist. A shivery thread of excitement hummed along her nerves at the sight of his fingers on her sleeve. Back and forth, they brushed against the silky material, an unconscious caress.

"I like this song," he said. "Macy Gray's voice hits me just right sometimes. Way down low."

"Me too." She tore her gaze from his fingers and found him watching her. "There's something really sexy about her style."

Boone didn't answer right away. His lashes lowered as he studied her mouth. "Tell me something, Professor."

She had to swallow before she could speak. "What."

"Do you..." He stopped, met her gaze, and straightened. "Do you want to dance?"

It wasn't what he'd meant to ask, and she wanted to know the real question preceding it, but the moment had already passed. "It's been a long time since I've danced with anyone."

"Is that a no?"

"That's an 'I might step on your toes'."

The tension in his features dissolved into an easy smile. "It's worth a shot."

Elizabeth paused, watched him slip from the booth and extend his hand. Then she said, "Boone, I'm going to be really honest with you. I don't think this is a good idea."

He frowned. "You mean dancing?"

"I mean any of this. I hardly know you. I'm thirty-six, I'm in the middle of a divorce...I'm your professor." She closed her eyes, shame flooding her limbs with a sick weakness. "So you see, you've really caught me at a bad time."

When she lifted her lashes, he was smiling at her. Warm, understanding, gently amused. God, he was an exquisite creature.

"If you don't want to dance with me, Elizabeth, you can turn me down. All the other stuff that's going through your head, I'm not responsible for. I wanted the pleasure of your company, I wanted to make you feel better about your broken-down car, and I've enjoyed being with you tonight. That's all."

"So we're still in a simple place?" She let him take her hand and draw her to her feet.

"Sweet and simple." He brushed a strand of dark hair from her eyes. "Macy Gray's halfway done. One dance, then we'll finish our drinks and I'll take you home."

Elizabeth nodded. "You're easy to like, Boone."

"I'd hoped you'd feel that way," he said.

Chapter Three

One dance eased into two, then three. Three slow, sultry ballads that gave Elizabeth a damn good reason for allowing herself the pleasure of Boone's embrace. She settled into it as though she'd stood within it a million times, excruciatingly aware of the heat radiating from his hard, young body, the tension in his muscles and the slightly quickened cadence of his heartbeat beneath her ear. He was tall and strong and he smelled like sexy, warm male—clean, a little smoky from the bar, and underneath, an earthy scent all his own that drew her nose to nuzzle the column of his throat.

Breathing him in, she felt shivery desire trickle through her insides, an innate knowing that if she wanted, her hands could learn the lines of his body, the shift of undulating muscles, his smooth, naked skin, damp with exertion and need…

No. Viciously, she stamped down on the alluring image. But the liquid heat between her thighs remained, pulsing with every beat of her heart. And when Boone drew back to meet her eyes, the want was written there, too, turning them to smoky malachite.

The song ended. They returned to their booth to find a fresh round of drinks waiting.

"I hate to waste good beer," Boone said. "Sure you need to be home this very minute?"

Elizabeth smiled. "Maybe not this very minute."

After finishing the Irish coffee, she exchanged it for chardonnay and seamlessly launched into another topic with him. Politics this time. He was a Democrat, she, a watered-down Republican. They argued. Discussed. Laughed. Shared smiles touched with unspoken promise.

Sitting across from Boone, Elizabeth forgot about the time, the easy music, the steady murmur of patrons around them. While Boone told her about seeing the Van Gogh exhibit, she sat enraptured by the sound of his easy, husky voice, the play of candlelight on his finely honed features. He was erudite, intelligent, funny. And so very sexy for a youngster of twenty-four.

Maybe an hour passed. Maybe two. When the pleasant, fuzzy warmth in her veins seeped into mild dizziness, she pushed aside her wine glass and sat back.

Across the table, Boone watched her with quiet discernment. "Ready to go?"

Somber now, she nodded, rose and reached for her coat.

"Let me." He held it for her while she thrust her arms into the sleeves. His palms lingered on her shoulders a beat too long, then slid away as he withdrew his wallet and dropped several bills on the table.

Elizabeth frowned at him. "If you pay for my drinks, this will officially be a date."

"I thought only a goodnight kiss had that kind of power." He put on his jacket and caught her hand. "Of course, I haven't walked you to your door yet."

She was too tipsy to be disconcerted by the threat. "What makes you think I'll let you?"

Boone only smiled and led her from the bar. Outside, the rainy haze had dissipated and the midnight sky sparkled with a million crystalline stars. When Elizabeth hunched her shoulders against the cold, he slipped his arm around her. She didn't protest. He smelled wonderful. It made her want to turn her nose against his throat and breathe him in. He was tall; she fit under his arm as though she belonged there. He matched his pace to her shorter one, his hand on her shoulder became a stroking caress as they walked.

Misplaced anticipation leaped inside Elizabeth's stomach as the Jeep came into view. Pausing at the passenger door with her positioned between his body and the vehicle, Boone withdrew keys from his jacket pocket and searched for the right one in the dim streetlight.

Elizabeth's breath, already shortened from the cold, now came in staccato rushes at his nearness. She faced him more fully, her attention glued to his hand as he fumbled with the keys.

How many women had those fingers touched? He was inherently sensuous, that much was obvious. But the innocence in his features made her sharply aware of his youth.

Her gaze lingered on the dark curve of his lashes as he studied the keys. Such long lashes. Such an expressive mouth. This man was more finely created than anything a fashion magazine could drum up. She thought of his hands on her naked breasts and felt her nipples harden beneath her sweater.

Fool, her common sense whispered. She'd been making out in the backseat of her boyfriend's 1983 Nissan Pulsar about the same time Boone was toddling off to kindergarten.

It didn't matter. She wanted him, the soft crush of his lips, his searching tongue in her mouth, the primal surge of his pelvis pressed tight against hers as the dance commenced. *The dance.* God, she missed the sweaty-hot weight of a man between her legs, the rush of supreme satisfaction when he drove into her, the sordid, feral words rasped between panting breaths as pulsing heat tunneled through wet, aching flesh.

This man could give her all of it, and she wanted it.

She wanted *him.*

Maybe it was the alcohol that allowed her to admit it. Any other more sober time, she was too conservative a person to entertain such taboo thoughts. But he was beguiling, and much too close.

He leaned around her to unlock the door, and the movement brought his shoulder close to her lips. Before she could stop herself, her fingers curled into the open sides of his jacket and she pressed her face against his throat, where the collar gaped and his flesh was warm and sweet.

A wild urge fulfilled. A mistake, one that couldn't be taken back. His breath froze, followed by the guiding, reassuring pressure of his hand at the back of her head. For a long time they stood in the odd embrace, Elizabeth breathing in his scent, exhaling humiliation. Boone holding her while he waited. Waited to see what she wanted. Waited for her to say it.

She couldn't. Her lashes never lifted as she raised her face and blindly sought his mouth, landed awkwardly on his chin, searching, until he cupped her jaw with both hands and opened his mouth over hers.

Deep. Soft. Hungry, as one would taste an exotic fruit for the first time, then settling to devour.

Oh God. Elizabeth's fingers closed around his wrists, held tight as lust swept through her with knee-weakening ferocity. A groan rumbled in Boone's throat, carried on his tongue as it dipped against hers, withdrew, waited until she sought it again with her own tongue and elicited a dance. Thrust, retreat, slow and sinuous, as though they had all the time in the world to learn each other's flavors. Beer. Wine. Heat and want.

Her back met the side of the Jeep with a thud, and Boone followed, palms hot on her cheeks as he held her face and kissed her, on and on, until the world tilted and the air in Elizabeth's lungs became his, the rhythm of her pulse matched his.

When kissing was no longer enough, his fingers skimmed down the arched column of her throat, tugged at the belt of her coat until it loosened, then rifled between the lapels, in search of a soft, giving breast, a tightened nipple, the undeniable evidence that she was as hungry as he. Despite the hard breath he expelled when his hand made contact with her breast, his touch was tentative, as though she might burn him if he ventured too far.

It wasn't far enough. With an impatient groan, Elizabeth covered his fingers with hers and flattened his palm over her breast, pushing herself into his touch, wanting to be swallowed by his exquisite caress, by his sultry lips, his unyielding embrace.

It was all the permission Boone needed. The wanton sound rising in her throat went silent as he swooped down to capture her lips again, voraciously this time. Bruising and wild, with plunging tongue and sharp intakes of breath. Blindly, he reached down and caught her behind the knee, hitched it up to hug his hip, and undulated against her, just once, a sinuous invitation to seek the hardness that brushed fleetingly against her.

Despite the barrier of their clothes, she could feel him—the steely, demanding length of his penis—and in response, her body softened even more, growing wetter with yearning.

When she whimpered and arched toward him, he surged against her again. Thrust, retreat, rhythmic and relentless, a provocative taste of what they both craved. She would come if he kept it up, shudder to orgasm from the simple, desperate rocking of his hard erection against her.

"Oh God," she breathed, fingers digging into his hips to bring him back to her. Mindless, she ground her pelvis into his, clinging to tough denim and craving the smooth, muscled flesh beneath it. "We have to stop."

She didn't mean it. Not really.

But the desperate, reluctant admonition and the wet sound of tires passing by on the otherwise deserted road seemed to rouse him, and he finally lifted his head.

His fingers slid from behind her knee, and having no choice, Elizabeth straightened away from the car door, legs wobbly.

His eyes were still closed when she focused on his features.

"Boone," she tried to say, but nothing came out except a whisper. She cleared her throat. "Boone."

"Shh." He laid his finger against her lips, caressed them. "Don't talk just now."

But she had to. She was already awakened to the reality of what she'd just done—making out with one of her graduate students—and anxiety compelled her to continue. "Please. You're too close. I can't think like this."

His lashes finally lifted and he stepped back, leaving her chilled.

"I'm sorry," he said soberly.

"No." She shook her head. "No, Boone. I'm sorry. I started it. My God, what's wrong with me?" The urge to cry surged in her chest, choked her words with tears and mortification. "I hardly know you. I mean…you're wonderful. Really. But this—I'm not thinking clearly. Last week at this time I had a marriage. I don't know what I'm doing."

"Elizabeth." He brushed back the hair that fell against her cheek as she bowed her head. "I'm not trying to take advantage of you. I know you're going through something. I could tell last night in your office. Your heart looked like it was breaking, and I couldn't get it out of my mind. I should've stayed away. But—I come into your classroom three times a week, and lately find myself wishing it were five times instead. I don't have any excuses for coming by your office, but somehow I slow down each time I walk by it." He shook his head and sighed. "I'm sorry."

"It's okay." She wiped her eyes on her jacket sleeve and offered a watery smile. "You did make me feel better. For a while tonight, I even forgot what a mess my life has become."

His green eyes searched hers. "Do you want me to take you home now?"

What other choice did decency allow? She nodded, and turned away from his painfully beautiful face to wait while he opened the passenger door for her.

They rode in silence broken only by her murmured directions. Elizabeth tried not to look at him, but each time they passed beneath a streetlamp, the sweep of light illuminated his solemn, troubled profile. She settled on looking at his hands.

They curved around the steering wheel, capable and strong. They'd held her face with such gentleness. Taboo or not, those fingers now knew the weight of her breast, knew how to pluck and entice and awaken sensations within her she'd nearly forgotten existed. She'd never survive it if he touched her naked skin.

Jewel's soft, cadenced poetry rose from the stereo and floated beneath the tension. Everything about this night spoke of seduction. The exquisite man sitting beside her, the lingering taste of his kiss, the warmth of alcohol in her veins, the chilled air that pushed two people closer in search of warmth. Everything but the dark, empty windows of her house when Boone pulled into her driveway and turned to look at her.

"You okay?" he asked. The green glow from the dashboard painted shadows across his features. Now that she'd experienced the sinuous slide of his tongue in her mouth, there was nothing innocent about him. The twelve years between them had dissolved the moment his lips touched hers.

"I'm okay," she said, her voice husky. "Thank you, Boone. For tonight, for distracting me, for making me laugh." For turning her limbs to mush with his touch. How long would it be before she'd forget such a searing experience? Maybe never.

Slowly, methodically, he set the parking brake and removed his seatbelt. "You know you don't have to worry about my discretion, don't you?"

Somehow, yes, she knew. "I'm not concerned. It's no one's business who I see."

"Then why can't you see more of me?" He reached to brush back a wave of hair from her cheek. "If you're worried about other faculty or students—"

"I'm worried about you, Boone. No one else. It wouldn't work."

"Not even for one night." His fingertip traced the curve of her ear, her pearl earring, raising chills on her skin. "You sure?"

Elizabeth closed her eyes, drew a breath for strength. The only thing that stopped her from inviting him into her bed was the thought of tomorrow morning. Her life was a dead end at the moment, and there'd be no place for Boone to turn around when time came. And it would come. The divorce from Stuart, the division of property and friends, a whole decade of wasted life. Enough to send a more seasoned man scrambling for escape. He would see it all, because with one kiss he'd broken down her fragile defenses and drawn her raw, wounded heart to a perilous place.

"I'm so sorry," she said, and slipped from the passenger seat into the cold, empty night, where no one could see her cry.

Chapter Four

Dry leaves scuttled across Elizabeth's path as she crossed the parking lot and climbed the stone steps to the art building. The crisp, smoky scent of autumn tinged the air and everything looked golden, dying foliage touched by the sinking sun. Her favorite time of year, but she could hardly breathe, her chest was so tight with outrage.

Her aunt had called that morning with news that Stuart was planning to marry Cecilia as soon as the divorce was final.

"And how do you know this, Aunt Barbie?" Elizabeth had asked woodenly. "You can't mean to tell me news of my break-up with Stuart has reached all the way to Annandale." Of course it had, compliments of Barbara Hayden. Elizabeth should have known better than to tell her aunt about the separation. The woman couldn't keep a secret to save her life, even if it belonged to the one and only child of her deceased sister. A nosy partner from Barbara's bridge group knew Cecilia's family and had corroborated the whisperings. The word was officially out.

"I just didn't want you to be surprised," Aunt Barbie said. "I know you pride yourself on your decorum, and to have people whispering about your loss..."

Her loss. Not Stuart's. Elizabeth seemed to be the only one who viewed it differently. She swallowed the fierce, fresh surge of anger and strode into the art building. It could be dealt with later. Right now she had a mid-term to administer, and within a few moments she'd be faced with another disconcerting issue—Boone McCrea.

Maybe it wasn't normal to sit through a meeting with her attorney and play Boone's kiss through her mind like a scratched record, but that's what she'd done the day before.

She'd sat on the Chippendale chair in her lawyer's staid office, heat creeping up her neck as she recalled Boone's possessive fingers against her breast, the unsteady jerk of his breath rushing between her lips, and—*oh*—the hard, hard press of his erection through all those clothes.

Sitting in that stuffy, formal office, she'd felt herself grow wet, her nipples tighten beneath her tailored blazer, as easily as if she were standing in Boone's embrace outside that bar all over again.

How could she have sex on her brain when she was supposed to be grieving the death of her marriage? Shame did nothing to thwart the desire twisting her insides.

She'd only seen him once since their impromptu date five nights ago. On Monday he'd been late for class, and had slipped in the back door to find a desk on the last row. Several times during the hour their gazes locked across the room, but he was always the first to look away. And Elizabeth had stumbled her way through the lecture, hot-faced and regretful.

She opened the classroom door, set her things on her desk, and glanced around the empty lecture hall. The test started in fifteen minutes, enough time for her to sneak upstairs and peek at Boone's painting. She'd wanted to look at it longer when he showed it to her on Friday night, but she'd been so utterly thrown by the subject matter. Amanda. Amanda Hastings with the unruly blonde hair, unruly body piercings, unruly sensuality. Boone had slept with her, no doubt. Maybe he still was, and Elizabeth had absolutely no right to care.

Voices echoed in the brick stairwell as she climbed the steps, and she hesitated on the first landing, heart pounding as she heard the upper exit door click shut. Quiet again. She made it to the studio, cracked the door, saw one girl working on a canvas by the display wall. No sign of Boone.

"Hi, Dr. Gilstrom," the student said when Elizabeth stepped into the room. "Are you looking for someone?"

Elizabeth smiled. "No. I just thought I'd take a peek at what some of the art students are working on." She sauntered around to view the girl's work. "Very nice," she said, and meant it. The landscape was half-finished, a snapshot glimpse of the verdant tree canopy above Washington with the National Cathedral rising in the distance. "It's lovely."

The girl grinned and turned to clean a brush. "I personally like landscapes. Not as exciting as some of the other stuff in here."

To say the least. Elizabeth bit back a smile and continued around the haphazard circle of easels, pacing herself to keep from arrowing straight toward Boone's canvas. When she finally got there, she took a deep breath and stared at it.

He'd worked on it since Friday night. Impossibly, Amanda's skin looked silkier, the shadows deeper, her need more consuming. Its intensity reached out and coiled around Elizabeth, tugging at deep places she'd nearly forgotten existed. She felt twelve years old again, when she'd snuck into her father's library and read choice excerpts of *Lady Chatterley's Lover*. Titillated, a little ashamed and completely enthralled.

Across the room, the student's voice pierced the thick air. "That's good, huh?"

"Oh. Yes." Elizabeth stirred and tore her gaze away from the canvas. "It's quite provocative."

"It's Amanda Hastings. Do you know her?"

"She's a graduate student," Elizabeth said.

"Yeah. She models for money." The girl laughed and shook her head as she reached to load her brush with paint. "All the guys in my program are lined up to hire her, but lately she's only been modeling for Boone McCrea." She paused. "You know Boone, right?"

"Yes," Elizabeth said. "He's hard to miss."

"No kidding. He could be a model himself. A real one. I wonder why he's wasting his time in art school."

"He's talented."

The student shrugged. "Yeah, but there's no money in art."

"There's the fulfillment of the creative drive," Elizabeth pointed out. "Sometimes that's more important." Hearing herself say it out loud shocked her. Good Lord—she'd chosen marriage to a promising neurology intern over the pursuit of her own goals as an artist. Security over creation. Image over love. Now she had nothing to show for it...only the faded memory of the brush's weight in her hand.

Breathing in the pungent scent of turpentine and linseed oil, she felt tears sting her eyes. It was too late to turn back. She couldn't keep her thoughts together long enough to even begin looking for her art supplies, buried somewhere in the garage of the home she and Stuart had agreed to sell.

"Well, keep up the good work," she said with forced cheer as she passed the girl and her skillful, if unexciting, landscape.

Downstairs, students trickled into her classroom. No sign of Boone yet. She checked the slides in the machine to make sure they were positioned correctly, glanced at her watch, then unclipped the pile of tests sitting on her desk.

As one last student slipped in, she bade them to take their seats, went to close the door, and nearly collided with Boone.

"Am I late?" he asked with a frown.

He wore the scent of autumn as though it were cologne. She tried not to stare at him, but he was such a welcome sight. Her gaze drank him in, a beat beyond awkward, before she said, "No, just in time." She averted her attention from his startling green eyes and motioned him into the room. "Have a seat, Mr. McCrea. We're about to start."

"Thanks, Dr. Gilstrom." Just sarcastic enough to bring her gaze back to his face. But he'd already passed her and made his way toward the back of the room, where he found a seat beside Amanda Hastings. The blonde welcomed him with a blinding smile, whispered something in his ear that made him laugh silently.

Elizabeth rubbed the tension throbbing in her neck and flipped out the lights. "Clear your desks and turn your attention toward the slide screen. All you'll need is a pen."

*****

Boone was the third student to complete the test. He rose from his seat, slung his backpack over one shoulder, and crossed the classroom to lay the test sheet on the desk in front of her. She'd been grading papers, and looked up at him when his hand came into view.

His long-sleeved T-shirt was the same verdant shade of his eyes, his features breathtaking and every bit as finely sculpted as she'd pictured them in her fantasies.

Elizabeth was a fool.

For a long moment, neither spoke. Then he leaned forward and whispered, "Hi."

An unbidden smile twitched her lips. "Hi. How do you think you did?"

"Aced it."

"Good." Warmth seeped through her veins for the first time in days. "Where are you off to now?"

"To get dinner. Then upstairs to the studio to paint. I'm almost done with the canvas I showed you."

Behind him people stirred, someone coughed. Elizabeth rose to motion him out into the hall. When they stood in the deserted corridor, she said, "I just wanted to say again that I…well, thank you, Boone, for Friday night. I was in a bad place, I acted inappropriately, and you were so understanding. So nice."

"It has nothing to do with nice," he said flatly. "I want to see you again."

"You can't."

He studied her for a moment, a frown creasing the space between his dark, graceful brows. "I think I can."

Elizabeth crossed her arms over her hammering heart. "Oh? How's that?"

"I think you can be persuaded."

"To do what? Boone, what do you think could actually come of us getting involved?"

Devious humor lifted the corners of his mouth, and quickly she added, "Don't answer that."

He shifted his backpack, glanced around, and shocked her when he leaned to brush his lips against hers. Once. He drew back just enough to see her reaction, then had the audacity to do it again, this time with a soft swipe of tongue. A brief caress which sent astonishment and sexual heat pumping through her veins.

She closed her eyes, drew a shaky breath of restraint. "I'm not going to have an affair with you."

"Then how about a cup of coffee after work tonight?"

"Boone—"

"If I promise to keep my hands to myself?"

The door behind them swung open and a student slipped out, offering an apologetic smile as he cut around them. When he'd disappeared into the stairwell, Elizabeth gave Boone a hard look. "No coffee. No more flirting. You're barking up the wrong tree."

"But how can you ask me to stay away when I know you're attracted to me?"

"Who says?" she shot back.

"Your eyes. They're all sleepy and sexy right now." He reached out and traced a finger down the bridge of her nose to her lips, which fell open in dismay. "Like they were when I kissed you Friday night. God, what I wouldn't give to do it again. And I think you want me to, Elizabeth. I might be young, but I'm not stupid."

"I didn't say that—" The door squeaked open again and Boone stepped back to let two students pass through, while Elizabeth turned away and forced herself to regain composure.

"This isn't a good time," she said without looking at him. "I have office hours after this. We can talk then, but nothing's going to change."

He didn't answer. When she turned around, Amanda Hastings had exited the classroom and stood waiting for Boone.

"Killer of a test, Dr. Gilstrom," she said, flashing a perfect, disarming smile. "Boone, you hungry?"

"Sure." He shouldered his backpack and glanced at Elizabeth. "I'll try to catch you during office hours, Professor."

"Fine." She forced a smile. "You'll be taking your chances."

"I'm bound to catch you at some point," he said, and the laughter in his voice promptly snatched away her reply.

*****

Elizabeth refused to admit she'd stayed two hours past her normal office schedule in anticipation of Boone's visit. She set aside the mid-term tests, capped her red pen and sighed. He'd left with Amanda for dinner. She'd stood there in the hallway and watched them go. Amanda, she discovered as she witnessed the sway of the girl's lithe, boyish hips in departure, had a generous tattoo across the low curve of her back. Boone's hand had covered it as he held the door for her and ushered her through.

Body art on a body that needed nothing to render it more beautiful.

Elizabeth groaned and let her forehead drop to the desk. She'd had a headache for days. It seemed to grow with every moment that she sat in the stark cubicle of her office and brooded over a man twelve years her junior. She was supposed to be dwelling on her broken marriage, struggling with images of Stuart locked in Cecilia's pale, graceful arms. But lately all she felt about that was utter annoyance. She wanted the divorce to be done. She wanted her life back, damn it.

A soft rustle at the door brought her head off the desk. Boone stood there, watching her with a somber expression. His dark hair was tousled from the night wind, his cheeks flushed from the cold. "It's late, Professor. You need to get out of here."

"Yes, that's the plan." She rose and shuffled her papers into her briefcase, ignoring the trembling excitement that fluttered in her stomach. "Want to walk me out?"

"That's a paltry consolation prize," he said. "What I really want could be considered totally inappropriate."

"Let's argue about it on the way."

His smile finally appeared, creeping from one side of his mouth to the other. A little shy, a lot sexy. "You think we'll argue?"

"I know it," she said firmly.

He waited for her in the hallway while she locked her office door, then he took her briefcase and walked beside her from the building and down the stone steps to the mostly deserted parking lot.

"Where's the Mercedes?" he asked as they strolled toward a gleaming maroon Acura.

"Mechanic's. This is a rental. They said it'd be at least a week before they're done with my car."

"That's too bad. Did you enjoy yourself Friday night?" The question came from nowhere.

Elizabeth glanced at his profile as they passed beneath a purple fluorescent light. "Of course."

"But not enough to do it again."

"Boone." She stopped and caught his sleeve to halt him. "Believe me, if this was just a matter of enjoyment, well—we wouldn't be having this conversation. I'd be sitting across from you in that cozy little bar as we speak. You're wonderful company. But I'm just not ready for—I'm not ready."

"Closed for repairs, I know." He caught her hand, studied it in the cold light. "You're shaking."

She didn't bother to deny it. He touched something within her, something more than sexual. He was a tender, bright, beautiful man...born twelve years too late.

"It goes against my grain to let this go," he said in a low voice. "But you're doing this whole 'my life is a mess' thing, and who am I to argue with such a compelling excuse?"

Indignation flared within her and she withdrew her hand. "It's not an excuse. My life is a mess. Why would you want to get involved with me?"

"Because it's you I'm interested in. I don't care about your divorce, or all the things that hold you back from doing what I know you want to do. It's just you, Elizabeth."

He reclaimed her hand and gave it a mild tug, bringing her against his chest. "I'm not asking for anything more than tonight. We can take it one day at a time. Just...give me the chance to know you. Don't turn away when what you really want is to say yes. 'Yes, Boone, I'll have a cup of coffee with you.'" He dipped his head to catch her gaze, his voice gently teasing. "'Yes, Boone, I'll come out with you tonight, no strings attached.'"

A helpless smile crept across her mouth, and when he saw it, he smiled in return. "That's a yes, isn't it?"

"I'll bet you were a stubborn pain in the butt when you were a kid," she said, laughing.

"Only when I saw something I really wanted." His thumb whisked across her knuckles, then he raised her hand to his lips. "Where do you want to go?"

Elizabeth shivered with delight. It wasn't often that a man kissed her knuckles with such tender reverence. "There's a Starbuck's around the corner. We could walk."

"I'll treat you to a cup of coffee." He tucked her fingers into the crook of his arm. "No alcohol this time to sway you in my favor."

It wasn't the alcohol that had swayed her last time. Ah, well. One last cup of coffee, shared with such an enjoyable friend. A pleasant end to a tumultuous day. It was just what she needed.

Chapter Five

The harvest moon hovered high in the sky when they returned to the empty parking lot. Elizabeth's watch read ten o'clock. They'd sat outside Starbuck's in the crisp autumn night for an hour, nursing steaming cups of coffee and talking about their lives.

Afterward, reluctant to head back, she'd suggested they take a walk. And they did, around three city blocks, lost in conversation. The easy sound of Boone's voice drew her in, wrapped her in warmth so she no longer felt the nip of the chilled night air.

Of course, he could recite the US Constitution and she would have been enthralled. But he spoke of his family—a large, loving brood—and of growing up in Rockville, right outside of D.C. He made her laugh, swept her out of her own bleak reality...and somehow forced her to take another look at it, to see that it was only as terrible as she allowed.

"Tell me something, Boone," she said as they sauntered across the empty lot toward her waiting rental car. "What makes you so unspoiled, so optimistic about relationships, when half of all marriages end in divorce?"

He shrugged and ruffled a hand through his dark hair. "I grew up with two parents who are still in love after thirty years of marriage." His eyes sparkled as he glanced at her. "Or maybe it's just the fresh hopefulness of my tender age."

She laughed. "Please. You're the oldest twenty-four-year-old I've ever met."

"Am I supposed to thank you for that?"

"It was a compliment."

Reaching out, Boone grasped her hand and they walked on, fingers loosely laced together. Elizabeth tried not to think about what it meant, or why it felt so right. Or why, suddenly, a strange tightness pulled across her heart, frustration and pleasure combined.

"I take it you're not seeing anyone," she said when the silence stretched between them. What she really wanted to say was, "*Are you sleeping with Amanda Hastings?*

Boone glanced at her, his gaze lingering on her face until she met his eyes and flushed at his knowing smile. "I was for a while. But now I'm officially unattached."

"I don't mean to pry," she said, her face hot.

His footsteps slowed. "Then why did you ask?"

Elizabeth hedged, took a step ahead of him, but the tug of his hand around hers halted her and drew her back to where he stood.

"I just like to know my admirers," she said primly. When he continued to scrutinize her, she rolled her eyes. "I don't know, Boone. You're very attractive." *How can I say this and still sound casual?* "I wondered about your relationship with Amanda Hastings when I saw the painting. It's very provocative. Anyone who looks at it will wonder."

"So ask me," he said, curling her hand against his chest.

She wanted to. The curiosity—and resentment—was killing her. She opened her mouth to impart the question, and came out with, "She has a tattoo."

Boone's brows lowered, and then a slow grin crept across his mouth. "Yes. She has several."

"Body piercings, too," she added.

"And this bothers you?"

More than she could explain. "I just don't understand why a beautiful girl like that would want to put holes in her body. She's perfect as is."

"Looks aren't everything, Elizabeth."

She scowled and removed her hand from his w
"Now you really do sound like a fifty-year-old."

"And you act like one. Why are you so settlec
middle-aged when you're far more beau
knowledgeable—than most women my age?"

She didn't have an answer, just stood there be
purple spotlight of the street lamp, hot all over with hu

"It's my turn to pry." He moved close to h
breaching her boundaries with his easy confidence ar
understanding. She half-hated him. "Tell me why
Stanley are getting a divorce."

"It's Stuart," she corrected in a dull tone.

His smile returned. "That's even worse. Okay–
what happened with Stuart."

"First he fell in love with being a renowned neuros
Then he fell in love with being rich. And finally he fell
with his surgical assistant. Someone younger and muc
beautiful than I." Her voice rose into the hollow night, so
and unfamiliar to her own ears. Hearing herself say i
revived the monster sadness in her center, so that it radia
in slow, painful waves.

"So you see, Boone," she finished in a trembling
lifting her head to lock eyes with him, "looks and you
everything in life. In mine, anyway. I've lost everyth
them."

He didn't reply right away. He watched her with
intensity, she stepped back. The tiny furrow between his
spoke of concern, understanding, sympathy. Beyond tha
couldn't guess his thoughts. She didn't want his pit
wanted…God. She wanted him. She wouldn't dissect i
Later, when the yearning came and swept over her in he
lonely bed, she could examine it. Kick herself for giv
before the going had even gotten good. And with a m
Boone, it would assuredly be very, very good.

Of course if he touched her now, she'd cry.

"I haven't known you very long, Elizabeth, but long ough to see that maybe this man who walked away from you ver deserved you to begin with."

"And there's someone out there who does? Oh, please, one. You're talking to the original romantic, and even I can't allow that one right now."

"You don't have to." He brushed his fingers against her eek. "I don't mean to upset you."

Elizabeth laughed, a short, mirthless sound. "God, you're e last person to upset me, and yet you've come along and rown such a wrench in my grieving process. One minute I ink my heart is broken, that Stuart has left me with othing…and the next, I can't wait until it's all final and he's one, and I'm free to—"

She stopped herself, acutely aware of how close she'd come blabbing out her attraction to him. Maybe he heard the nspoken declaration beneath her flustered words, because his rown deepened and he stepped closer, and all she could think do was get to her car, get away clean and unscathed, before he unraveled completely.

She moved, somehow made it to the Acura, the only vehicle arked in the sprawling lot. Another slow, trembling breath, and he found her composure.

He followed and stood by, quietly waiting as she retrieved er keys from her briefcase.

"Well." She straightened her shoulders and faced him, keys lutched in her hand. "Boone, I just want to say—"

"Don't say anything." His eyes glittered, reflected the treetlight. With one step, he backed her against the driver's oor. "Unless it's to tell me not to kiss you. And you'd better nean it if you say it."

She stared at him, silent.

"That's what I thought," he said, and ducked his head to nd her lips. His mouth was soft, undemanding as it moved

against hers in gentle exploration. Then he drew back to meet her eyes. "Kiss me back, Elizabeth."

She tried to swallow, couldn't. Tears welled in her eyes, clung to her lashes. Big, fat drops of humiliation. "How can I? This is wrong. I'm a mess, and this is wrong."

"You're so unhappy," he whispered, his hands cupping her face. A tear trickled to her cheek and he followed it with a single finger, trailed the moisture down to her jaw, then caught it on his fingertip and brought it to his mouth.

Elizabeth watched, mesmerized, speechless, as he tasted it. Her sadness, her frustration, as though taking it into himself. It was the sexiest and most poignant gesture anyone had ever offered her.

While she stood in stunned silence, he nudged her chin up, lips hovering over hers. "Let me give you this one pleasure, Dr. Gilstrom. One kiss. Will you let me?"

Her eyelids slid closed. Desire roiled in waves through her most secret places, burning her as though she'd never been aroused before. "Yes," someone said. Someone choked and vulnerable and strange…not Elizabeth Gilstrom of the steely will and unwavering morals. "Please, yes."

Her briefcase slipped from her fingers and thudded against the concrete as she rose on tiptoe to fully claim his mouth. There was nothing sweet or gentle about it this time. It stretched far beyond a simple kiss and into a mating of mouths—wet, ravenous, wholly sexual.

Elizabeth kissed him with all the soaring need that had simmered inside her since she could remember, a need Stuart had never come close to touching with his clumsy, selfish hands. Strips of her disguise peeled away in the wake of Boone's young, fearless passion, following suit as he slipped the coat from her shoulders so it joined her briefcase at their feet.

Then his palms slid down her back to her bottom and hitched her against the car door, parting her legs so he could move between them. Instantly she felt his arousal press against her, granite and insistent, against the fast-dampening place where she ached for him.

She'd never felt emptier, hungrier in her life. She wanted to rip aside his jacket, yank the shirt from his jeans and slide beneath it to feel his hot, muscled body. Taste every inch of him. Take him inside her and let the sheer ecstasy of his flesh within her carry her irretrievably away.

"Wrap your legs around me," he murmured against her mouth, and the utter wantonness of doing so sizzled through her so hotly, she had no choice. Her knees wouldn't hold her up any longer. When she did as he asked, he hoisted her as though she weighed nothing and thrust against her, burning her through layers of denim and gabardine and cotton.

"God," she whispered, her breath coming hard as his mouth scalded the side of her neck, her throat. His hand slid up her ribcage to cup her breast while he bent his head and drew on her nipple through her thin sweater. The moist heat of his mouth seared her, made her squirm against him for more. More contact. More pleasure. More of this torturous game that made no sense and only guaranteed the most mindless carnal delight.

She sank her fingers into the glorious thickness of his hair, buried her nose against it, breathing in the scent of heat and faded shampoo, and held him. Tight.

"Closer…" He groaned. "I need to be closer to you."

"How?" Desperation choked her reply, left her breathless and aching as his hips rocked against hers, a poetic and unyielding demand. "We can't have sex right here, Boone. Not like this. Not ever."

"Then touch me. Let me touch you." He let her slide down his body until her feet gained ground, then he caught her hand, kissed it, led it between their bodies to the hard proof of his desire.

Elizabeth couldn't think. She closed her fingers around his erection, traced the long, rigid shape of him through his jeans, and lifted her lashes long enough to read the passion in his face.

His eyes were closed, head thrown back as she stroked him through his jeans. The moment—the sheer, personal beauty of it—imprinted itself forever on her brain. Beneath her fingers, his penis throbbed.

His lips found the crown of her head, one hand working its way under her hair to cup her neck. His other hand slipped between them and fumbled with the thin leather belt she wore. Before she could protest, he had unfastened it and loosened the button and zipper of her pants.

Alarmed, overwhelmed with wanting—and the futility of it—she caught his wrist. But it was too late...and too good. His fingers slipped inside the elastic of her panties and burrowed through damp curls to her aching center, parted the soft folds wet with desire, and stroked, just once, enough to elicit an involuntary whimper from her throat.

All she could do was cling to him. "You can't do this," she groaned, her fingertips digging into his shoulders. "We can't..."

"You feel so good," he whispered against her forehead, his thumb rotating gently on the tiny, aroused nub of her clitoris. "So wet. I want to put my mouth on you. I want to taste you, Elizabeth."

She shivered from head to toe at the direct contact on skin so sensitive, at the caress of his bold, sultry words washing through her. He said something else wicked enough that a blush spread through her entire body. Something more he wanted to do to her with his mouth, his tongue and his hard, hard cock—but she couldn't assimilate the information, couldn't separate the promise of his whisper from the rhythmic pleasure of his touch between her legs. The blood was pounding in her ears, the cold air not cool enough to soothe the heat building within her, heat and tension, tighter, higher...

He found the slick entrance to her body and pushed one finger inside her, then ever so subtly stroked...and stroked...so gently, so *damn gently*—and sent Elizabeth soaring. The astonishing climax tore through her in a slew of wild electric jolts, and Boone clamped his mouth over hers to drink in her cry of amazement.

She was still shuddering against him, limp and exhausted, when blue lights flashed behind him.

"No..." She buried her face against Boone's chest, wishing she could crawl inside him and hide. Slowly, decorously, he withdrew his hand from her panties, closed her pants, and wrapped his arms around her to shield her from the approaching security cart.

"Evening, folks." The guard pulled to a stop behind them. "Mind if I ask what you're doing out here at this time of night?"

"Winding things up, sir." Boone's voice sounded steady and confident as he spoke over his shoulder. Elizabeth burrowed harder against him, where his heart beat a comforting rhythm. She could picture the guard peering around Boone's big frame to catch a glimpse of her, and there was nowhere to run.

"She okay?" the guard asked. His voice sounded disturbingly familiar. It was Ernie, probably, or William. She knew the guards by name; they often walked her to her car when she stayed late at work. Thank God the Mercedes was sequestered at Turner Imports. It would have shrieked her identity. She'd never been happier about a broken-down car than at that moment.

"She's fine," Boone said, and to corroborate, Elizabeth loosened her hold on his back and half-heartedly waved a hand.

"Alrighty," the guard spoke with just a note of warning in his tone. "You kids have a good night."

"Thank you." Boone waited until the whine of the cart disappeared up the hill, then he caught Elizabeth's chin and tilted her face up to meet his laughing gaze. "I can't remember the last time I got busted for making out in a public place."

She closed her eyes. "You would think I'd know better."

"Me too. Truthfully, I didn't see anyone around. The parking lot looked deserted."

A new wave of heat flooded her face. "At least you had the wherewithal to even check. We could've been in the middle of the Capitol Rotunda and I wouldn't have noticed another soul."

"I'll take that as a compliment." He pressed a kiss against her tousled hair and stepped back to allow her space to tidy herself.

She tucked in her blouse, refastened her belt, smoothed her hair, all without meeting his eyes again. The time for humiliation had somehow come and gone without her feeling a single bit of it. All she knew was that she'd just experienced her first orgasm in at least three years. Good God—had it been that long? The last time had occurred—miraculously—with Stuart, after a particularly rowdy faculty Christmas party, when she wobbled home and tackled him before he could issue his usual protest.

She felt raw, suddenly. Naked. Resentful that this man had broken down her disguise and exposed her for the needy, fragile being she'd become. She couldn't think straight. All she wanted was to flee. Heart thudding, she leaned to retrieve her coat and briefcase from the ground, but Boone captured her hand.

"Are you going to talk to me?"

"Of course," she said, still without looking at him. "But I have to get home. I'm never going to wake up in the morning, and I have a department meeting—"

"Elizabeth. Don't."

She used her keys as an excuse to turn away, and slipped them into the Acura's lock.

Behind her, Boone was silent, but she felt the heat from his body so close, still radiating desire. She'd taken her pleasure and offered him nothing. She had nothing to give.

"Where's your Jeep?" she asked finally, without turning around.

"The weather was nice today. I rode my bike."

She swallowed, staring over the hood at the light bouncing off the slick yellow parking lines that stretched acres beyond. "Let me give you a ride home, Boone."

He shifted behind her, moved aside. "That'd be great. Then you can call us even and walk away."

Chapter Six

She knew where he lived now.

She'd driven him home in silence laden with frustration. Hers. His. He didn't want to talk, and she didn't try.

Following his brief directions, she turned onto a wooded road that curved around three landscaped roundabouts. Every house they passed grew larger, until he said, "This is it," and Elizabeth slowed down, staring at the mansion that sat an acre off the road.

"This is your house?"

"My uncle's. Follow the driveway around by the tennis courts. I live in the garage apartment."

The "garage" was as large as the house where she'd grown up. A brick staircase led up to the gabled second story, where a warm light burned behind sheer curtains.

"What a beautiful estate," she said, awestruck.

"My uncle's been good to me. I'm staying here until I graduate."

Swallowing her astonishment, Elizabeth glanced at him. His tone was polite, distant. Thirty minutes ago he'd offered her the most incredible pleasure, touched her inside and out. Now it seemed like miles stretched between them. As it should be. So why did she feel as though she'd made the mistake of a lifetime?

The dashboard lights limned his profile when he turned his face away and reached for the door handle. "Thanks for the ride, Professor."

"You're welcome." There was so much more she wanted to say, but the knot in her throat swelled until she could only manage, "Goodnight, Boone."

"'Night." He climbed out of the car without looking at her again, locked the passenger door and gently closed it.

Elizabeth sat there and watched him ascend the stairs to his apartment with quick, easy strides. The moonlight spilled across his dark head and broad shoulders as he unlocked the door and opened it. Only then did he glance back at her, and she couldn't read his expression.

With a shuddering sigh, she threw the car into reverse and backed down the long, elegant driveway.

And now she knew where he lived, and it kept her awake, picturing the interior of his home, the size of his bed, the golden gleam of his skin against white linens. Pressing a palm to her breast, she counted the beats of her pulse and remembered the press of his lips against her hair as she caressed him in the parking lot. She'd wanted to wrap her hands around him, stroke the silky-hot skin of his penis, feel the surge of life and blood beneath her palms. And now it was too late.

A groan of sheer misery rumbled in her throat. Her fingers seemed to move of their own accord as they skipped down her body and tugged up her nightshirt, drawn to the juncture of her thighs, where Boone's touch had revived sleeping nerve-endings, infused them with relentless yearning.

Masturbation would solve nothing, of course. Elizabeth told herself she was simply curious to see her body's reaction to the mere thought of Boone, but her hips jerked at the tentative contact, and after a moment, her hand settled between her thighs. It might not solve anything, but it eased the ache. Scarce droplets of water to a parched and dying soul.

A picture of Boone's face darted through her heated mind; her stomach fluttered, muscles clenched as a potent wave of arousal slammed into her. God, she was as wet from thinking about him as he'd made her with his touch.

Inexplicably shamed, she held her breath and slid a finger through the moist folds of her own flesh to caress herself, a paltry substitute for what she really wanted.

The climax came quickly, brief, cold and hardly enough to quell the tension in her pelvis. Only one man could heal this pain. The one who'd caused it in the first place.

She bit her lip and sighed as the aftershocks of orgasm faded away. He'd made her feel alive, beautiful, safe. He'd brought her excruciating pleasure and then with the same easy confidence, wiggled them out of a potentially mortifying situation with the security guard.

In the dark, an unbidden smile crept across Elizabeth's lips. Desire made a woman do reckless, dangerous things...and for the first time in years, she felt the soft wings of freedom brush over her.

* * * * *

Stuart called on Thursday morning.

"You can talk to my lawyer," Elizabeth told him. "I'm hanging up."

"Wait! Liz, please wait."

With a sigh, she leaned her hips against the kitchen counter and eyed the gurgling coffee pot. It was too early to deal with Stuart, and she hadn't had her morning jolt of caffeine. "I have no desire to talk to you."

"I know. I know, Liz. I don't blame you. But I thought maybe you and I could hammer out a few things before we have the joint meeting with our attorneys. Just to save time and awkwardness."

She laughed. "Awkwardness. That's a good one, Stu. Leaving your ten-year marriage for a busty love goddess guarantees a bit of that, I must say."

"Don't be like that. I want to discuss the house sale like adults. We need to iron out the details."

"What specifically did you want to iron out? I like the agreement we have. I never wanted this house. It was yours from the beginning. Either we sell it and split the money, or you buy me out. Maybe Cecilia could do something flashier with the interior. You never did like my love of traditional furnishings."

She glanced around the stark, chrome-and-tile kitchen and tried to envision the redhead stirring a steaming pot of something delicious and domesticated, while Stuart sat at the granite-topped kitchen table, bouncing a chubby baby on his knee.

The scenario curdled her stomach, despite its improbability. He'd never wanted children, and she hadn't argued. Anything to avoid conflict and its icy aftermath. Another self-denial she now regretted. She did want a child. More than one, and right now it felt like a pipe dream.

"I could go to a sperm bank," she said thoughtfully, interrupting Stuart's explanation of how he wanted so-and-so real estate agent to handle the sale.

He paused in the midst of his diatribe. "Sperm bank?"

"I did want children. I lied about it, Stuart."

"I'm sorry, Elizabeth. I don't see what this has to do with selling the house."

"It has nothing to do with selling the house. It has to do with me."

He blew out a frustrated sigh. "I don't follow."

"I know. You don't know how." An image of Boone glided across her mind's eye and gave her stomach a good, hard jolt of yearning. "You can iron things out with my lawyer. That's why I pay him."

"Wait a minute. Don't hang up."

"I'm hanging up."

"Liz!" The urgency in his tone brought the receiver back to her ear. "Are you there?"

"Barely," she said with a sigh.

"Cecilia and I…it's not the grand love affair you think."

"Oh?" She studied her nails. Once impeccably manicured, they were now bitten to the quick, and soon to be paint-stained, because she planned to stop at the art supply shop on the way home from work to pick up a canvas. Her urge to paint had returned somewhere in the night, between sexually charged dreams of Boone. "I'm sorry for you, Stuart. Especially if you're planning to marry her. Watch out, you might end up with another nasty divorce on your hands."

"Who told you I'm planning to marry her?" He sounded aghast.

"Good news travels fast when you're related to Aunt Barbie."

"I'm not planning to marry Ce-Ce. I'm not even divorced from you yet. Why would I be making marriage plans when—"

"Ask Ce-Ce, since I believe she's the one who's spreading the information, with a little help from my Aunt Barbie's cronies. Small world, huh? And now I do have to go. Goodbye, Stu." She hung up and slumped by the phone, her heart whacking against her ribs in dull, uneven thuds. But she didn't cry. She crossed the kitchen, poured a cup of coffee, and went out to the garage to search for her lost art supplies.

*****

Elizabeth dreamed of Boone McCrea that night. He sauntered across her field of vision as though he'd just stepped out of a waterfall, naked, golden skin beaded with moisture, dark hair wet and swept back from his face. Her imagination produced an impressive, detailed portrait of his lean, graceful limbs, the sleek line of his spine, the carved musculature of his backside as he turned for her examination.

Elizabeth was fairly certain that even her sex-starved mind couldn't paint him more exquisite than the real thing, but she settled into the dream, into the coiling desire that tightened her nipples and burned through her pelvis, swelling soft skin too-long hungry for a man's attention.

In her sleeping vision, he faced her, his features tense with need, and wrapped a single hand around his impressive erection.

I think about your mouth on me, his voice echoed in her mind like a faraway whisper. *Look what you do to me, Professor.*

His fingers caressed his penis, faltering at first, his brows furrowed as he studied her from his misty, sleeping world. *Do you dream of me, Elizabeth? Do you think about this?* His fingers fisted more tightly around his shaft and his eyes slid closed, head falling back with pleasure.

Even through cloying layers of sleep, Elizabeth heard herself gasp. This was more excruciatingly erotic than any conscious fantasy she could have produced. Clinging tight to the image, dry-throated and breathless like a covert voyeur, she watched him pleasure himself with ever-quickening strokes, until his straining muscles shuddered, and a groan of release tore from his throat.

Elizabeth! His dark head dropped forward, shoulders jerking again, again, again, with each quake his surreal climax drove through him.

In the vibrating silence, the mist gathered around him and he sought her gaze again, green eyes like bright jewels in the gray miasma.

The dream was ending.

"No," she pleaded, stepping toward him. "Boone—"

The sound of her own voice shattered the night and hauled her to wakefulness with as much solicitude as a bucket of icy water dumped over her head.

"Christ," she whispered into the dark, both relieved and disillusioned as she stared at the dance of shadows on the ceiling.

Kicking off the sheets, she let the cool air sip the perspiration from her skin. Then she laid awake the rest of the night, eyes wide, shell-shocked from the force of the sexual dream, and from the realization that she'd shuddered through her own involuntary, nocturnal orgasm with the help of a mere fantasy.

God, the real thing would kill her.

* * * * *

It was hard not to stare.

Elizabeth stood frozen in the art building entry, her gaze fixed on the dark-haired man in the green soccer jersey and shorts, walking hand-in-hand with the slender blonde across the campus quad. Boone played soccer, she hadn't known. Boone was dating Amanda Hastings, she hadn't known that, either. At least not totally. Last week in the parking lot, he'd denied being involved with anyone. But he obviously was.

He was holding her hand.

Thank God, her common sense added. It was for the best. He wasn't interested and available and focused on her after all.

"Ouch," she muttered under her breath, simply because the mere idea hurt so much.

He didn't see her standing in the art building entrance. A few seconds more and she might have collided with them on the nearby sidewalk. Thank goodness for small mercies.

The back of Boone's jersey said "Bethesda Community Soccer," and under that, "McCrea" and "04". His retreat looked as good as his approach—strong, tanned legs and thighs, a hint of well-defined, muscled buttocks beneath the loose soccer shorts.

It was far too easy to recall the Boone in her dream, stripped bare and fully aroused. Far too easy to picture Amanda's lithe, golden body thrashing under his sensuous touch. Far too depressing. Despair grabbed Elizabeth by the heart, and for a moment, she couldn't remember why she'd even stepped out of the building.

John Weinburg, an associate art professor and one of Elizabeth's favorite colleagues, came through the glass doors behind her and paused to offer her a wide smile. "Heading home for the night?"

"Thinking about it," she said. "John, do you know anything about community soccer leagues in this area?"

"My son plays for Alexandria. Game tonight, in fact."

Her knees weakened inexplicably. "Is his team playing Bethesda, by any chance?"

"That's right. You must know Boone McCrea. Did he tell you about the game? It's supposed to be a hell of a match."

"No one told me. I just…I saw his uniform and wondered about it." She paused, tried to drink in the realization that she was actually capable of finding the soccer field and attending the game, just to torture herself by watching Boone in all his young, masculine glory.

Maybe if she were really lucky, Amanda Hastings would save her a seat.

Hysterical laughter bubbled in her throat and she managed to swallow it. "I'm a soccer fan," she told John Weinberg. It was only half a lie. She'd played on the girls' team in high school, but hadn't attended a game in fifteen years. "Maybe I'll drop by the field and watch for a bit."

He nodded with enthusiasm. "Look for me. I'm on my way to pick up my wife, and we'll be there in about half an hour."

"Where's the game?" she called after him as he started down the steps.

"Bethesda," he said. "Graystone Park off River Road. We're sitting on the east side of the field."

When he was gone, she closed her eyes and sighed. What was she doing?

Falling, whispered a small, inimitable voice…the one in her heart.

* * * * *

"You have Boone McCrea in any of your classes?" John asked Elizabeth over his wife's frosted curls as they huddled on the wide bleachers and braced against the mid-October wind.

"My 506 Art History," she said with careful disinterest. "You?"

"He's one of my more skilled painting students. He attended undergrad at George Mason, but he liked our graduate art program better. More and more I'm thinking we're the lucky ones in the deal. I'm looking forward to his private show in the spring."

Betsy Weinburg glanced at her husband. "Who are we talking about?"

"Number four, playing for the enemy." He nodded toward Boone, who was trotting across the field to rejoin his team. "You know, the kid who painted that Appalachian landscape you love so much."

Betsy gave a shiver of delight. "Oh yes. How could I forget? Very talented. And such a gorgeous young man," she added under her breath.

Resisting the urge to smile, Elizabeth hugged herself against the chill and leaned forward to search the crowded bleachers. There was no sign of Amanda Hastings, which didn't mean she wasn't there…but Elizabeth humored herself and pretended she wasn't.

Alexandria's league apparently didn't stand a chance against Bethesda. The match was exciting though, its spectators passionate. Elizabeth tried to remain inconspicuous, but when Boone scored a goal, she leaped to her feet with the rest of the Bethesda fans and let out an ear-splitting whistle. Whether he saw her or not, she didn't know. He smiled in her direction, but his attention didn't linger and a moment later he was back in the heart of the game.

He was magnificent to watch. Even between plays, when he stood in the white floodlight and braced his hands on his knees to catch his breath, he absorbed her. Everything about him was beautiful, from his dark hair, curling and damp with perspiration, to his lean, muscled physique, to his easy smile. She could see it from where she sat, and the sight of it made her ache. He was flushed and healthy and vibrant. Full of life, good humor and promise. Watching him made her forget a dour man named Stuart Gilstrom had ever existed.

When the game ended, Elizabeth bid the Weinburgs goodbye and slipped out to the parking lot, where her newly repaired Mercedes waited for her, gleaming under the streetlights.

Maybe now that she'd reveled in her attraction to Boone, she could let go. What a lovely distraction he'd been. She breathed in the clean, crisp night and felt like a new person. He'd revitalized her with his misguided pursuit, and she'd forever be grateful to him for reminding her that she was a desirable—and still young—woman.

She slipped her key in the ignition, pulled her seatbelt into place, and tried to start the engine.

Nothing happened. The Mercedes was dead.

Heart pounding, Elizabeth shook her head and tried again. This wasn't happening. She'd done something wrong, left the headlights on, or forgotten to put it in park. No, everything looked in order. She pulled out the key, took a calming breath, and inserted it again. The dashboard lights came on, and the "check engine" light, a smug red glow that told her the mechanics at Turner Imports had failed her for the first time in three years of customer satisfaction.

"Damn it, damn it, damn it!" Clutching the steering wheel, she pressed her forehead against its cool surface and inadvertently sounded the horn. Two men leaving the game threw her an amused look and kept walking.

For a while, Elizabeth sat in the cold leather interior, watching for the Weinburgs. But they'd left right after her to meet their son, and were probably long gone by now. She had no cellular phone, either. She'd taken great pleasure in canceling the contract the day after Stuart moved out, since he'd used it as a sort of electronic leash to keep tabs on her whereabouts. So now what?

Boone, said the provocative voice she'd grown accustomed to ignoring where he was concerned. And if she caught up with him, what would be her reason for being at Graystone Park in the first place? How painfully obvious. How mindless. How…how completely infatuated she was with him. No more beating around the bush. She'd just have to tell him…if Amanda Hastings wasn't standing at his side, a beautiful trophy for a game well played.

She locked her traitorous car, drew her sweater sleeves down around her chilled fingers, and trekked across the parking lot toward the soccer field. When Boone appeared between the bleachers, she immediately spotted him. He was walking with two teammates, a duffel bag in his hand.

Elizabeth cut between two sport utility vehicles nearby and hesitated. It was now or never. "Boone?"

He stopped, squinted at her. "Elizabeth?"

"Hi," she said, trying her damnedest to avoid the curious gazes of his companions. "I know this is an odd coincidence."

"Yeah." He ruffled a hand through his hair in a confounded gesture. "A little."

Oh God, it couldn't get more painful than this. "Do you think…could we talk for just a second?"

"I'll see you at practice," he told his friends after a pause, and they went on, throwing one last look in Elizabeth's direction as they disappeared among the parked cars.

Boone approached her, the surprise fading from his features. His hair curled damply against his forehead, clung to his neck. He was flushed, muddy, beautiful, and obviously suspicious. "Did you see the game?"

"Yes." She drew herself up and forced her gaze to remain on his. His eyes were so very green tonight. Meadows danced through them. Rich, lush fauna. "The game was great. You were great."

He nodded, took a breath, released it, as though he didn't know what to say next. "So…are you heading home now?"

"I was." *Just tell him the truth, Elizabeth. And for God's sake, be honest with yourself.* "I came here tonight because I wanted to watch you play. And then my car wouldn't start." No real epiphany, but it felt good to say it anyway.

His frown deepened. "The rental?"

"The Mercedes. The mechanics finished with it more quickly than they initially thought—and now I see why. I think they stuck a bandage on the problem and turned her loose."

"Oh. I'm sorry."

She waved aside the matter. "I know you're heading out of here now, and you probably have plans. But could you give me a ride to the gas station about two miles up the street? I can use the phone there."

"No," he said.

Elizabeth paused. "No?"

"No, I won't give you a ride to the gas station. I'll give you a ride home."

"But what about—" She bit her lip and winced.

"What about...what?"

"I thought...I thought maybe you weren't here alone tonight."

He shifted his weight from one foot to the other and shouldered his duffel bug. "Who'd be here with me?"

She closed her eyes. "I don't know. And I really didn't plan this little fiasco, in case you were wondering."

Boone didn't answer, and when she opened her eyes, he was smiling. Just a little. A sexy, knowing smile that spoke of amusement and delight. "I have to admit, Elizabeth, it does look kind of suspicious."

"I know. But do you honestly think someone with my decorum would come up with such a weak plan as this?"

"No," he said. "I suspect you're far too creative."

Her cheeks warmed. "I'm glad we've cleared that up. And I accept your ride offer, as long as you let me give you money for gas."

"You must get weary doing the right thing all the time." He reached out to grasp her hand. "Come on, St. Elizabeth. I'm parked right over here."

Elizabeth hesitated. His offer of a ride home was starting to sound suspiciously like a date. "That's fine," she said after a moment of weighing the risks and coming up with a confused tangle of desire, anticipation and dread.

* * * * *

"Watch your step," Boone told her as he led the way up the narrow brick staircase to his apartment. "I forgot to leave on the outside light."

She waited, shivering on the step below him, as he fit the key into the lock. Her gaze landed on the smooth curve of his backside, lingered, and quickly darted upward when she realized where she'd focused. His jersey clung to his wide shoulders and hinted at the hard muscle beneath it. He was taller than Stuart's five-foot-ten stature by more than a couple of inches.

"Sorry," he said, casting an apologetic smile over his shoulder. "The lock sticks sometimes."

A moment later Elizabeth followed him over the threshold, closed her eyes in the darkness and breathed in the warm scent of Boone's home. Leather, faded cologne, maybe a little dust.

He crossed the room and turned on a reading lamp. "Make yourself comfortable," he said, throwing the keys and duffel bag on a granite counter that flanked a small galley kitchen. "I'll just be a minute."

She watched him disappear down a shallow hall beyond the kitchen. When he was out of sight, she moved toward the burgundy leather sofa and perched uneasily on the edge. It felt strange and titillating to be sitting in his home, where he practiced all the most personal rituals. She leaned forward to peer down the hallway at a door that was half-open. His bedroom, probably.

Inexplicably she thought of Amanda and shook off a pinch of dismay.

"Did this place come furnished, or do you just have reall expensive taste?" she called, her gaze taking in the dark lines primitive antiques and rich, masculine upholstery.

"My taste in furniture is questionable, I've been told, a yes, fortunately this apartment came furnished." His v floated from the back room. "My uncle used it as an office years. His studio's downstairs."

Elizabeth's eyebrows shot up. "Your uncle's an artist?"

"The proverbial variety. Volatile temperament inclu Boone reappeared, shirtless and barefoot, and round corner into the kitchen. "Want something to drink?"

Holy—

She stared. At his sculpted, naked torso, at the clean symmetry of his wide shoulders, the smoothness of su skin stretched taut over muscle and sinew. Better dream. No comparison, in fact.

Alarms wailed in her head and she shot to her drumming. "I'd love a glass of water."

He opened the refrigerator and braced a hand freezer door. The pale light spilled over his feature turned his skin to marble. "You sure? I've got Gatorade. And…a semi-flat liter of Mountain Dew."

"Water's fine." This was ridiculous. She'd seen man before.

But one like Boone? The seductive little voice her mind sounded smug. Of course not one like explained the hot rush of blood that now burned

She forced herself to approach the counter. to bite her. He was only as dangerous to discipline as she allowed.

"Okay with you if I jump in the shower handed her a glass of ice and a cold bottle of Ev

Illicit visions darted through her mind water into the tumbler. "Absolutely. I'm not in

He backed toward the hall. "You can turn on the stereo in the cabinet while you're waiting. I have a pretty good selection of CDs."

"Thanks," she said, and took a long, thirsty swig of Evian to quench her nervous tension.

A moment later, the sound of running water floated to her ears. The slide of shower curtain rings across a rod. The thud of a shampoo bottle hitting the shower floor. She folded her arms on the counter and buried her hot face against them. Who knew hat listening to the sounds of a man bathing could be so sexy?

That thought sent her scurrying across the faded Persian ug to the weathered oak sideboard, where she found Boone's ollection of CDs. A hundred or so, impressively varied. Alanis Iorissette, Jimmy Buffett. James Taylor's *New Moon Shine*, still its wrapper. Elizabeth smiled at that and wondered if he'd cked it up after their conversation in the college painting udio. Mozart, Sting, Creed, the Grateful Dead. The enomenal, silky-voiced Luther Vandross. Just what she eded to sooth her flustered nerves. She gingerly opened the e, set the CD in the disc player, and pressed the button.

If she closed her eyes, it sounded as though Luther ndross was performing a private concert for her ears only. stood in a charmed trance, letting his liquid vocals roll over in sensuous waves.

In the next room, the man she desired, possibly more than d ever desired anyone, was naked and clean and wet. A rush nsation flooded her senses, turned her muscles soft, brought nerve under her skin to life, until she tingled from head to And in her center, a yearning, aching need coiled and ned.

Vhat are you going to do, Elizabeth? You can have him if you im. He won't push you away.

ut what about the inevitable consequences? And what about la Hastings?

Amanda Hastings wasn't here...Elizabeth was. And screw the consequences. She'd ended up in Boone's apartment because she wanted it, wanted him. *Reach out and take what you want.* There was no one to stop her anymore.

Down the hall, the bathroom door opened and a column of light spilled across the fringed runner. Boone emerged, his gleaming shoulders water-beaded and dark hair dripping. A white towel slung low on his hips was all that separated Elizabeth from realizing her fantasies.

"You like Luther Vandross," he said, pausing in the hall.

She nodded, took a step toward him. "This music...it's just...so..."

"Sexy."

"Yes." Another step. "It's good music for making love. I've always liked having background music for that sort of thing."

For an instant, time seemed to freeze. A stranger had spoken those words. Someone other than the restrained woman Elizabeth knew herself to be.

Boone's smile softened, his gaze searching hers. "Me too."

"Really?" Two more steps. "What's your favorite lovemaking music?"

He clasped his hands behind his back and appeared to consider the question. "Some of Sting's newer stuff is pretty mood-inspiring." His gaze flickered back to her face. "What about you?"

"Luther Vandross." She stopped a couple of feet from him, shivering as the scent of shampoo and steam billowed to greet her. "Although I haven't personally made love while listening to this particular album."

His brows rose. "Oh?"

"No. Have you?"

"I haven't," he said huskily, leaning his backside against the doorjamb, "yet."

The toes of her tasseled loafers brushed the runner's fringe. She swallowed. Her pulse hadn't seen this much action since she ran the Capitol Hill marathon in 1998. "Boone?"

"Elizabeth?"

"I'm so out of practice."

"You're doing fine," he said.

She gazed at him, wide-eyed with trepidation and undeniable need. "Do I have to tell you what I want?"

"You don't have to do anything."

The two feet between them felt like the Great Divide. "But I want to. That's my problem. I want you to know I'm not desperate. I didn't think I was, but you make me feel that way. Desperate. Crazy." She shook back her hair, tried to grasp at dignity pulverized by desire. "Am I...do I seem crazy to you?"

Wordlessly he held out his hand, and she took it, let him lead her across the space that separated them. "You're beautiful to me," he said, hooking a finger beneath her chin to study her eyes. She drowned in his, all shifting shades of jade and shadow. Water spiked his lashes.

"Will you kiss me?" Her fingers encircled his wrists and clung.

"Yes," he whispered. "Close your eyes."

Her lashes fluttered closed, breath trapped in her throat, as Boone's lips drifted over her face. Forehead, eyebrows, nose. Skipping over her lips to her chin. His breath brushed her skin, desire trickled downward, hints of the wild, fierce downpour to come.

Warm fingers gently braced her throat, holding her face still for his delectation. God, oh God, how could this man be only twenty-four and know that this kind of devastating tenderness was more erotic than any frenzied crushing of mouths?

The scent of shampoo and soap rose between them. Elizabeth's breasts brushed his chest, nipples tight beneath a layer of cashmere and lace.

His arousal pressed against her stomach through the towel, but still he didn't move to embrace her. Just held her face, his gaze searching. "I'm going to fall in love with you, Dr. Gilstrom," he whispered. "Is that okay?"

"I think so," she said. "Yes. Oh Boone. I want you so much."

The delicate ties that held them apart unraveled at that moment, sent them rushing together, lips and tongues and arms enfolding. Elizabeth was wild, starved for him. For the minty taste of his hot mouth, the flex of his muscles beneath his smooth, damp skin, the sinuous, restless shift of his hips against hers as his hands slipped beneath her sweater and molded her spine. They broke apart long enough for him to draw the sweater up and over her head, leaving her hair in wild disarray, and she didn't care, she felt beautiful and alive under his hands.

"Your jeans," he said against her ear, mouth searching, tongue leaving a damp trail of adulation.

"Your towel," she replied, and he laughed, a short, breathless sound.

"Ladies first." His hands slid over her breasts, fingered the lace of her bra until her nipples tightened beneath it, then slid down her stomach to the button on her Levi's. "I can't wait to touch you." And he did, in short order, without waiting for her to shimmy out of the jeans or the sensible cotton bikinis she wore every day of her life.

He pressed her back against the wall; his palm slid inside the elastic and shaped itself to her desire, fingers searching, finding, circling her clitoris and teasing the moist entrance to her body that so ached to be filled.

Elizabeth hadn't imagined she would climax from such a brief and gentle foray, but a quick, fierce orgasm shuddered through her and she cried out against his throat, against the place where his pulse beat in triple time beneath his skin.

His lips brushed her hair when he spoke. "Well, that was easy."

Despite her embarrassment, Elizabeth managed a breathless laugh. "I have years of sexual frustration on you, Mr. McCrea. Are you equipped to deal with such a special case?"

"You tell me." He caught her hand, kissed her palm, then led it down his smooth, bare chest to his groin. His hard shaft surged in response to her touch, and she caressed it through the towel, watching the pleasure weight Boone's lashes.

"It'd be so easy to just make love right here, in the hallway," she murmured.

"Later. I want you in bed first."

She didn't argue.

Boone helped her step out of her shoes, then her jeans, and when she bent to retrieve them, he said, "Leave them." Taking her hand, he led her into the bedroom, where a single bedside lamp burned a dim golden arc against the wall. While she sat on the edge of the unmade, queen-sized mattress, he took the receiver off the hook and set it beside the phone. Then he faced her, caressed her hair, her cheek, smiled into her eyes.

"I need to touch you," she said, her hands rubbing his hips through the rough terrycloth wrapped around them. "I need to taste you." The towel unknotted from his waist with little effort, and she drew it away, unveiling his hard, muscled stomach and harder erection, impressive and demanding as she closed her fingers around it.

Silk over smoldering steel. It jerked in her hand like a live creature as she stroked it from base to head, and she glanced up to see his reaction. Boone was watching, eyelids heavy, features dark with tender need. He combed her hair back from her face, letting the thick strands slide through his fingers.

Better than any old dream.

Elizabeth closed her eyes and took his penis in her mouth.

The distant, mellow croon of the stereo hovered around them, a sweet accompaniment to the uneven rush of his breathing.

At first she merely sampled him, revealed in the flavor and scent of his hot flesh beneath her tongue, the tightening of his thigh muscles with each slow, suctioning retreat of her mouth.

Holding him between her lips, she slid both hands around to his buttocks, and found them as hard and muscled as she'd imagined, the skin as smooth and resilient. When she drew more firmly on his penis and dragged her tongue across its swollen tip, the muscles under her palms hollowed and flexed in response, and a faint sheen of perspiration misted his skin.

His hands left her hair, trembling now, and slipped down the back of her neck, searching for the clasp on her bra. The garment loosened and the straps slid down her arms, but she couldn't be bothered, so intent was she on showing him the same delight he'd shown her twice. Two times with Boone in a handful of days, and he'd brought her more pleasure than she'd ever experienced in her life.

She wanted him inside her, pushing against her very core, chest to chest, heart to heart. Wanted to feel the thrust of his hips beneath her hands, the shudder of his lean, hard body when he climaxed. Too much desire. She wouldn't be able to get enough of him.

With a murmur of sheer delight, Elizabeth drew him into her mouth yet again, as deeply as she could take him. Her tongue simultaneously danced along the underside of his shaft, where the vibration of blood surged in tandem with the ever-quickening beat of his pulse.

Above her, his breath ripped from his chest in violent, sporadic pants. "Oh…" he whispered, "oh…God…stop!" His hands cupped her face to free himself from her lips and he dropped to his knees before her, his hands shaking as they grasped her thighs. "You're going to make me come if you keep that up."

Elizabeth didn't care. She wanted him to come, over and over, as many orgasms as his young body could relinquish. With an intensity bordering on desperation, she craved the hot jolt of his ejaculation against the back of her throat, the hard shake of his muscles in response. It was something she hadn't shared with her ex-husband, an intimacy he'd never allowed. Stuart hadn't particularly liked oral sex...giving or receiving.

She'd been so starved. How could she have ever lived without this pleasure?

As Boone knelt before her, her hands swept down to recapture his arousal, her lips finding the warm, moist curve of his neck, where the tendons stood out with the stress of withheld desire. "Boone—please let me."

"I will. I will," he whispered, gently removing her hand and lifting it to his reverent kiss. "But we have all night."

One night couldn't possibly be enough. Now that they'd started, she wanted it to go on and on until she'd expended every last ounce of lust and need and searing desire that had built in her since the moment he'd first walked into her office.

Letting him urge her back against the rumpled, Boone-scented pillows, she drew off her bra, let it fall among the sheets, and held out her arms. He knelt over her, mouth hot and hungry as he sought her kiss.

Chapter Eight

Elizabeth didn't allow herself to feel self-conscious in her thirty-six-year-old woman's body. This night was too precious to taint it with uncertainty and hesitation. And the way Boone looked at her, the way his gaze skimmed worshipfully over her naked skin in the golden wash of the lamplight, made her feel more beautiful than she ever had at a lithe twenty-one.

Bracing his hands on either side of her, he met her eyes, smiled into them, and eased himself down her body, mouth trailing a path of flames over her breasts, her stomach, to the soft curls of her mound.

"My turn," he murmured, and slid his hands between her thighs to press them apart.

Cool air brushed burning wetness, and Elizabeth instantly stiffened at the unequivocal exposure. "Boone—"

"You're beautiful," he whispered, gently nudging her fingers aside when she tried to cover herself.

"But—"

"I've thought about doing this so many times..." He dipped his dark head to brush his lips against her inner thighs, one, then the other, and back again. And when Elizabeth finally breathed again, he directed his searching mouth to her open, vulnerable flesh.

The fleeting kiss against her aching center shuddered through her, head to toe. How could something be so tender and decadent at the same time? Hot desire pooled low in her stomach and overflowed, sluicing into her pelvis, her thighs, swelling the tender, throbbing place where he now suckled her with lips and tongue.

Elizabeth's inhibitions caught fire, flamed, sizzled to a fine line of cinders, dwindling remnants of her repressed past. All she could think was, *nothing is better than this. I was made for this…*

And Boone was so damn good at it.

Her fingers wound into his thick, soft hair, caressing and grasping, following the slow wag of his head as he dragged his tongue back and forth across her quivering flesh. Sparkles danced behind her eyelids and her thigh muscles quaked as the pleasure built…and built…

Boone shifted on his elbows, glanced up at her with dazed, hot eyes, and returned to his ministrations, first lightly, then with more determination, his tongue a slick-rough spear of fire as it lapped at her, plunged inside her, then licked over her again, as though she were something savory, a delicacy to be relished for long, splendid hours.

She would die from the pleasure.

Over and over he bathed her with his tongue, in an ever-quickening rhythm, until Elizabeth no longer heard the whimpers torn from her throat, nor the low croon of the stereo floating from the living room. Her senses filled with the thunder of blood and pleasure and freedom, and then her hips arched off the mattress, bucking beneath his hands and mouth as she came, and came, and came.

*****

Someone was weeping and laughing at the same time.

Me, Elizabeth thought, and felt not one bit ashamed as she shivered with each aftershock of orgasmic pleasure. Her senses had only started to return to her, but the reality to which she awakened was too sweet to be anything but a dream.

The sound of rustling sheets brought her heavy eyelids open. Somnolent, she watched Boone edge up on the pillows beside her, his hair rumpled from her clutching, his green eyes sleepy and mouth curved with satisfaction.

"No fair," Elizabeth tried to say, but all that came out was a husky, indiscernible murmur.

"Stay just as you are," he whispered, rolling on top of her, and her over-sensitized nerve endings sent yet another jolt of pleasure through her as the hard tip of his erection nudged her slick folds.

"What are you going to do next?" she drawled, all stretchy and languorous as her thighs bracketed his hips.

"Anything you want." His voice sounded even. But when he dipped his head to capture her mouth, the barely restrained passion in his kiss, the plunge of his tongue and the desperate thrust of his pelvis against her spoke of fast-dwindling restraint.

She tasted herself on his lips and decided not to be embarrassed. Everything about him was so free, so untethered. He would teach her how to breathe again.

"What do you want me to do?" he whispered, the provocative question caressing her ear. "Just say it, Elizabeth. Say the words."

"I want you inside me."

His breathless laughter rushed over her in provocative waves. "Tell me another way. Not the poetic, polite way. Tell me what you really want me to do. I like to hear it."

She paused, sought his face for reassurance, titillated and mortified at the same time. "I don't ever use that word."

"But don't you think about it? Do it," he whispered, his tongue tracing her bottom lip. "Do it for me, Elizabeth."

It was such a small thing to ask. Elizabeth reached between them and traced a languid finger over the swollen head of his shaft. "Boone," she said, wrenching the forbidden phrase from some deep, shadowed place beneath layers of propriety, "I want you to fuck me."

"God, Elizabeth…" he groaned, half laughter, half desperation as he lunged against her. "Yes. You make me so hot."

His lips covered hers with sweet, aching fervor. Lacing their fingers together, he raised her arms above her head and pinned them against the pillows, forcing her breasts to arch, pebble hard, against his chest.

The thought of protection darted through Elizabeth's mind, but she didn't speak, just flowed with the graceful rocking of his body, and gradually became aware of his right hand rummaging in the night table drawer. He would take care of it, she thought driftingly. He would take care of her.

He sat back on his heels, his gaze never leaving her face as he rolled the condom over the head of his straining penis with deft fingers.

Before he could move from his position, she sat up, nipped his throat, her fingers tracing a path of chill bumps down his ribs to his hips, where they clutched and drew him to her.

Grasping the crook of her knee, he pressed her wide, led himself to her, and sank slowly inside her, deeper, deeper…until he was completely encased in liquid heat, and they both gasped with the searing pleasure of it.

Boone paused, every muscle held taut. "Oh," he said, lashes sinking closed as his head listed to the side, "unreal."

Oh yes. It felt too good. The wet, molten drag of his erection through her tender, lust-swollen tissues, the firm pressure of his groin against her clitoris with each downward undulation. Elizabeth bucked under him, spurring him on, eschewed his attempt to pace himself and forced him to drive down into a wild, erratic rhythm.

Wreathing his arms around her waist, he shifted her onto her hip, found leverage on his left elbow and thrust into her from the side, again, again, fierce in his abandonment, every feature flushed and tight with rapture.

The bed scooted against the floor, squeaked under the fervent act taking place on its broad expanse. Elizabeth braced one hand against the wall above her head, pushing back at

Boone's thrusts with equal vigor while a ferocious voice in her head chanted, *deeper…deeper.*

As though sensing her need, he complied and quickened his movements, a breathless groan of exertion and pleasure escaping his lips. "Elizabeth—oh yes."

The sweet sounds of a man's complete helplessness in the climb to ecstasy. She wanted to revel in it, store away this moment of supreme feminine triumph, but her orgasm washed over her with alarming suddenness.

She hadn't seen it coming, had only sensed the unruly tension building within her while she savored the driving plunge of his body. Now it shuddered through her, fierce, astonishing in its power, and Boone took her cries into his mouth, breathed them in, before he surged against her one last time, then clutched her tight.

Elizabeth counted the hard shudders of his climax, smiled against his damp shoulder as he buried his face in the curve of her neck and uttered a hoarse, vulnerable sound. Her name, maybe. Something unintelligible that told her how very good it was.

"Boone," she whispered at last, stroking the wet, curling hair at the nape of his neck. "I'm going to fall in love with you, too."

*****

Sunlight poured through the sheers, blinding and cheerful. Elizabeth opened her eyes and squinted at it, lost for an instant.

Boone. His scent was all around her, but he wasn't beside her. The cheerful male/female chatter of two morning radio hosts floated to her ears, followed by the soft clink of glass and the splash of water in a sink. He was in the kitchen.

She stretched, snuggled into the soft pillows and glanced around the room. The walls, painted a soft, buttery yellow, held an array of framed photographs. Family gatherings, a collage of high school candids, football pictures. Two beautiful, dark-haired teenagers in spaghetti straps, holding bouquets of white roses and smiling Boone's smile. God, was his whole family this gorgeous?

"Boone?" she called, wondering if he'd hear her sleep-husky voice over the yammering of the radio.

A rustle of newspaper, the scraping of a chair across tile, and he appeared in the doorway, a joyful fantasy come true in Looney Toons boxer shorts and nothing else.

"Morning," he said, a slow, shy smile creeping across his mouth.

"Good morning." Inexplicably self-conscious, she sat up, brushed her hands through her disheveled hair, and hugged the sheet to her breasts. "Are you a coffee drinker?"

"I'm an orange juice drinker." Before she could groan, he added, "But I'll pull out the coffee maker just for you."

"No hurry. I'm still asleep. My wake-up process takes a solid five minutes."

He rubbed a hand over his bare chest and sauntered toward her. "Mind if I watch?"

"Be my guest."

He sat down on the mattress beside her. "You have the biggest, brownest eyes I've ever seen. You're a beautiful woman, Dr. Gilstrom."

"Please," she said, but delight curved her mouth. Then, more soberly, "Last night was amazing."

"Mm-hm." He leaned in, brushed his lips against hers, then kissed his way down the side of her neck to her shoulder. "It doesn't have to end yet, does it?"

Her head listed to the side, heavy with pleasure. "Technically the night *is* over."

"But I'm not finished with you."

"Thank God," she sighed, and let the sheet drop to her lap, exposing her breasts to his warm, cupping hands.

He leaned to nuzzle one hardened nipple, then withdrew to study her face. "Spend the day with me, Elizabeth."

"I have a lecture to give. You have a lecture to attend," she said sternly. "Don't you dare skip my class this afternoon."

"I'll be there. I'll sit in the back and think about all the places on your body I didn't taste and touch last night."

"I didn't think you left a single stone unturned. And I have the sore muscles to prove it."

He traced a finger across the tops of her breasts, reddened where his beard stubble had chafed her. "Is my youthful exuberance too much for you?"

"Oh no," she whispered. "Never." Her nose found its way into the warm curve of his neck and they sat like that, drunk on love's potential, until Boone finally stirred and sat back to look at her.

"Last night put ideas in my head. Romantic notions. But I won't ask where we're going with this yet."

"I might be able to tell you if you answer one question for me."

"Shoot," he said, caressing her cheek with the back of his fingers.

Elizabeth closed her eyes, pulse racing. She had to know. She stood on the precipice of the deepest chasm, and one step in the wrong direction might shatter her. "What's your relationship with Amanda Hastings?"

He didn't answer right away, just sat there, his green gaze searching hers. In the sunny glow filtering through the sheers, he looked younger than any twenty-four-year-old she knew.

After a beat, he sighed and straightened. "I dated her for a while."

"What's a while?"

"Three or four months. We broke up over the summer. I think of her as a good friend, Elizabeth. That's all."

"But that painting..."

"Yes, the painting. I started it when she and I first began seeing each other last year. I guess you could say I was caught up in the moment."

"It'd be hard to avoid," Elizabeth said dryly. "My God, Boone. The girl is gorgeous."

"She's beautiful. But I told you before, to me, looks don't mean everything."

She made a face at him. "Spoken like a true Adonis."

Boone smiled, moved forward to kiss her. But she wasn't done.

"So it was an intense relationship?"

His brows drew down. "I suppose. At times, anyway."

"Was it a full-blown affair?" She retrieved the sheet, covered her breasts and pinned the linen firmly beneath her arms. "I know I'm asking too many personal questions."

"It's okay," he said gently. "If you need to know these things to feel comfortable with me, then ask. I have no secrets."

Elizabeth didn't hesitate. "So you slept with her."

"And after a few weeks, when I figured out it was all we had going for us, I called it off. She's a nice girl, bright and kind-hearted. But she wasn't for me. And now we're friends."

"Friends who hold hands," she ventured, watching his face.

Boone returned her steady gaze. "Elizabeth, don't accuse me of lying in that roundabout way of yours. You and I have a long way to go before we know each other, and you're just going to have to trust me."

She released the breath she was holding and nodded. "I do trust you."

"I'm not Stanley."

"Stuart," she said, and they both burst into laughter.

He caught her chin and kissed her lips, a lingering, tender caress. "I won't hurt you," he whispered.

"Okay," she said, tears pricking her eyes.

"Want that coffee now? Or a long, hot shower?" He tugged the sheet loose from its mooring beneath her arms and trailed his fingertip down the slope of her breast to her nipple. "Or how about we just go back to bed and see how many more dirty words the learned Elizabeth Gilstrom, PhD knows?"

She shivered, her flesh tightening to arousal beneath his caress. "Can't I have all three?"

Boone pressed her back against the pillows, lifting his hips obligingly while she tugged his boxers down his thighs. "Oh, Professor," he murmured as she closed her fingers around his erection, "you can have whatever you want from me. Haven't you figured that out yet?"

* * * * *

In all of Elizabeth's thirty-six years—including an arid decade of marriage to Stuart—she'd never had sex under the hot beat of a showerhead. The mere, thrilling idea of it sent trembles coursing through her as she stood naked behind Boone in the bathroom and waited for him to adjust the water temperature.

"I've never done this before," she told him as he held aside the curtain for her.

"Just think of how you're helping the environment," he replied. "Haven't you heard the old adage, 'Save water, bathe with a friend'?"

Steam billowed around them inside the spacious tile stall and enfolded them in a humid embrace as Elizabeth ran her hands over Boone's wide shoulders, following the water's path down his muscled chest to his abdomen.

"You're the beautiful one," she said, letting her gaze roam the golden texture of his skin, dark where the sun had touched, pale in the more tender places. "I feel drugged just looking at you."

Boone smoothed back her dripping hair and kissed her until they were both gasping. "Turn around," he said. "I'll do your back."

And more, it turned out, with the slightly invasive help of a condom he'd thought to set on the shelf by the shower.

"Bend forward a little," came his breathless instruction behind her, and she complied, bracing her palms against the chilled tile wall. The water drummed down on them, as merciless and rhythmic as their driving desire. Boone dipped his knees, guided himself to her slippery-wet opening, and drove home.

This sexual position was another first for Elizabeth, and the first plunge he made inside her wrenched a sound of surprised pleasure from her throat. Each thrust jolted through her like a charge of electricity, so that her gasps came in breathless rhythm with the firm movement of his pelvis.

His wet, soapy hands cupped her breasts, caressing, exploring, while behind her he rotated his hips in slow, sinuous circles. She felt the sliding movement of his penis all the way to the top of her head. "Oh my God."

"You feel so good," he whispered, and catching her hand, led it down her torso, between her thighs to the slick, hot place where their bodies joined. "Come with me."

"Where?" she asked foggily, and when he didn't answer, she turned her face slightly to catch him laughing. Embarrassment washed over her in waves of fiery heat. "I didn't know what you meant, Boone. I may be older, but I'm not as—as sexually sophisticated as you."

She tried to withdraw, but he held her fingers tight between her thighs, keeping contact with the steady thrust of his shaft inside her.

"I'd be happy to educate you." Between her thighs, his hand guided her fingers up and around her swollen clitoris. "Come with me, Elizabeth," he repeated softly.

Mutual orgasm was something she'd only read about, and hadn't thought possible for herself, but Boone broke down her antique notions with his lack of inhibition, pushed aside her barriers with his gentle insistence.

Her head dropped back against his chest. "If you want this to be mutual," she said breathlessly, "you'd better catch up."

"I'm with you." His mouth hovered against her ear, his free hand encircling her throat. "Is now good for you?"

"Yes. Boone!" Stars danced behind her eyelids, rapture stripped her ability to stand under the convulsive waves rolling through her muscles, and Boone held her tight against his hot, hard body, moving like a piston inside her.

In the midst of it, she turned her head, arched back and took his quick, panting breaths into her mouth, his fierce, final thrust into the heart of her womb. And drifted in the wrenching sound of his pleasure as it echoed off the surrounding tile.

* * * * *

Elizabeth moved in a dream state, withdrawing clothes from her closet and spreading them out on the king-sized bed. Her muscles complained pleasantly. The silk blouse sliding over her skin made her shiver, every nerve alive as though for the first time. When she glanced down to button it, she saw a tiny red mark on the pale slope of her breast and smiled. Graffiti. *Boone McCrea was here.*

Her staff advisory meeting was scheduled in an hour, but the thought did nothing to hurry her. She wouldn't be able to concentrate anyway. Her fellow instructors would most likely question her changed demeanor. What had happened to Elizabeth the Solemn? Elizabeth the Droll and Somber? She had nothing to say for herself.

After a half-hearted attempt at lunch and yet another interlude of lovemaking—this time in the hallway, as Boone had promised—he had dropped her off at her house and left to run errands, giving her a chance to prepare for the day and to call Turner Imports. Then he would return to pick her up and take her to campus. She didn't know what people would think if they saw her in Boone's Jeep. She didn't care.

Never in her wildest imaginings had she known sex could be so untamed, so concurrently frenzied and tender and excruciatingly pleasurable as it had been with Boone. The woman in the mirror smiled back at Elizabeth with flushed, softened features, with glowing eyes and kiss-reddened lips. A happy woman, well loved and content to her very soul. Age didn't matter, nor sexual prowess. Only this piquant joy that colored the world around her a sweet, golden iridescence, rendering it a place where true love could be found.

Elizabeth found she couldn't even be cross with the manager at Turner Imports when she called to complain about the Mercedes. The man, a jolly Hispanic fellow, apologized profusely and blamed it on himself, since he was responsible for the quality of the mechanics' work. She immediately forgave him and made arrangements to have a tow truck return the Mercedes to his care. All was well with the world.

And then Stuart showed up.

Chapter Nine

He rang the doorbell. Stuart never rang the doorbell.

Thinking it was Boone returning early—and that they could quickly christen her king-sized bed with a round of lovemaking that Stuart's overly-firm mattress had never seen—she rushed down the stairs in the silky shirt and nothing else, and threw open the door.

"Liz," Stuart exclaimed, his black eyebrows nearly disappearing into his hairline.

Instantly her enthusiasm crashed to the ground, incinerated. "Whom did you expect?"

"Whom did *you* expect?" he shot back, lips thinned with displeasure.

Good question. Supremely self-conscious, she stepped back and allowed him into the slate-tiled foyer. "You could've called."

"I did. Your cellular phone's been disconnected. I just came from the real estate agent's office…here's her card."

Elizabeth took it and glanced down at the toothy, ultra-coiffed blonde pictured on the business card. "Say, Stu, she looks like your type."

"Stop it," he snapped. "Put on some clothes and then we'll talk."

Upstairs, she jammed her legs into a pair of tweed pants and tucked in her beige blouse, anger vibrating every nerve in her well-loved body. Only Stuart had the power to rob her of the fragile joy she'd found in Boone's arms. Love and hate were so very entwined. Now that she'd crossed the line with her former husband, she could hardly look at him without feeling nauseated, and there was no going back.

He was pacing the living room Oriental when she descended the stairs.

"What do you want?" she asked, resting a shoulder against the door molding.

"Jane Vestley thinks she can sell the house for at least ten thousand more than we'd thought," he said. "I want to use her for the sale."

"Be my guest. It doesn't matter who you use, just as long as we get this over with."

Stuart narrowed his eyes. "You look different. What did you do, dye your hair?"

Automatically her hand went to her head, but she shook off the rush of self-consciousness he magically invoked with the single, off-handed remark. "I've done nothing different."

"You look rested." The idea seemed to disturb him.

Elizabeth smiled. "Anything else?"

"I need the rest of my things."

Turning on her heel, she crossed the foyer and opened the coat closet, grasped the handle of a bulging, cumbersome suitcase, and hauled it to the middle of the floor. "Anything else?"

"All my things are in that suitcase?" Two red spots appeared high on his clean-shaven cheeks. "Clothes, documents, everything?"

Elizabeth threw a pointed glance at the fireplace.

"Oh Christ, Liz. You didn't burn anything, did you?" Panicked, he started across the living room and squatted by the marble hearth, peering in at the mysterious lump of ashes in the grate. "Elizabeth, so help me God—"

"I burned our honeymoon photograph album. I didn't think you'd mind." She glanced at her watch, raised her eyebrows. "Is that all you wanted? I'm on my way out the door to class."

Scowling, he rose and swept by her to grab the suitcase in the foyer. "You were always disagreeable. I just didn't realize how much until now."

"It's a good thing you didn't waste any more time finding out," she said pleasantly, and reached for the doorknob to usher him out.

Boone stood on the other side with a smile that said he'd hurried to get back to her. "Hi."

She tried to reply, to warn him, but only managed to draw a breath before Stuart peered over her shoulder. "May we help you?"

For a moment, no one spoke. Boone's gaze darted from Elizabeth's burning face to the man lurking behind her, and she could see the realization flashing before his mind's eye. His smile faded and his brows lowered. "I'm here to take Elizabeth to work."

"Who are you?" Stuart demanded.

"Boone McCrea. Her student. Who are *you*?"

"Her husband."

Boone glanced back at Elizabeth, his green eyes searching hers. "You still need that ride to work, Professor?"

"Yes. Stuart was just leaving. Let me grab my things." She hated to abandon Boone like that, leave him subject to Stuart's x-ray vision, but everything inside her screamed to act casual. Ducking under Stuart's arm, she dashed upstairs, collected her briefcase, and flew down again, praying for peace.

"Why does Elizabeth need a ride from you?" she heard Stuart ask Boone as she flung open the door and stepped out.

"Why do you need to know?" Boone's response was cool and easy, without an ounce of give.

Elizabeth stepped between the two men. "The Mercedes is in the shop, Stuart. Not that it's any of your business." Her smile felt like a paste-on as she nodded at Boone. "Ready?"

He didn't answer, just flipped his key ring around a finger and strolled ahead of her toward his Jeep, where he waited for her at the passenger door.

Elizabeth followed him down the walk. "Lock up, will you, Stu?"

"I'll be in touch," Stuart said, his black gaze drilling between her shoulder blades.

* * * * *

"He just showed up," she spoke through gritted teeth, staring out at the houses they passed as Boone maneuvered the Jeep out of her neighborhood and onto the highway. "I was so ill-prepared. It's like he has radar. Is it going to be like this from now on? The moment I'm happy, he'll just *pop up*. God only knows what kind of rumors he'll spread, just to be vindictive."

Silence greeted her tangent, and she turned her head to examine Boone's profile. A muscle flicked in his jaw, his hands white-knuckled on the steering wheel.

"I'm sorry I rocked the boat," he said.

"No, Boone." She reached out and touched his arm, curved her fingers around his smooth, muscled biceps. "There's no boat to rock. Stuart left me, remember? What I choose to do with my life is none of his business."

"I don't give a damn what he thinks. He's a bastard. It's you I worry about." He glanced at her, his gaze troubled. "You acted so freaked out. Do you know how nervous you looked?"

"A typical response to my ex-husband," she said quickly, trying to brush off his sober observation.

But Boone shook his head. "I didn't know what to say, Elizabeth. Standing there on your doorstep, it occurred to me that maybe I've been too quick with this." He swallowed and moved his hand away from the console before she could grasp it. "I'm assuming—no, realizing—that maybe you don't want people to know about us. That maybe people *shouldn't* know about us."

Elizabeth opened her mouth to argue, but no words would come. She wasn't ashamed of her relationship with him, but she wasn't ready to announce it and weather the resulting storm, either. She didn't exactly know what consequences instructors paid for having affairs with their students. There were no guidelines, no one to ask about a situation like hers and Boone's. Maybe it would cost her job. And she had no idea if the sweet promise of things to come with Boone was enough collateral to sacrifice her security.

He, too, lapsed into silence. Eventually they pulled up at a stoplight beside a banana-yellow Cabriolet filled with tanned, unruly teenaged girls. Boone ignored the redhead behind the steering wheel when she gave her horn a little push and flashed him a come-hither smile. He busied himself inserting a Creed CD into the stereo, while Elizabeth glared at the teenagers over his dark head.

And suddenly, the years between twenty-four and thirty-six stretched wider, wider…until Elizabeth felt as though she sat beside a stranger. The man who had driven her to ecstasy over and over in the last few hours, the man who had touched her and tasted her and offered her his heart seemed more distant than any span of age could ever place him.

"Boone?"

"Yeah?" His sculpted profile revealed nothing.

"I don't know what to say," Elizabeth muttered.

He didn't meet her eyes again.

Thirty minutes later, he pulled the Jeep into a sparsely populated section of the faculty parking lot, turned off the stereo and set the brake. "I'll let you out here."

She swallowed against the lump in her throat. He was dropping her off in a place where she wouldn't be seen climbing from his car. "You don't have to do this."

"It's the one thing I wondered about where you're concerned." His gaze fixed on some far-off spot beyond the windshield. "The only thing that stopped me when I thought about pursuing you. But last night I decided it was worth the risk. Maybe I was wrong."

"What are you saying?" She sat forward, grasped his chin and forced him to meet her eyes. "Boone, what are you talking about?"

"The repercussions if anyone on campus finds out about us," he said. "Maybe we should think this over a little more carefully. Sex does funny things to people, especially the kind of sex you and I had last night."

"You think we're rushing?" It stabbed through her, swift and breathtaking.

"I've never been one to mind rushing in. I do whatever my heart tells me. But after seeing your face—and your husband's…"

Panic clenched her stomach. "He's not my husband."

Boone closed his eyes, sighed, rubbed a weary hand between his brows. "You're going to be late for lecture."

"Are you saying you don't want to continue what we started last night?"

"I don't know."

"Please don't do this, Boone." Tears choked her words. She couldn't help it. The mere idea of losing him was more intense a pain than anything she'd ever experienced. She was falling in love with this man. And now that her heart was on the line, she wasn't about to remind him of that obviously inconsequential detail.

Anger clawed its way up from deep within her. Rage to the rescue.

"Your timing is lousy, you know." Her voice rose in the Jeep's silent interior, pinched with the effort to withhold tears. "It makes me suspect you just wanted to get your ol' college professor in the sack. Quite a feat, huh? How do I know one of your buddies didn't put you up to it? If so, I hope you won a sizeable till to make all this trouble worth your while."

"Come on, Elizabeth. Stop it."

Her wry humor faltered and she glared at him through swimming eyes. "You just expect me to trust you now? God, Boone—most men your age are out there doing all sorts of damage to tender hearts everywhere while they sow their wild oats. Why should you be any different?"

"Because I am." He spoke firmly, his troubled gaze steady on hers as he draped his forearm across the steering wheel. "I'm different. The way I feel about you is different, Elizabeth, and you know it."

A silence born of indignation and frustration simmered in the space between them.

Then he stirred and reached down to turn the key in the ignition. The engine rumbled to life, a subtle and hurtful cue for Elizabeth's departure.

"I need some time to absorb all this…and so do you. Up until last night, you fought this thing between us like the plague. You need to back up and decide if I'm what you really want, Elizabeth. Because I'm nothing like what you've known before, and your whole life will change if people find out. People will judge you for all the reasons you fear. Then this thing will be real, and if you don't…"

He stopped, wrapped his fingers around the steering wheel and looked away from her. "If we get to that point, and then you decide you don't feel the way for me that I do for you, you'll hate me for it. You'll hate yourself, and you'll break my heart."

Elizabeth just sat there, watching his beautiful, troubled face while waves of grief clenched her stomach. Damn him. Damn him for his decency and patience and for acting different than any other man who'd walked through her life.

She hated him for it. She hated him for making her fall in love again, and then leaving her in limbo like this to face her own fears.

Amidst her building fury, a frantic need to taste his lips, to reestablish her own power in the situation, drew her over the console.

In the back of her distressed mind, she heard him say, "Elizabeth…" An encouragement, a rejection—it could have been either. It didn't matter.

Scrambling to her knees, she crushed her mouth down on his, with broad daylight, the parking lot and the world surrounding them an intrusive, faraway audience.

Any reticence on Boone's part melted away when her tongue dipped against his, and his hands grasped her waist, drawing her toward him as though he were as defenseless against the passion between them as she.

There wasn't enough room for Elizabeth to straddle him, but he fumbled with the seat adjustment anyway, slid it back and reclined it, pulling her down with him at an awkward angle. Her hand slid between them and jerked open the buttons of his Levi's, yanked at the waistband of his boxers. He was already hard when she freed his penis and closed her fingers around it.

Distant voices, youthful and female, carried to her ears from outside the Jeep, and she didn't care. All that mattered was this, the feel of his cock in her hand, the power it granted her, a deceptive, injurious power, because she would hurt ten-fold when she was done exerting it.

"People are walking by—" Boone tried to say, but she opened her mouth against his and drank in his protest. She stroked him, quick and steady, instantly establishing a strong rhythm that would drive him to orgasm in a matter of breaths.

Boone's head arched against the car seat, his left knee banging once against the driver door as his fingers buried themselves in her hair.

"Not like this," he whispered against her lips, gentling the ravenous, brutal thrust of tongues, the pressure with which she ate at his mouth. "Not in anger, Elizabeth."

She drew back an infinitesimal distance and looked at him with stinging, blurred eyes, her hand's rhythm unfaltering on his erection. "How does it feel to be so out of control, Boone? To know you have no power over what someone else does to your body, your desires?"

He grasped her hand, stilled it, even as his body shuddered in subconscious protest. "I'm not the one who hurt you, Elizabeth. Don't take this out on me."

She tried to jerk away, but he caught her wrist. "I'm not the one who left you," he said firmly. "Touch me out of love, out of caring, because you want to bring me pleasure. Because it brings you pleasure. But not to get back at the people who've hurt you."

Hot tears squeezed between her closed eyelids and she swallowed hard. "You're no different. No better."

"I am." His hand left hers, lifted to brush the loose wave of hair behind her ears. Then he reached to turn off the engine. "Come here. Let me show you."

"No."

But she didn't fight him when he sat up and drew her over the console onto his lap. His attention focused on her face as though life had stalled all around them, as though the sunlight didn't spotlight them in the middle of the parking lot, and they weren't in danger of being caught by a passing student or campus employee.

Elizabeth acquiesced woodenly, allowing him to hold her, cursing him for stripping her down to vulnerability. He wielded tenderness like a weapon, and it ravaged her fragile hold on her emotions. "What are you doing?"

"Touching you the way I want to be touched. Put your hand on me again." He cradled her head in the crook of his neck, fingers working between them to free her belt and the zippered placket of her pants.

Before she could think, protest, scramble away, his hand had wedged itself inside her pants and between her thighs, his gentle touch easing beneath the elastic of her panties.

One stroke and Elizabeth nearly forgot why she hadn't wanted this. Her fingers curled around his penis again, slid up and down, then faltered as unbidden waves of pleasure assaulted her senses.

"I won't come," she said between clenched teeth, a final, rebellious declaration before ecstasy pulverized her ability to argue.

In reply, his finger burrowed inside her, and he pressed his lips against her damp forehead as he stroked and caressed her shamefully wet flesh, her aching heart.

Somehow, as though her hand had a mind of its own, it resumed its pulsing rhythm on his hard shaft.

Boone groaned his satisfaction, and the power that suffused Elizabeth this time was crystalline and euphoric, a woman's triumph in her lover's pleasure.

The heavy desire flooding her pelvis wound tight, tighter; the movement of her fingers on him quickened, mirroring his caress within her body.

Several thunderous heartbeats passed and his hips shifted beneath her weight in strong, primal response to her touch.

"Faster," he breathed, free hand clutching her hair to hold her lips against his throat. She bit him gently, drawing on the warm skin of his neck, tasting the salt and sweetness of his flesh, until ecstasy grabbed her consciousness and all she could do was strain for more, and more…

Elizabeth's orgasm came first, shuddered and bucked through her with piercing potency. Boone followed, his shaft surging within her hand as hot, pulsing droplets jetted against her fingers and up the front of his shirt.

Only the harsh tear of their breathing rent the silence. The scent of semen and desire, Elizabeth's perfume and Boone's warm skin filled the air. Despite the humid interior of the Jeep, she shivered.

After a moment, she shifted off his lap with little aplomb, her anger gone, passion drained, leaving nothing but a spiraling sadness.

He *was* different. He was the only man who'd ever made her feel complete. And despite his good intentions, the excruciating intimacy they'd just shared hadn't dissolved the distance between them.

She found a wad of napkins in the glove compartment, handed Boone several, cleaned herself up, then methodically fastened her pants and belt. When she was done, she turned to regard him, watching the smooth, muscled skin of his stomach disappear as he tucked in his shirt and buttoned his jeans. Last night she'd kissed him there, in playfulness, then in sensual exploration.

"I'm late for lecture," she murmured. "I have to go."

Boone didn't reply.

Elizabeth opened the passenger door, turned to slide out...and felt his hand at the nape of her neck, gently beseeching.

"Kiss me goodbye," he said hoarsely.

She couldn't help herself. She leaned back and met his lips, too choked to breathe, to soak in the warmth of his mouth, the hungry, desperate way he kissed her. His hair was thick and silky beneath her fingers, and she couldn't appreciate what might be her last chance to caress it.

"Let me go," she choked, jerking from his embrace. And when she climbed out of the Jeep and fled across the parking lot, he didn't follow.

*****

He skipped lecture. He *skipped* it. Not just on Wednesday after dropping her off, but Friday, too. And all weekend—silence. He knew how to reach her, but he hadn't called. He hadn't come by, and she didn't know what he wanted. Space? Or her?

On the following Wednesday, Aunt Barbie called.

"How are you, dear?" she asked in a careful, concerned tone she usually saved for the infantile, the elderly, or the just plain mentally unstable.

"I'm great." Moving like an automaton, Elizabeth rummaged through a tackle box of old oil paints and pitched several dried-up tubes into the trash as she talked. "The house is on the market, Stuart's totally moved out, and…oh, yes. I had a brief fling with a much-younger man, but it didn't work out."

Aunt Barbie's surprised silence gave Elizabeth a solid jolt of satisfaction. When it crossed her mind that the older woman might have keeled over with a heart attack, she added, "Oh, Aunt Barbie, I'm just kidding."

"That's not funny, Elizabeth."

A humorless smile twisted her lips as she examined an unopened tube of Alizarin Crimson. "Not even a little?"

"Stuart says you had one of your male students out at the house a few days ago."

"Stuart's jumping to conclusions. Besides, the *man* who was at my house was there to give me a ride." A partial truth, and the best she could manage. Feeling guilty, she added, "Anyway, he's a grad student, only twelve years younger than I am, as compared to Cecilia Aldorf being—what, twenty years younger than Stuart? People in glass houses, and all that good stuff. Stuart's a hypocrite."

Aunt Barbie sighed, a weary sound of resignation. "Don't even joke about fooling around with some young boy. People will believe you. A woman of your age and social status just doesn't—"

"Women of my age and social status do all sorts of naughty things. I've been a very good girl all my life, Aunt Barbie. Don't you think that in my time of crisis, I deserve to leap off the deep end?"

"You're worrying me," Aunt Barbie said in a hushed tone. "You sound like someone I don't know."

"I *am* someone you don't know. When I'm ready to introduce myself, I'll call you." And quietly, firmly, Elizabeth hung up the phone.

Chapter Ten

The campus gallery hummed with polite laughter and steady conversation, as fifty or more faculty members and students roamed the brick-walled room, studying the gargantuan, abstract canvases of a visiting Croatian artist whose name Elizabeth could hardly pronounce.

She had agreed to meet John and Betsy Weinburg at the opening reception, unable to face a weekend filled with more loneliness, more of Boone's silence. Now she regretted it; weariness seeped through her bones, despite the fact that she'd taken a long, hot shower before returning to campus for the opening reception.

"How about a glass of wine?" John asked, as the trio lingered in the entry and scanned the milling crowd.

"I'd love one," Betsy said dryly. "It's the only thing that gets me through these bizarre abstract shows."

Elizabeth smiled. "You two go on. I'm going to give the show a cursory glance, maybe say hello to a few people and sneak out."

"Are you all right?" Betsy, maternal and quick to worry, pressed a palm against Elizabeth's cheek. "You feel warm."

"Just tired." More than she'd realized. Maybe thoughts of Boone and what could have been wouldn't keep her awake tonight after all. Being depressed expended an exorbitant amount of energy.

"I'll catch up with you before I leave," she told her friends, and when they had disappeared in the crowd around the hors d'oeuvre table, she began her dutiful trek through the display of contemporary canvases.

After making small talk with several colleagues, she stopped before a ten-foot-wide painting of bold geometric shapes and let her gaze drift over the other attendees. A niggling part of her had been worried she might run into Boone, but he would jump out in a monochromatic crowd like this with his dark hair and wide shoulders, and so far she hadn't seen him.

Offering a passing couple a distracted smile, she rounded a display wall and ran headlong into Amanda Hastings.

"Hi, Dr. Gilstrom," the blonde chirped. "Were your ears burning? Boone McCrea and I were just talking about you."

Elizabeth opened her mouth to respond, and found herself struck dumb when Boone approached from behind Amanda's shoulder.

His burgundy crewneck sweater electrified the green of his eyes. He'd gotten his hair trimmed some time in the last few days, and the idea filled Elizabeth with an inexplicable resentment.

For a moment, they just looked at each other. Then, aware of Amanda's confused regard bouncing between them, Elizabeth broke the connection and affected a polite smile.

"Well, well, Mr. McCrea. You've been skipping class."

"It's been a rough week," he said, his voice low and humorless. He obviously wasn't going to make this easy on her.

"I told him to talk to you, Dr. Gilstrom," Amanda shifted her weight to one chunky-heeled boot, her myriad silver bracelets jangling on her slender wrists as she cast Boone a doleful glance. "His uncle's sick, and Boone's been at the hospital all week with him."

Boone frowned. "Give me a minute to talk to the professor, Mandy, and I'll catch up with you. Why don't you go grab a beer?"

She shrugged. "Sure. I'll get one for you too."

When she had dissolved into the crowd, Boone's gaze pivoted to Elizabeth. "Care to take a stroll, Professor?"

She nodded, an incongruent mixture of concern and frustration tightening her throat. Why hadn't he come to her in the past week, told her what was happening in his life?

The anger that had built within her during his absence dispersed in tiny particles, blown away by confusion. She tried not to look at him as they sauntered around the show with heavy silence hanging between them.

Finally Boone said, "I know you don't understand."

Her jaw tightened. "Right. I don't."

"I told you we needed some space, but I wasn't purposefully avoiding you, Elizabeth. My uncle's heart attack just sidetracked me."

"You should've told me he was in the hospital," she said, annoyed at the telltale burning behind her eyes. "I would have understood."

"I know. I'm sorry. I didn't want to pile it on you with everything else you've got going on."

She slanted a doubtful look at him. "So you skipped an entire week of class, and worse, had sex with me several times directly preceding, without bothering to call after. If I hadn't run into you here, Boone, would I have heard from you again?"

"Of course." He stopped and faced her, his expression softening. "I couldn't stay away, even if I wanted to."

"When would I have seen you again?"

His brows lowered, and he actually had the audacity to look hurt at the suspicion in her voice. "I can't say exactly, but I would've called you."

"Well, that's a relief. Thanks for throwing me a tidbit. It's big of you."

She bit her lip and fell silent for fear of bursting into tears. Somewhere deep down, she wanted to believe him, but the wounded part of her, the part that had once trusted Stuart so blindly, wore a hardened shell.

Boone could have called, could have left her a voice-mail on her answering service, could have even sent a message through Amanda, damn it, because obviously he'd been in contact with *her* all week. But when it came down to the truth, he just hadn't bothered.

Elizabeth's feelings hadn't been important enough.

They paused at a triangle-shaped canvas, standing so close that his arm brushed hers. The familiar, clean scent of him drifted to her, enticed her senses, and automatically an unbidden curl of desire wound in her belly.

"I have a feeling," she said without looking at him, "that you don't wish to continue what we started last week."

Boone glanced at her, but she didn't meet his gaze. If she looked into his troubled, sensitive features, she'd cry.

"You're wrong, Professor. More than anything, I want to continue what we started last week. It's all I think about."

"So you're saying that your uncle's illness is the sole reason I haven't seen or heard from you?"

"I'm not saying that," he murmured. "Nor do I feel mistaken about putting distance between us while you sort out what you really want."

Anger snapped through her, sharp and refreshing. "You mean this silence has been all for my sake?" She gave a short, humorless laugh. "And you say *I'm* a martyr."

"Elizabeth—"

She finally looked at him, struggling to keep her voice low and controlled. "I'm too old to play games, Boone."

"It's not—"

"Why are you here with Amanda?"

It was his turn to look incensed. "Oh, come on."

"Are you seeing her, Boone?" Irrational jealousy bit into her, pulverizing her common sense with rapier claws. "Is she your rebound girl? Someone should clue her in so she can save face."

"I'm not going to explain anything to you when you're in this mood," he shot back. "If you want to fight, do it with somebody else. Your husband, for example. He's still hanging around, and he still cares, from the looks of it."

"I don't care if he crawls back on his knees—he's the wrong person for me. And it's becoming more obvious by the second that you are, too."

In the single, unguarded moment that her tight words ricocheted between them, Elizabeth saw Boone flinch.

Instantly regret rushed through her, made her stumble, desperate to take it back. She didn't mean it. Boone was more than right for her—he was the only man she wanted in the world.

Before she could retract the vehement declaration, he turned to study the painting, his profile shielded by a calm veneer that chilled her. "Funny how childish people can be, no matter how old they are."

Color flooded her face in a warm rush. "Isn't it my turn now? You've already had your chance to handle things poorly, just like a typical twenty-something."

His fingers closed around her elbow. "Stop it," he said through gritted teeth. "You're pissing me off."

Her pulse picked up speed, the knot of desire coiling tighter in her stomach. "Let go of me."

"Why?" His gaze narrowed on her burning face. "Afraid your esteemed colleagues will figure out what the honorable Dr. Gilstrom's been doing with one of her students? Come on, Elizabeth. Own up to your reckless behavior. No one's as perfect as you look. It's a long way down from the pedestal you've placed yourself on."

She stared at him, open-mouthed at his vehemence. Not wounded…amazed. Amazed that the color washing his cheeks, the bite in his words, were born of passionate emotion, a passion she'd stirred in him.

She stopped tugging at his hold, her attention rapt on his face. He *did* care. A bizarre flood of elation and sexual heat sluiced through her, and suddenly his grip around her arm eased into a silky caress, his regard a heated examination that swept down to her breasts and lingered, until her nipples tightened beneath the silk blouse, as though he'd touched her with cupping hands.

Boone stepped closer to her, his chest rising and falling with harsh, uneven breaths. His lashes dropped, lips parted, and she closed her eyes, braced for his kiss, oblivious of people passing by, of curious eyes and whispered speculation.

Just as suddenly, his fingers drifted away and cool air wafted across her features. She jerked awake. Boone had moved back. His green gaze swept the room over her head, then returned to her face, intense with a determination only a lover could understand.

He was thinking the same thing as she—sex. With her. Now.

But where?

After a terse moment of consideration, he tugged her toward a nearby corridor that led to the restrooms.

Elizabeth's heartbeat leaped into an erratic jig. "What are you doing?"

"Giving you what we both obviously need."

"What's that supposed to mean?" She tugged free, but kept walking toward the shadowed end of the hall, where the reception jazz music faded, and the sound of her own panting breath shattered the air around them. She knew what he wanted, what he planned, and she desired it just as much.

Never was a passionate rendezvous more inappropriate or poorly timed. And the anger between them had exploded into a need that drew her toward him like a dancer to rhythmic melody.

He paused between the ladies' and men's rooms to grasp her hand. "Your place or mine?"

"You're out of your mind," she retorted.

Ignoring her stubborn response, Boone pushed open the ladies' room door, leaned to check for feet beneath the stalls, then pulled Elizabeth none-too-gently inside and shut the door behind them, clicking the deadbolt into place.

"But someone could try to get in!" she hissed.

"Then you'll have to bite your tongue when I make you come," he said, and promptly pressed her up against the door, his hot, insistent hands pushing up her sensible wool skirt to bare her thighs.

Trembling with a mixture of excitement and panic, Elizabeth slapped at his fingers until he caught both her wrists in one hand and pinned them above her head.

He kissed her, tongue sweeping her mouth until she ceased struggling and softened beneath his ardent assault. She'd never seen him riled like this, never knew he could be so dark and volatile, and it stoked the fire between them, surged her pulse until it seemed molten blood would explode through her body.

In desperation he rocked against her, barricaded by her panties and the jeans he struggled to unfasten with one hand.

Elizabeth thrust back, angry, wild with pent-up emotion and starved for the feel of his hard body. She had no idea the frenetic press of his erection against her, even through layers of clothing, could stimulate her to orgasm. But her body, soaked with want and strained to the shattering point, arched and mimicked the cadence of his driving movements. Within feverish seconds she quivered under the steady friction and a fierce spasm of ecstasy shuddered through her, wrenching a cry from her throat.

It wasn't enough. Squirming from Boone's captive grasp, she shoved down her own panties, then helped him free his arousal with greedy, shaking fingers so she could stroke his shaft, the burning satin skin and granite rigidity that pulsed with every beat of his heart.

He bore the sinuous caress for a terse few seconds, then his hand closed over hers, guiding her into a firmer stroke, base to tip, again, again. A man showing a woman how to satisfy him. Elizabeth had never been taught, and beneath his tutoring her sensuality unfolded, her fingers dancing over his penis as though she'd been born to touch him.

"Oh..." his forehead dropped against hers, his breath leaving him in a rush. "Elizabeth..."

Abruptly, he jerked her fingers aside.

Now he would fill her, drive into her. Finally, finally. Elizabeth closed her eyes and braced for the lush invasion.

Instead, he guided the tip of his penis to nudge and tease at her wet entrance, then directed it to circle her clitoris, gliding on the moisture of her need.

She arched toward him, whimpered when he retreated. "Boone...now..."

"Say 'please'," he panted against her open lips.

"Oh God...*please*."

Crushing his mouth down on hers, he blindly found the wet, hot portal to her body, bent his knees and thrust inside her.

They both cried out.

Boone gave Elizabeth no reprieve. He plunged into her again and again, driving her against the door in hard, rhythmic thuds, his breath seesawing in perfect accompaniment to hers. No tender, solicitous caresses, no rationale. No condom.

For the first time in her life, Elizabeth didn't care. She hooked a leg around his buttocks and drove him on with mindless lover's words, counterthrusting, clinging to his shoulders and existing solely on the scent of his skin and passion.

Her fingers dug into the damp muscles of his back beneath his sweater, her teeth sank into the tender flesh of his throat bared by the crewneck. He tasted a little salty to her lapping tongue, clean, all male. She wanted to eat him alive, to draw him into her and hold him. Her young, beautiful, passionate lover.

In the midst of the tempest, he pulled back to met her gaze, his features flushed with exertion, muscles clenched. "I'm going to come."

"Yes," she whispered, threading her fingers through his hair as her own climax mounted. "Yes."

"Inside you."

"Yes."

"We can't—" He tried to withdraw, but she wreathed her arms around his waist and tugged him back, and his shaft slid wetly into place as though he'd never left her.

"It's okay, Boone," Elizabeth urged, pleasure stealing the breath from her words. "Come inside me."

He flattened his palms on either side of the door, thrust hard, and gave a violent shudder, his ejaculation pulsing in hot jets deep within her.

The searing, flooding pleasure of it, the primitive satisfaction of giving him his release and the starving need that had propelled them to this place of desperation, exploded over Elizabeth's senses and shoved her, too, into a spiraling orgasm.

Boone clutched her and his forehead dropped to her shoulder, a final shiver quaking through his body and into hers, as though they were joined not just sexually, but limbs, muscles, nerve-endings, souls. Then he sagged against her, and she held him, inhaling the uniquely male scent of his essence, of perspiration and soap and passion.

When he could speak again, he lifted his head and gazed at her with troubled eyes. "I'm sorry."

"Don't be sorry." She sighed and drew his head into the crook of her neck. "It was incredible."

"I couldn't hold back. It was over so fast."

A smile flitted across her lips. "Short and sweet. And every bit as satisfying."

After a somnolent moment, he straightened, eased her leg off his hip and reached behind him to grab a couple of paper towels. He handed her one and they cleaned up in silence, then he fastened his jeans, scraped his fingers through his hair, and said, "We used no protection."

"I know." Even though Elizabeth had remained on the Pill after Stuart left, the fact that she'd thrown caution to the wind so mindlessly bothered the conscientious place inside her. How could she be so careless?

"Don't worry about it, Boone." She mustered a fleeting smile. "I'm a big girl."

He straightened his sweater, waited for her to tuck in her blouse, then nodded at the door. "No one tried to get in."

"Good thing," Elizabeth agreed, painfully aware of the return of distance between them. They had coupled like animals in heat, and now no reassurance was forthcoming from either of them.

She fidgeted in the awkward stillness. There was so much she wanted to say, but all she could mete out was, "Amanda is probably looking for you."

He nodded. "There's nothing between Amanda and me, Elizabeth. You have to believe me. She's a good friend."

"But she wants more."

Boone didn't respond. It was the truth, they both knew it, and he had nothing to say.

Neither did she; defeat had caged her sentiments.

The chasm between them stretched and yawned.

"I'll slip out first," she said, motioning to the door. "When the coast is clear, I'll let you know."

Myriad emotions played across his features, too ephemeral for Elizabeth to grasp their meaning. "You don't want anyone to catch us," he said, like an afterthought. More of an observation than a question.

"It would create quite a stir." Her throat tightened with dismay.

Nothing had changed. All the passion in the world wasn't going to put them on the same page.

They stared at each other, Boone's expression indiscernible, Elizabeth's eyes stinging with tears of regret.

After a moment he said, "Go on," and stepped closer, holding the door ajar for her while she peeked out.

The corridor was empty. They slipped out of the restroom, walked in silence toward the gallery, and when they reached the threshold, Boone caught her sleeve.

"Elizabeth…"

"It's okay," she hurried, looking away from his probing gaze. "You don't have to say anything, Boone. Please. It's so painful. Let's just leave it at this."

He started to reply, but Amanda appeared like a golden nymph in the crowd, and Elizabeth stepped away from him, slipping from his grasp.

Somehow, she had to let him go.

"There you are," the blonde set a plastic tumbler of beer in Boone's hand. "So have you forgiven him, Dr. Gilstrom?"

Elizabeth smile was born of sheer irony. One small action—walking out of the bathroom with Boone beside her for all to see—would have sealed their relationship.

Instead she'd shattered it with her reticence.

She was the sorry one.

Chapter Eleven

The rain fell endlessly, turned the world gunmetal gray and washed away the crisp scents of autumn. Water pooled in shallow puddles at the edges of the sidewalks, overflowing in gutters clogged with brown, fallen leaves. The campus became a swampy, steel-colored landscape that fed into Elizabeth's despondency as though the weather itself monitored her mood.

She clenched her jaw and stared out the window at the rain pelting the evergreen shrubs. Ten minutes after class ended, she still sat at her desk in the empty lecture room, too distressed to do anything else. She wanted to go home, but big-toothed, big-boobed real estate agent Jane Vestley was showing the house to some unsuspecting couple who'd never known a true aggressive sell before today. While they were being victimized, she had nowhere to go, and all she could think about was Boone, absent from class yet again. Absent from her life.

A soft rustling from the doorway brought her head around, and her heart nose-dived at the sight of Amanda Hastings lingering just outside the classroom. "Dr. Gilstrom?"

Somehow Elizabeth dug deep enough to locate a polite smile. "Miss Hastings. Are you here to discuss our suspiciously absent Boone McCrea?"

"No. But he's planning to drop your class."

Elizabeth's heart jolted as she took another look at the young woman's somber expression. "Did his uncle pass away?"

"No." For once, Amanda's midriff was under wraps, her slender figure clothed in a skin-tight, ribbed sweater and jeans. She took a few steps inside, hesitated, then crossed to the desk and carefully laid something on the planning book.

Pearl earrings. Elizabeth's.

"I found them at Boone's apartment," Amanda said hollowly. "I've never seen the same design anywhere but on your ears. May I ask you a question, Dr. Gilstrom?"

Elizabeth stared at the earrings, her mouth dry, heart thrashing behind her breast. "I can't promise you I'll answer it."

"Fair enough." The blonde retrieved a chair by the wall and dragged it over to sit down across from Elizabeth. "I'm going to be really direct."

"Go for it," Elizabeth said, numb.

"Are you the woman Boone's been seeing?"

The silent seconds ticked by, while Elizabeth weighed which hurt more, her embarrassment at being found out by Amanda Hastings, or her shame at having ever doubted that Boone was worth the sacrifice she might have to make for his love.

She drew a breath and met Amanda's gaze. "Did he tell you?"

A little sound escaped the blonde's throat, so soft Elizabeth wasn't sure she'd heard it. "He wouldn't tell me anything. I live in the apartment complex behind the gymnasium. I was out running a couple of weeks ago and I saw you two in the parking lot. I couldn't believe it—I had no idea he was involved with anyone. But it was dark, and I wasn't sure who was with him until now."

Mortifying images of the torrid embrace she'd shared with Boone in the parking lot shimmied through her mind. Maybe Amanda had only seen them walking together, before Elizabeth turned to putty under his hands. Elizabeth wasn't about to ask.

"Then at the gallery show last Friday night—you both acted…well, I just never imagined it'd be you. After we ran into you, Boone clammed up. He had nothing else to say the rest of the night. We had plans to go out, but he just wanted to home after that." Distaste edged the younger woman's soft voice. "Do you love him then?"

Elizabeth closed her eyes. "Why?"

"Because I do. And if you don't, I'm asking you to leave him alone. Something's happened to him in the last few days. He's not himself." She shifted on the seat and looked away, as though she couldn't stand the sight of Elizabeth any longer. "I suppose you're wondering what I was doing at his apartment when I found your earrings."

"It's none of my business."

"But I know you're curious."

Elizabeth tried to swallow the lump in her throat and failed. "You're right. I would like to know."

"I was checking on him because he's been so quiet lately. That's what friends do, and that's all we are. But we used to be more, and my feelings for him haven't changed."

Her cornflower eyes narrowed on Elizabeth's face. "I don't know what's going on, Dr. Gilstrom. He won't tell me. But Boone's hurt, and that makes it my business. I love him, and I can guarantee I've felt that way about him longer than you have. He was never hurt or unhappy with me, and now he's miserable, and I think it's because of you. So if you don't want him, back off. How can I be any clearer than that?"

Her ferocity both surprised and impressed Elizabeth.

"You're right," she said finally, fingering the earrings on the desk in front of her. "Backing off would be the right thing to do."

She picked up the pearls, studied their unique, incriminating setting, let them roll on her trembling palm. When was the last time she'd eschewed doing "the right thing"? Elizabeth Gilstrom, Queen of the Right Thing. She felt her abdication coming, a wild hurricane of rebellion with Boone at the eye.

Rising, she forced herself to meet Amanda's scrutiny head-on. "May I ask you a question, Miss Hastings?"

"I guess."

"What do you plan to do with all this mind-boggling information you're now privy to?"

For a long time Amanda said nothing. Then she stood, returned the chair to its original spot by the wall, and shouldered her purse. "I don't even want to think about it. I'd never do anything to hurt Boone. Maybe he doesn't love me anymore, but he's my friend." She paused at the door and added, "That means I'd do anything to protect him."

Even report an instructor for immorally fraternizing with a student. Maybe there was a penalty for such a breach of conduct, maybe not. For Elizabeth, the bigger penalty lay in a life spent without Boone.

Amanda's threat skimmed over her head and dissolved. It didn't matter who knew. All she cared about was reclaiming the man who held her heart in his sensitive, artistic hands.

"Thanks for the wake-up call, Miss Hastings," she said, opening her purse to set the pearls inside. When she straightened again, Amanda was gone.

* * * * *

2002 Fall Faculty Art Show, the flier read. *For information on entering your work, contact John Weinburg at *2306.*

Elizabeth sat back and stared at the announcement she'd dug out of her campus mailbox. If ever there was a time to break free from her five-year artist block, this was it. Time to reclaim her life, her past...her future. She'd bought the paints, the canvas, set up a corner in the clean, empty garage.

Time was ticking, Jane Vestley was a real estate agent possessed. She'd performed countless showings of the house for the last three days, her maniacal determination spinning around her like a separate entity. The house would sell soon. And Boone was nearly beyond Elizabeth's reach, his silence like a vast, spiraling hole in her heart.

It was time.

Boone was bound to appear on campus sometime. Elizabeth spotted his Jeep parked by the art building on Tuesday

and found him in the art studio, perched on a metal st
front of his easel, his gaze glued to the canvas.

When she cleared her throat, he looked up, stared at h
an endless moment, then returned his attention to the ca
"It's done," he said.

She crossed the room, drinking in the sight of him
greedy eyes. His hair was swept back from his face as th
he'd shoved his fingers through it a hundred times in th
few minutes. His jaw seemed sharper, his features even
chiseled. The shadows under his eyes spoke of exhau
Maybe he'd been sleepless, too. She didn't like to envisio
unhappy and restless. Everything feminine in her want
reach out and comfort him.

"May I see it?" she asked when she reached him. A
nod, she slid around the easel and into his private works
where the scent and warmth that was wholly Boone s
through her senses and enfolded her in yearning. "It's
incredible."

The finest, most sensuous painting she'd ever se
student produce.

He turned his face toward her, so close that his
brushed her hair. "You look tired," he said softly.

She swallowed, kept her gaze fixed on the imag
Amanda sprawled and inviting. "So do you."

"I've been painting non-stop since Saturday. Finished
one and started something new, an abstract this time. W
your excuse?"

"I haven't been sleeping." The flat-out truth. If she tu
toward him even slightly, their mouths would col
"Something about heartache keeps a girl wide-eyed at night.

When it became painfully obvious that he couldn't mus
response, she added, "I have a favor to ask you."

"Oh?"

"The faculty art show is coming up in two weeks, a
want to enter a piece in the exhibition."

"That's great." Boone finally shifted back toward the canvas. She could breathe again, although the driving rhythm of her pulse stole nearly as much of her oxygen as his nearness. "What's the favor?" he asked.

"I want you to model for me."

His silence proclaimed his surprise. After a moment, he released a soft sigh and reached to shut off the glaring work light positioned at his left shoulder. "If you paint me and hang it in the gallery, people are going to talk."

"I couldn't care less."

"I don't think that's true."

"You don't know me well enough to say that," she said evenly. "Just because you take a woman to bed doesn't mean you know her heart."

He glanced down at his hands, paint-stained and calloused. "I guess not."

The awkwardness and yearning between them swelled. Restive, Elizabeth focused on his features and repeated, "I'd like you to model for me."

"And I appreciate the effort you're making to smooth things over between us, Elizabeth, but—"

"I don't want to smooth anything. I want to paint you. Your face fascinates me." She paused. "I'll pay you for your time."

Boone looked at her for the space of several heartbeats, and for once, she didn't let her gaze drift away from his direct regard. She stared back at him and read the uncertainty in his eyes, the wounds Amanda had spoken of. She'd hurt him with her reticence. And God help her, if he allowed it, she'd make it up to him with every ounce of passion that burned inside her.

"There's no charge," he said finally, the dry, familiar humor creeping back into his voice. "So what do you have in mind?"

Elizabeth crossed her arms over her breasts and finally returned her gaze to the canvas. "I don't know yet. Why don't you come to the house tonight and we'll talk about it."

"I can't," he said. "I have plans."

All her confidence liquefied and seeped away. "Oh. Of course. I didn't mean to sound presumptuous. When would be good for you?"

"How about tomorrow night? Soccer practice is tonight and then I have to study. My art history professor gives too damn many pop quizzes."

The urge to weep surged through her, a mixture of relief and adoration for him. The time for being bold was fleeting. If she met his eyes now, she would shatter. "Sounds like a real shrew," she said when she could speak again. "Tomorrow night is good, then. Eight o'clock?"

"Yeah. I'll stop and pick up dinner on my way over. Chinese okay with you?"

Raw turnips would have been okay with her. All she needed in the world was Boone, the sweetest sustenance she'd ever known. "That's fine." She shouldered her purse with a trembling hand. "Okay, then."

Before she could move away, he caught her fingers, drew her back to him. While she watched, mesmerized, he raised her palm to his lips, laid a gentle kiss on its center, and closed her fingers around it. "You doing okay, Dr. Gilstrom?"

"I'm..." She shook her head, tears clinging to her lashes. "I've got to run. Don't skip class tomorrow, Mr. McCrea. There's a pop quiz with your name on it bouncing around in my head."

He smiled. "I'll be there."

Chapter Twelve

Elizabeth didn't give a pop quiz to her art history class on Wednesday. She was too shivery and discombobulated by Boone's dutiful appearance in the back row. He hadn't sat with Amanda this time, she noted, only grabbed the nearest empty seat a minute after lecture began.

When the class ended, he slung his backpack over one shoulder and slipped out with the rest of the students. He was keeping his distance. Elizabeth didn't know whether to feel disappointed or touched. Did he still want her? Only a matter of hours, and then she would find out.

When she got home at five o'clock, she shooed Jane Vestley out of the house, placed a James Taylor CD in the stereo, and took a long, soothing shower. The hot water drizzled over her head, down her breasts, slid between her thighs like a lover's caress. She would never again stand beneath a showerhead without an erotic short film of Boone's lovemaking flashing before her. The slide of the soapy washcloth over her skin raised chills in its wake. Every cell in her body was alive, thrumming with desire and anticipation.

After toweling off, she rubbed a sweet-scented lotion into her skin, dabbed a new perfume on her pulse points, and went in search of an outfit suitable for both painting and seduction. Her beloved gray sweatpants, she decided. Boone had requested once that she wear them. She pulled a snug, long-sleeved T-shirt over her breasts, knowing full well that if she moved just right, the hem would ride up and expose her stomach. Maybe she had fifteen years on Amanda Hastings' golden physique and no navel ring to brag about, but she'd performed one hundred sit-ups nearly every night for the past decade, and now was her chance to show off the toned results.

She stroked a brush through her hair in an attempt to tame it, but it was wavy tonight, unruly. Like her emotions, like the desires pulsing through her veins.

Downstairs the doorbell rang, and this time it wasn't Stuart hulking on the other side.

Boone was looking back at the driveway when Elizabeth opened the door, and he turned to offer her a smile. "I see your Mercedes has recovered."

"Yes. Turner Imports is back in my good favor, too."

"They never left mine," he said, and the electric innuendo shivered through her. It hadn't occurred to her to appreciate the mechanics' oversight that one incredible night last week.

"Come in," she stepped back to allow him entrance.

He set the bag of Chinese food on the kitchen table and withdrew six small cartons. "You hungry?"

"Starved."

"Me too," he said, but after she'd retrieved two plates and they seated themselves to eat, they merely picked at the steaming, fragrant food, their gazes playing a provocative game of tag across the table.

Their conversation was stilted with shyness and pent-up desire. They talked briefly about next semester, about the Smithsonian, about a group of Elizabeth's former students showing their work in a gallery on H Street.

A lot of words with no real truth spoken, but verity hung in the air, thick and sweet, and the searching looks they shared grew longer, filled with silent sentiment and need.

"Well," she said finally, when the tension between them stretched taut enough to snap, "ready to begin?"

"Sure."

He took their plates to the sink and followed her through the door that led to the garage, where Elizabeth's makeshift studio awaited. A six-foot-long, plywood platform draped in pale blue material was positioned by the easel. Boone studied it, then glanced at her. "Mind if I get comfortable?"

"Whatever you need to do," she said.

After removing his tan hiking boots and socks, he sat on the platform's edge, watching her as she turned on a work light, adjusted it, and retrieved a camera from her work table.

"I'm going to take some photos for reference," she told him, "in case I want to work on the painting and you're not available."

"So I just sit for now?"

"Actually…" She reached behind him, adjusted the material across the wood, and felt the cool draft of air kiss her bare abdomen where her shirt had pulled free from her sweatpants. When she straightened, his gaze was fixed on the strip of exposed skin.

"Lie down for me." Her words were husky, and his eyes darted back to her face, dark with need. They stared at each other, both breathing in quick, uneven rushes.

Without waiting for her to ask, Boone reached behind his head, grabbed a fistful of his navy blue sweatshirt, and drew it up and off. His cheeks were flushed, dark hair ruffled as he bunched the garment into a makeshift pillow and set it on the platform behind him.

Elizabeth tried to swallow and failed. Her mouth had gone dry at the sight of his bare torso, so beautifully honed and golden in the work light's beam. How would she get through this session without devouring him? One minute at a time, she told herself, and stepped back on wobbly knees as he stretched out on the platform before her.

"This okay?" he asked, his green eyes sleepy. The glow from the lamp gilded his lashes, tipped them with gold.

"It's great." She held the camera to her eye, then lowered it, tilting her head as her eyes sketched an imaginary composition. "It needs something, though. Maybe more skin."

His dark eyebrows shot up. "Really?"

"Yes. May I?" She moved forward and gingerly unfastened the fly of his jeans. Just the top button at first. *Ah, what the hell,* she decided, and undid the remaining four buttons. Heat radiated from his body, licked the skin of her fingers. He smelled like shampoo and desire. "That's better. Now make yourself comfortable."

"You've helped a lot," he said with a quiet laugh.

She snapped an entire roll of film, then set aside the camera and studied him again, knowing in the back of her mind that she was using the opportunity to drink in every detail of his amazing body for the sake of sheer delight.

In return, his gaze followed her as she moved to prepare her palette. She felt him watching her, sensed the sexual content of his thoughts, and wondered if he knew she was as aroused as if he'd touched every inch of her.

When she turned back with charcoal pastel in hand, he'd laid his fingers across his stomach, down low where his jeans opened. Elizabeth bit her lip and sketched out a quick image on the canvas, her gaze returning again and again to that hand, and the subtle, back and forth movement of his fingers just inside the fly of his jeans, teasing himself, teasing her.

The charcoal snapped against the canvas and she cast him a look of desperation.

Boone smiled and slid his hand back to a safer place on his chest. "How about some music? Do you have a radio out here?"

"A CD player." She held her chalky, trembling hands behind her back. "What do you say to a little Luther Vandross?"

"Someone once told me it's good music to make love to."

"I'll have to keep that in mind," she said shakily.

Moments later, the sultry vocals filled the garage and fed the excitement dancing on the air, like a match to seeping fuel.

Elizabeth started over, sketching Boone's figure in quick, energetic lines, her fervor fed by erotic recollections of the way he tasted, the texture of his skin beneath her hands, the hard jerk of his breath against her ear when he climaxed inside her with nothing between them but her uncertainty.

Finally, thirty minutes into it, she'd captured him on canvas. She reached for one of the wide, flat paintbrushes she'd recently purchased and removed it from its package. When she glanced at Boone, his eyes were closed.

"Are you sleeping?" she said softly, moving toward the platform.

"No. I'm remembering."

"Me too."

His lashes lifted and he stared at her. "What do you want, Elizabeth?"

"You." The brush trembled between her fingers. "More than I've ever wanted anyone or anything."

"Come here." He tucked an arm behind his head and held out his hand, watching her, waiting.

She reached him and grasped his fingers, sat down beside him, thinking she'd never seen a finer work of art than the whole of his features. "You're so beautiful, Boone."

"So are you." He raised his head to seek her lips, but she drew back, laid a gentle hand on his chest.

"You said to me once, 'Let me give you this one pleasure.' And now I'm asking you the same. Let me pleasure you, Boone. I feel like I've waited forever."

"Are you sure, then, Elizabeth?" His green eyes bore into hers, intense, shimmering with need. "Because I am. About you, your goodness, your value. About falling in love with you. I'm sure. Are you?"

Her chin trembled, and she rolled her eyes at her pitiful lack of control over her emotions. "Boone McCrea, I've never been more sure of anything than I am of this night, and you. I'm absolutely sure that I'm head over heels in love with you. And you're going to ruin this highly provocative moment if you make me cry."

Wordlessly, he let his head fall back on the rumpled sweatshirt, his hand resting at his side. Silent permission to proceed, and the look in his eyes told her she could take—and give—as much as she needed.

Beneath her palm, his heart beat a heavy, quickened cadence. She gazed at the brush in her other hand, at its silky, feathery tip, and touched it to the pale line inside his open fly, along the low waistband of his boxers, where his tan ended and a dusting of dark hair began.

Holding her breath, she drew the brush along that line of tender skin, up toward his navel, circled it, watched the abrupt contraction of his stomach muscles.

"Wow," he said on a moan, his fist bunching the material at his side.

Elizabeth leaned closer, dragged the brush in soft zigzags up the center of his chest, then around his left nipple, which had tightened like her own beneath her T-shirt.

In response, a blanket of chills spread over his skin, raising the fine hairs on his torso and arms. Still, he lay in quiet desperation, at her mercy, his eyes closed, jaws clenched.

She drew the silky bristles along his throat, watching the bob of his Adam's apple as he swallowed beneath it.

"I've always been told I was talented with a brush," she said into the silence, and when his lashes lifted, she met his gaze with a helpless smile.

"If they only knew," he murmured.

"Shh. I'm not done."

Groaning, he turned his face away and she continued her sweet torture, stroking the brush back down his body to the waistband of his Levi's. "Take them off," she said after a moment.

"I'm not going to survive that damn brush if I do."

"For me," she whispered, and dropped a slow, persuasive kiss on his parted lips.

Boone lifted his hips and shoved his jeans down his legs and off, taking his boxers with them. Then he braced himself on his elbows to watch her ministrations, his eyelids heavy, chest rising and falling in rapid rhythm.

He looked so young to Elizabeth, so vulnerable. And he was...but so was she. She felt reborn, untouched, new.

She combed the wave of hair off his forehead, exchanged slow smiles with him, then ran the paintbrush in a lazy, searing circle around the tip of his erection.

Boone released a harsh, pent-up breath and grabbed her wrist. "Don't get me wrong, Professor. I like the brush. No, I love the brush. But this is going to be over so much faster than either of us wants."

She sat up, eyebrows raised. "Are you telling me to stop?"

"God, no. It's just a warning."

"Then thanks for your thoughts, but I know what I'm doing."

"I love you, Elizabeth."

"I love you, too." And she proceeded to caress him with the sable bristles, stroking down the straining line of his penis to his testicles, where she ran the brush over soft, vulnerable flesh, around and around, then up again.

Boone let his head fall back on the platform and pressed the heels of his hands against his eyes in desperation, his muscles quivering, hips straining toward the delicate, gossamer kiss of the brush. "Touch me. Put your hands on me."

"Say the words." Elizabeth leaned forward, let her breath waft over his engorged erection. "Not the polite, poetic way, either."

"Wait. Oh...Christ." He lifted his head, expression flushed and terse. "Elizabeth..."

"Say it for me, Boone." Her tongue darted out to catch the silvery droplet of semen glistening on the tip of his penis, swirled around him, letting his essence seep into her, an aperitif to tantalize her senses.

He gritted his teeth. "Fine. Just...suck me, Elizabeth. Make me come in your mouth."

She smiled, rubbing her lips over the swollen head. "It's my fantasy, you know. I've dreamt of it."

Boone reached out to cup her jaw with a tender hand, his eyes shining like fine jadeite in the dance of light and shadow cast by the work lamp. "You can have anything you want, Elizabeth. I'll give you everything and more. This is only the start."

Letting the brush drop to the floor at long last, Elizabeth wrapped her fingers around his steely arousal and took him fully into her mouth, and instantly his hands found her hair, slid through the strands and clutched.

Senses raw and alive, she breathed him, tasted him, suckled him like he was pure sustenance, stopping when she sensed his orgasm rushing too quickly in the hard race of blood beneath her stroking hand.

Only when perspiration slicked his skin and his hips rose in a rhythmic dance to meet her mouth, only when his every breath was a tortured groan, did she let her lips slide down to the hilt to engulf him totally.

His shout of release fractured the night.

Swallowing his essence, Elizabeth closed her eyes and drank him in, and found herself—finally, finally—made whole again.

Chapter Thirteen

"I had no idea you were this skilled with a brush," John Weinburg said, staring at the portrait of Boone beneath the gallery lights.

"That's what Boone said," Elizabeth replied, straight-faced.

"He makes a striking subject matter. You could turn this portrait into a poster and my wife would be first in line to buy it."

She cocked an eyebrow and laughed. "He's very handsome. And such a good person." Her gaze darted to her colleague's face, uncertainty a mild pinch in a steady existence of joy. "I suppose you know about Boone and me."

John drew a breath and shrugged. "Oh, there's talk. But you're both adults, so I have nothing to say. I like the man."

"I'm painting again because of him." She looked back at the canvas, where Boone's green eyes shone like polished gems. "And he came along right when I needed him most. I feel so very lucky."

"He's just as lucky to have a smart lady like you, Elizabeth. I'm sorry for what happened with you and Stuart. But you're a different woman these days." He smiled. "Betsy says you glow."

Shy pleasure washed a fresh wave of warmth through her cheeks, and she rolled her eyes. "Oh, brother. I do?"

"You look about sixteen. It seems to me that this young man is just right for you." He put his arm around her shoulder and squeezed. "You've brought so much to our faculty and students. I really wish you'd reconsider your resignation."

"Thank you, John." She slipped her arm through his and strolled with him toward the refreshment table, where white-aproned servers were setting up a colorful array of hors d'oeuvres in anticipation of the opening's attendees. "So much has changed in my life. It's time to move on."

"And what are your plans?"

"I don't know," she said. "The divorce will be final in a few days. Stuart and I sold the house, so I guess I need to make a decision about which route to take."

"You'll stay in the area, of course."

"It's my home," she said with a smile. Only half a truth. *Boone* was home.

While John excused himself to greet incoming visitors, Elizabeth sauntered around the brick-walled campus gallery, gazing at the faculty's individual creations with admiration. Moments later, though, she returned to Boone's portrait, tugged to it by the invisible thread that stretched between the canvas and her heart.

"What a distinguished looking soul you've painted," his warm, low voice came from behind her. Slipping his arms around her waist, Boone let his lips brush her ear. "And to think, he was about to explode for want of the artist."

She covered his hands with hers and smiled. "My dear Boone, no one will begin to guess what I put you through...and then all the creative ways you returned the favor."

He pressed a kiss to her temple and turned her to face him. "Hi."

"Hi." The sight of him caught her breath as though it were the first time all over again. "I'm glad you could make it."

"Sorry I'm late. But I brought someone with me I want you to meet."

"Really?"

"Over by the food." He motioned toward the crowded table, and when Elizabeth's gaze followed his finger, she found herself staring at none other than Ferber Fielding, grumpy-old-artist extraordinaire, and one of her least favorite people in the creative community.

"That's Ferber!" She squinted at Boone. "What's he doing here?"

"He came to see the exhibit. And that's *Uncle* Ferber. To me, anyway."

Astonishment burned her cheeks, and for a long time all she could do was stare at him in dismay. "Boone! Why didn't you tell me you were related to Ferber Fielding?"

"I knew you didn't like him," he said with a sheepish smile. "But it's just a matter of time until you run into him at my apartment. Then God only knows what sort of inappropriate comment he'll make to you, even though underneath he's just a soft-hearted old curmudgeon." He bit his lip to hold back his laughter, but it was useless. "Ah God, Elizabeth. I'm sorry. If you could just see your face. You look like the world's come apart."

"He's a mean old man," she said with a groan.

"Only to a choice few. Everybody else, he ignores." He hooked an arm around her neck and pressed a kiss against her hair. "Have a little mercy, Professor. He's suffered a lot since his heart attack."

She eyed him. "Has it mellowed him?"

Boone held up a thumb and forefinger. "Maybe a little. He knows you well. Couldn't stand your husband."

The magic words.

"Really," Elizabeth said, mollified at last.

"Really. And I believe he has a proposition for you."

Clinging tightly to Boone's arm, she allowed him to lead her over to a soapstone sculpture, where Ferber Fielding stood scowling over his small, plastic plate of hors d'oeuvres.

Boone patted him on the back. "What do you think of that sculpture, Uncle Ferber?"

"Second grade-ish," the old man muttered. His watery eyes scoured Elizabeth from head to foot. "Well, Miss Elizabeth Gilstrom. I thought you'd fallen off the face of the earth."

"How are you, Ferber?"

"Too busy to waste my time at this dilettante opening." He raised his chin, glanced around and, locating a nearby waste can, dumped his plate. "Food's lousy, too."

She stared at him, speechless.

"Tell Elizabeth why you're really here," Boone said patiently.

"Oh. Yes. I bought the Binoche Gallery downtown."

Elizabeth glanced at Boone. "I didn't know it was for sale."

"It is when you're Ferber Fielding," he said, rolling his eyes.

"That's right. There's money to be made in the art community if you're not a sniveling, starving coward." Ferber yanked a handkerchief from his cardigan pocket, blew his nose, and tucked it inside his sleeve. "So I hear you're out of a job," he told Elizabeth.

"I resigned from my teaching position here at the college, yes."

"I need a gallery director. Boone thinks you'd be perfect, and since he's the only smart one of my sister's kids, I'd be willing to discuss this further."

"But what about the existing director?" Elizabeth asked, weak with astonishment.

Ferber adjusted his half-moon glasses and stared at her over the frames. "I'm cleaning house. Incidentally, I know your work well. You dropped out for a while, but I see you haven't lost your touch. That portrait of my nephew is the only thing worth a damn in this exhibit and even better, it's raising a few eyebrows. I like a little scandal. Looks like you and Boone have rocked the boat at this stuffy asylum."

Elizabeth didn't know whether to laugh or cry.

"So?" Ferber demanded.

"So..." She found her composure, straightened her shoulders and leveled a look at him. "I'll consider your offer, Ferber, and thank you for asking."

"Don't think too long," he said gruffly. "And when Boone asks you to marry him, for crying out loud, say yes immediately." He poked Boone's arm. "Where's my umbrella, boy? I'm catching a cab."

"Wreaked enough havoc, huh?" Boone cast an amused look at Elizabeth over his uncle's bald pate and walked him toward the exit.

She was still standing in the same spot, shell-shocked, when he returned. "Like I said, he's a lot of bark and no bite. Believe me, Elizabeth. He'll turn you loose at the Binoche and it'll be your oyster."

She moved closer to him, a slow-creeping joy infusing her soul. "He won't be breathing down my neck and arguing every decision I make?"

Boone shook his head. "He's getting too old for all that. He's loved the Binoche since he was a kid. It's too bad he can't run it himself." He smiled down at her, caressed her cheek with gentle fingers. "He likes you."

"My God," she muttered. "Who could ever tell?"

He gave a rueful laugh. "You know, I think he actually proposed to you for me. Didn't you hear him say something about marriage?"

Pleasure crept up Elizabeth's neck in the form of a hot blush. "I thought I was imagining things."

"He knows me too well. Reads my intentions like a book." His gaze softened to a clover-green caress. "Speaking of my intentions, how long do you want to stay at this thing?"

"I'm ready to go," she said, recognizing the sultry droop of his lashes.

His hand enfolded hers and they strolled with careful decorum from the reception, down the darkened sidewalk, past students and faculty alike who would no longer have to speculate at the nature of the relationship between the art professor and her graduate student.

They made it as far as her Mercedes before they flowed together, mouths devouring, hands sliding, cupping, caressing.

"I love you, Elizabeth," Boone whispered against her neck. "You're everything to me."

"Oh, Boone." She sank her fingers into his hair and clung to him, throwing back her head to give his sweet, gentle lips access to her throat. "I love you, too. You make me so happy."

"How happy?" Laughter edged his voice. "Happy as in, we'll actually make it home before we jump each other's bones, or happy as in, let's get in the car and get naked *now*?"

"How about both? You're young and strong, with lots of stamina." She let him back her up against the Mercedes door, her laughter and words muffled by his kiss.

Boone clutched the lapels of her coat and nuzzled the curve of her breast. "We got caught out here once before."

"In this very spot, if I remember correctly."

"That's right," he said dolefully. "Officer Friendly's untimely arrival resulted in the worst case of sexual frustration I've ever suffered."

"Let me make it up to you." She drew him closer until the weight of his body pressed her against the car door, then wrapped one leg in sinuous provocation around his thigh. "No one's around," she whispered, undulating against the instantaneous rise of his erection beneath his khakis. "We're out here in the dark, where we can't be seen. How about a quickie? An appetizer before we go home and do it right?"

"Oh, yeah." His hands slid down to her buttocks and rubbed in slow, enticing circles, so that her skirt's silky lining teased the sensitive skin of her backside. "Unbutton me," he instructed, breath quickening. "I'll keep a lookout."

But his diligence lasted only until she freed his arousal from his fly. When she stroked it, he groaned and his head fell back, eyes closed. "Oh, that feels too good."

Without relinquishing her hold, Elizabeth used her free hand to shimmy up the hem of her conservative tweed skirt, beneath which she wore only a black lace garter belt and stockings—decadent gifts from her insatiable young lover. They made her feel sexy, but what was even better, they gave him access to her body at fervent, delightful moments like this.

Panting now, all laughter forgotten, Boone guided her leg up around his waist, took the tip of his penis in hand and rubbed it against her aching, swollen folds until her fingers dug into his shoulders. When a groaning protest tore from her throat, he bent his knees and eased into her, an inch at a time, filling her until Elizabeth bit back a scream of impatient need.

With slow, measured thrusts, he drove into her, his lust-darkened gaze locked on hers until her eyelids drooped with pleasure. Liquid heat gathered in her stomach and spilled downward, into her womb, washing him in her desire, in heat and love and want.

His muscles trembled and he hoisted her higher, thrust harder, his features a mask of rapture as he clutched her bare buttocks and quickened his rhythm.

"God," he whispered, lips moving against the damp tendrils of hair at her temple. "I'm going to come inside you. You feel too good..."

The low warning was all Elizabeth needed to topple her into the hot, pulsing river of her own ecstasy. She sank her fingertips into the tough muscles beneath his sweater and bit back a sob, riding each quake that coursed through her, her own inner contractions setting fire to his orgasm.

Boone braced a palm against the car door, the other clapped tight against her bottom, and thrust deep into the heart of her one last time before he cried out to the chilled winter sky, his body jerking in quick, relentless shudders.

Heat exploded inside Elizabeth, a fluid mixture of pleasure and warm satisfaction, and in the aftermath, she drifted in complete contentment. When he finally sagged against her and she could find the breath to speak, she said, "Is anyone coming?"

"Besides us? Don't think so." His sleepy reply elicited a laughing groan from her, and she straightened beneath him, tugging her skirt back into its proper position.

She felt sticky and decadent and more than a little pleased with herself. When they got home, they would climb into the shower together, and the lovemaking would start again, slower this time, less desperate and more intense. The thought made her shiver anew with anticipation.

God. Boone had made a monster. No—he'd done more than that. He'd reminded her what it meant to be alive. Every cell in her body vibrated with love and well-being.

While he fastened his pants, she stood on tiptoe and wrapped her arms around his neck. "I can't get enough of you."

"Yeah?" He tugged her snugly against him. "Show me."

She was straining toward his smiling lips when a shock of blue lights whirled behind him. "You've got to be kidding," he groaned.

The security guard's cart whined to a stop nearby. "Evenin', folks. Haven't I seen you here before?"

This time, Elizabeth stepped out of Boone's shielding embrace, standing bold and singular in the lazy blue strobe as she waved a hand at the man. "Hi, William," she said, a mixture of elation and embarrassment dancing within her. "We were just leaving."

About the Author

ℌ

Writing romance comes naturally to Shelby Reed and has flavored most of her work since she first fell in love with Jane Austen's stories years ago. She strives to write about real women with contemporary issues, who manage to find love despite the trials and tribulations of today's single female. When not churning out fiction, Shelby utilizes her B.A. in Art as a portraitist, works part-time as an editor, and considers herself a full-time author since she recently quit her day job to throw herself headlong into writing. She lives in the flavorful deep south with her husband, two rambunctious dogs, and a house full of manuscripts and artwork in various stages of completion.

Shelby welcomes mail from readers. You can write to her c/o Ellora's Cave Publishing at 1056 Home Avenue, Akron OH 44310-3502.

Also by Shelby Reed

Holiday Inn

Midnight Rose

Seraphim

The Fifth Favor

Zeke's Hands

Madison Hayes

ƐD

Trademarks Acknowledgement

The author acknowledges the trademarked status and trademark owner of the following wordmark mentioned in this work of fiction:

MapQuest.com: MapQuest.com, Inc.

Chapter One

There were several things wrong with Zeke Rutherford, perhaps the foremost of which was the fact she worked with him. Not the least of which was the fact that, at twenty-three, he was way too young for her. Add all that to the fact that he was tall—too tall—at six-four. *Six-four,* she mused as she swung in her chair. He looked taller.

"Ms. Walker. Sara?"

Sara swung to face the doorway of her small office, and raised her eyes the length of Zeke Rutherford—and reminded herself she didn't like having to stretch for a kiss.

It didn't take a big man to satisfy her, she further reminded herself. Her current boyfriend was living proof of that fact. *One of his fingers should do nicely, though,* she thought. Geez. His middle finger was as long as—Ericson's dick. Sara fought the urge to lower her eyes down Zeke's body as she wondered just how much living proof he might have to offer.

"Would you review these expenses with me? The form's pretty straightforward," he said, pushing into the room before she could respond. "But it's my first attempt and I'd like a senior engineer to take a look at it."

He probably didn't notice her wince at the word "senior". She took a breath and wished her office were larger, because when Zeke Rutherford was in it, there wasn't room to breathe.

The form *was* straightforward, and certainly nothing a recent graduate of Cal State couldn't handle, but she stood and smiled, reaching for the papers in his hand. With eleven-point-five inches of maneuvering room on the length of the paper, she couldn't manage to get the sheaf out of his grasp without brushing his fingers. But then he had big hands she reasoned, with long fingers—long, thick, made-for-a-woman fingers.

Realizing she was staring at his hands, she cut to his face and quickly realized that was a mistake.

She gazed into eyes that couldn't decide whether they were gold or brown, but were decidedly nice, particularly when they were backlit with laughter as they were now. Perhaps she stared a bit too long because his lips turned up at the edges and her eyes were now drawn in that direction. His lips were extraordinarily full and that shouldn't have looked good on a man, but somehow it did—on him anyhow. Very ordinary brown hair curled around the bottom of his ears. *Very ordinary*, she reminded herself. Perfectly ordinary. Geez.

She dropped into her chair and scanned his numbers while he pulled a chair close to hers in her very small office. Which felt like it was rapidly shrinking. She nodded her head. "Looks good. Looks perfect," she said. And it was. She pushed it at him, anxious to get him out of her office.

He leaned forward over the form, and she watched his long finger slide to a number on the page. At the same time, she felt his knee slide against her thigh.

Oh, man. The guy was all legs. Pulling back in her chair, she increased the margin between their bodies.

"Then I've expensed these batteries properly? They shouldn't be charged to the client?"

His voice was warm and deep, causing a tingle to generate along the length of her spine. A little shiver of excitement originated at the nape of her neck and shot down her backbone accelerating along the trunk route on its way to the juncture of her legs. A juggernaut of warmth pulled in between her legs, parked and started cranking up the RPMs. Her fingers tightened on the desk's edge as the reverberations raced through her body and rattled her heart.

Yes, yes, anything, she thought. *Just move along, Cal State*. She gave him a supportive smile. She was old enough to be his—babysitter, twenty years ago. "Looks perfect," she repeated, and watched his back out the door. *Perfect*, she thought, and concluded she had been born exactly eleven years too soon. For—although there were several things wrong with Zeke Rutherford—everything else about him was perfect.

Chapter Two

"Pull over! I mean it, Sara. Pull over now!"

"Sorry, Ericson. Am I driving too fast?"

"You always drive too fast, Sara. Pull over and let me out."

"Just let me get around this guy." She passed the sports car like it was standing still, whipped her head around as she whipped the jeep into the right lane then eased her foot off the accelerator until the speedometer read seventy.

"Shit, Sara. The speed limit here is forty-five."

"Yeah, I know," she said, frowning. "I don't know why. You can easily do seventy down the canyon."

"Yeah, well, you can do seventy down the canyon without me. Let me out."

She glanced at the passenger seat. "You can't get out here. We're miles from any bus route."

"I'll hitchhike."

"That's dangerous!"

"Compared to commuting with you? I'll take my chances. There's a convenience store up ahead."

* * * * *

"I'll call you." Ericson slammed the jeep door, and Sara watched the back of his gray suit enter the convenience store. She never much liked that suit, anyhow. She pulled back out onto the road. So much for Lover Number Nine. At the rate she was going, she'd soon need more than two hands to count them off.

Murphy, Collins, Frizzel, Manisci, Williams and Stringer, Jackson and Martinez.

And that brought her to Number Nine—Ericson. She'd long since given up on the romantic notion of true love, settling down. She'd been disappointed too many times for love to be considered a real option.

Murphy was Number One. She looked at her thumb. What a one-time disaster that had been. Collins, Number Two. She'd wanted to marry Collins. She'd wanted to marry Frizzel, Number Three.

By then she was in college. She obtained a BS in engineering as she worked her way through three more lovers. *Not that it was all work,* she thought with a grin. Manisci was nice, too nice, actually. Williams was hot, but a confirmed bachelor. And Wills couldn't decide which of his three girlfriends he wanted to be a confirmed bachelor with. She'd obliged him by narrowing his choice down to two. Stringer was the first man she slept with that she didn't love and had no intention of marrying. That was a big step in her life. She should have done it earlier. She still had fond memories of Stringer—but—the guy did so many drugs, she wasn't sure she knew who he was.

After graduation, there was Jackson. She'd been so attracted to him, she didn't immediately realize he was impotent. Then there was Martinez. It was just sex. For Martinez, at any rate. And after she'd invested three years there, he dumped her and married an aerobic instructor he'd known three weeks. For a long time after that, she'd steered clear of men.

Which brought her to Ericson. Ericson was smooth, good-looking in an east coast way and only a little taller than herself, which made him perhaps five-seven. Always immaculately dressed, his condominium—his life for that matter—was similarly arranged.

God, his job was boring. He was a lawyer. Sara tried to pay attention when he launched into one of the monologues he considered conversation, but the fact was, his work was just plain boring. And his hands! How could a woman get excited about a man who'd never in his life had dirt under his fingernails? *Not that she liked dirty fingernails,* she thought, frowning at her own chipped nails on the jeep's steering wheel. She liked a guy who cleaned his fingernails, but a man had to have done something to have anything to clean in the first place. She smiled to herself. She liked a guy who worked for a living. Worked hard. Hard enough to have finger creases stained dark with the not-easily-eradicated evidence of that work.

She made an abrupt left and pulled into the parking lot in front of the long, low building where she worked, shoved the door open then pulled it closed again as a long black truck pulled in close to hers. Opening the door again, this time just a crack, she squeezed out of the jeep and onto the pavement.

Zeke joined her on the sidewalk.

"Geez, Zeke. You don't give a girl much room."

"Sorry, Sara. I just got it. It's bigger than I realized."

Her eyes cut to his as she checked his face but if the innuendo was intentional, he did a good job of hiding it. His arm came around hers as she reached for the office door, and she watched his hand fasten around the handle. Stared at his thick knuckles wrapped around the glistening steel shaft and groaned inwardly at the fantasies it evoked. She caught at a breath and shook her head, trying to dislodge the mental image of Zeke's hand wrapped around his cock and feeding it into her…

"Graduation present?" she forced her voice to be hard.

The door didn't open, and his hand was still on the handle. Impatiently, she flicked her eyes at his face.

His eyes, too, flickered with impatience. "I bought it."

She continued ruthlessly, "No college loans to pay off? Your parents pick up the bill?"

His fingers tightened around the door handle, and he gave his head a curt shake. "I worked my way through school. At an auto shop. I still work on my own vehicles…in my spare time."

She watched his hand as he opened the door for her. Gazed at the dark creases that striped his long fingers. Shit! How could you graduate Cal State top of your class and hold down a job repairing cars at the same time?

The guy was brilliant, hard-working, as well as a nice young man. He didn't need her abuse. It wasn't his damn fault she couldn't look at him without imagining his long body stretched over hers, those hands gliding into her damp, full sex, his rough fingers tweaking her button until she was pushing herself against his body, begging for his full entry.

Poor kid probably hadn't known what had hit him.

Sara knew her cutting comments hadn't been fair. But if Zeke thought she didn't like him, maybe he wouldn't notice how much she wanted him.

* * * * *

Zeke Rutherford couldn't understand how Sara could be so supportive and helpful in most instances then out of nowhere come off like he was some sort of jerk kid. Like she was...trying to remind herself...of what?

He snorted to himself. She was probably just warning him off, probably didn't want him coming on to her. Shit! Was it that obvious? His eyes slid to the placket at the front of his jeans as he shook his head. Yeah, it was probably obvious.

But then, Zeke had the distinct impression that Sara Walker had no idea she was hot or exactly how hot she was. Most of the time, she showed up at the office in loose, nondescript clothing. But every now and then—every now and then—she'd slip up and turn up in a top that was a shade on the tight side or pants that actually fit. She had a pair of dark green pants. Zeke prayed for green pant days. God, she had a nice ass.

Every now and again—purely by accident, he was sure—she'd walk in with both green pants and tight top—all at the same time. Man, she had nice tits. God, he'd like to rub his dick all over the rough tips of her nipples.

Leaning back in his chair, the computer monitor blurred as Zeke imagined what sort of response that would elicit—in her—as the soft skin of his hard erection came into contact with her pink nipples.

Brown nipples.

Peach.

Whatever.

Crap, he thought, with a lurch back to reality, he still had thirty more logs to process.

He usually picked on women his own age and closer to his own size. Generally, he preferred blondes, and Sara's hair was shorter than he liked on a woman. It wasn't her looks, although with light brown hair and blue eyes, she was nice enough to look at. And it wasn't the fact that she had to safety pin her sweaters to keep them closed across her chest.

It was probably her personality. Working conditions at Schueller Engineering were stressful, to say the least. The work constantly required last-minute emergency mobilizations, testing under extreme conditions then the results analyzed and reported overnight—sooner if possible.

Sara's encouragement and casual laughing manner helped to soften the bleeding edge they all worked on. Not that she didn't have passion. She could flare up on occasion, only to laugh it off two minutes later. He'd seen her laughing with tears of frustration still in her eyes.

He leaned back in his chair and stared at the computer monitor. Sara Walker was going down, he decided.

On him.

With that thought in mind, he picked up his printouts and stepped out of his office. A few strides put him outside Sara's door where he halted before entering. Zeke swallowed his next breath.

Sara stood with her elbows resting on the table behind her desk. Her perfect, heart-shaped bottom was prettily presented and begging for a stroke—or two—or perhaps a whole series of strokes. Zeke watched her foot snake backward to catch at her chair as she absentmindedly maneuvered the chair to meet her bottom. Stepping into the room, he leaned over to catch the back of the chair and navigated its curving bottom to meet hers. He had to smile. Sara was so focused on her work, she wasn't ev aware of his presence. He slid his hand up the chair th separated his hand from her body.

"Sara?"

Dragging her attention from the reams of data spread on the table, Sara turned toward the voice, and came face-to-face with a man's fly. She didn't have to raise her eyes to identify whose fly filled the landscape so completely—she'd have known that stretch of jeans anywhere. For two long mesmerizing seconds she stared as Zeke stood beside her, his dick two inches from her mouth.

"Do you have time to review these plots with me? They're just preliminary."

"Take a seat," she growled, and gave him what she hoped was a pleasant smile.

Pulling up a chair, Zeke wondered why she grimaced. The woman looked like she was in pain.

"Sorry to intrude," he said, having lost his confidence just a notch. "Looks like you've got about as much as you can swallow without me shoving a lot more in your face. I don't mean to make it hard for you," he mumbled, "but I could use your—"

She blinked up at him, her eyes enormous, full of pale, breathless wonder, staring at him as if from a trap of her own device. Gradually, he realized what he'd said—his exact words. Realized how she might have taken those words. And thought—just maybe—he knew why. His confidence ratcheted back upward about the same time his cock followed suit.

Chapter Three

"Can you go to Dallas on Wednesday?" Karl Schueller stood in the door of Sara's office.

"Sure," she answered, never removing her eyes from her computer monitor. "What is it?"

"Column integrity in a parking garage."

"How many?"

"Three columns on four levels. You can do it in a day."

She made a face. A long day, maybe.

"Take Zeke with you."

Sara's eyes widened as she swung them on her boss. "What! No! I don't need a Sherpa. I work alone."

"You could use Zeke's help. It's a lot to get done in a day."

Geez. Was Karl trying to kill her? Yeah, she could use Zeke's help—any day, every day, all day long—and several nights thereafter. And she wasn't talking about testing columns. Although…she wouldn't mind testing out the integrity of Zeke's column. She didn't expect she'd find any fault with it or failing, for that matter. She had to guess Zeke would have one entirely competent structural member that would support her through orgasm without compromise.

She refocused on her boss. "I'll get a helper at the worksite. My Spanish is improving." She leaned back in her chair. "*Dome la muerta*."

"What!"

"*Dome la muerta*. Take the hammer," she translated.

"Tome el martillo," he corrected her. *"Dome la muerta*...sounds like...give me death." Karl continued impatiently, "We need to train the new engineers, Sara. And this is a perfect opportunity."

"I'll take Nick, then."

Karl gave her an intolerant stare. "Nick? He's no taller than you. We're talking columns here. Take Zeke." His tone was final as he took a step down the hall.

Sara stifled her frustration. "Tell him to let me know when he's got his reservations," she called out after her boss.

* * * * *

She'd waited and made her reservations after she knew Zeke had made his, planned her arrival at the airport to allow her just enough time to clear security before the plane would be boarding, dawdled on her way down the concourse and arrived at the gate to hear her name in close association with final call. Swinging her field computer in front of her, she made her way down the plane's aisle knowing 16C would be mid-plane on her right. Not knowing Zeke Rutherford would be sitting in 16B, mid-plane, also on her right.

Until she sat down, then he'd be on her left.

With a tight smile, she swung the heavy computer up to the overhead bin, bobbled it a bit and watched Zeke's arm rise in front of her face to balance the computer as she shoved it into the bin. "Thanks," she said, feeling not one bit thankful.

Dropping into her seat, she tightened her seatbelt with satisfaction. Over a hundred flights and never a seatbelt she didn't have to tighten after the passenger before her. She'd always considered herself a bit heavy up until she'd taken this job. But the work, the demanding schedule, the stress, excitement and physical demands of testing in the blazing sun, freezing rain, snow, dangling off the edge of a dam, balancing on the beam of a monorail track—all with no time for lunch—had whittled her down to her present size six.

"I called the travel agent back—Carol—and asked her to seat me next to you."

Sara nodded grudgingly, trying to ignore the knot this young man put in her stomach. She'd like to think he was as hot to park his chassis next to hers as she was to park hers...in his lap, actually. The parking metaphor evoked an intrusive image. She couldn't help thinking of the broad, gleaming head of a parking meter—preferably with the red warning fully extended and threatening to expire right up into her slot.

She'd like to think Zeke Rutherford had parking on his mind. But the poor guy probably just wanted to pick her brain about project details. Zeke didn't disappoint her. Or actually, did disappoint her—with his next statement.

"I thought you could prep me on the test procedure. It's always so crazy at the office and there's never enough time for training."

She gritted her teeth. He was right, of course. He was a young, junior engineer and she was a senior engineer with ten years of experience. It was time she started acting like one.

The plane was starting its descent when he finally put his notebook away, apparently satisfied with her instruction.

Licking her lips, she took a breath of relief. She closed her eyes and left them that way for a while, ignoring the small clipped sounds coming from beside her. Finally curious, she tipped her head back and sneaked her eyelids up. She watched as Zeke clipped his middle fingernail down to the quick and moved on to the next.

"You keep your nails short for a woman," he observed.

Which meant he knew she was watching him.

Lifting her eyelids, she raised her hands and nodded at the short nails. "They get in the way otherwise. You?"

He smiled slowly, his eyes backlit. "I keep my nails short for a woman, too."

She laughed. "Any woman in particular?"

"Yeah," he said, and moved his eyes from her hands to her face.

Her smile died as she started it and she stared, caught in his gold-brown gaze.

While she was trapped, he reached for her hand and spread her palm out against his own. It made a poor showing against his. Cocking his head, he observed their hands together.

"Small," he said. Turning his hand on hers, he used his thumb to curl her fingers around his long, thick forefinger. He turned his backlit eyes on her. "A perfect fit," he said.

Zeke drew his finger slowly through her hand, as he made some quick assumptions. It was only a rough estimate, but he had to assume she'd be a perfect fit in other ways as well. Probably every way, in fact. Every possible way he could think of putting it to her. When her fingers shook, he was inclined to wrap them back up in his hand. But, kindly, let her go instead.

Consideringly, he frowned at his empty hand before his eyes slid to Sara's left breast. That would work, he decided. Looking at each finger, individually, he knew where he'd like to put each joint—individually, and jointly. When he stretched his hand out, he pictured it riding behind her, hooking the bottom of her heart-shaped ass, and pulling her groin in tight against his sex, thick and crowded inside his jeans. His cock thickened at the thought, the thought of Sara on his dick, fitted tight and hot, and wet and perfect.

The moment her hand was free, Sara reached up and opened the air vent to blow down on her.

Zeke leaned back in his chair and smiled.

Geez. Could it get any hotter in here? Sara grumbled to herself. Airplanes were always hot and stuffy. Over a hundred flights and she'd never…been this goddamn hot. It wasn't fair! The guy was flirting with her. She was having a hard enough time keeping her hands to herself without his leading her on, sucking her in!

She had a spike of flaming desire shoved so far up inside her she could feel it scorching her breastbone. Scraping a hand through her hair, she mentally calculated how many inches it would take to stretch from her vulva to her…heart. Because that's what it would take, right now, to satisfy her. Approximately twelve inches of Zeke Rutherford stretching into her deep enough to reach her heart.

She shifted in her seat as the lips of her labia slid against each other, hot, wet and just about drooling for something more to slide against. Something thick and hard to suck up inside her—something substantial to salivate about. Damn. She couldn't believe she could get this hot over a little suggestive hand play, a little juvenile flirting.

Leaning forward, she peered out the window, relieved to discover the plane was almost on the ground. The plane bucked on rough air and the seat jolted beneath her. When she gasped, Zeke brought his eyes around to hers. The plane hit the ground hard, bounced and Zeke's hand automatically reached around her wrist. The force of the landing rocked the seat hard against her inflamed pussy, rubbed her labia up against her clit. Her hand twisted in Zeke's grasp as, mouth open, eyes locked on Zeke's, she dug her fingernails into his hand and came.

Blood roared in her ears as the jet engines roared into reverse.

Zeke watched her eyes as she blinked up at him. "Are you okay?" he asked with a puzzled frown. "I thought you'd flown—"

"Hundreds of times," she filled in a few blinks later. "Never landed that hard before," she told him as she shook her head. *Never fallen this hard before, either,* she thought.

Chapter Four

"Do you like it in the front or behind?"

Startled, she cut a look at him.

Zeke smiled slowly as he reached for the rental car's radio. "The music."

Pulling out of the rental car gate, she suppressed a smile. "I don't know. I didn't know you could have it…in the rear."

"Really?"

"I've always had it in the front."

One of his long fingers circled around the outside of a knob. "I think you'll like it from behind."

She was still smiling two minutes later as she braked at a red light. "Oh, yeah," she said with breathy admiration. "Look at that."

They were stopped at a light on the south side of Dallas. With tight-jawed irritation that came out of nowhere and threatened a long stay, Zeke watched the well-dressed man in the crosswalk. But he wasn't going to be baited.

"Isn't that something?"

Despite his resolve, he flicked his eyes at her. Her eyes glowed as she stared through the windshield. Shit! The guy wasn't that good-looking. At least he didn't think so.

"Don't you just love cranes?"

Now his eyes followed hers to the Dallas skyline. Masts extended and loaded, three massive cranes hovered over a construction site up ahead. His eyes slid back to her face. "Yeah." His lips relaxed into a smile. "Don't you just," he echoed.

She turned her eyes on him and he wasn't displeased to find that some of that blue glow had shifted to himself. It warmed him right to the tip of his…tip.

She grinned. "I knew you'd understand."

"Yeah," he said, stretching his arms behind his head as far as they would reach within the confines of the SUV. "Yeah. We're made for each other. You adore a piece of heavy equipment with a huge mast. Just like me."

She made a face at him that demonstrated her disapproval at the same time it revealed her amusement. Accelerating away from the light, her head turned to the right, and then the car abruptly followed as she pulled onto Blair Street and alongside the parking garage.

Zeke looked at his watch. "It's six-thirty. Do you think anyone's still working?"

She shrugged. "We can poke around a bit either way, lay out a plan for tomorrow."

"It looks dark in there," he said, dipping his head to peer out the window.

"We can use the car headlights."

Running several preliminary tests, it was nine o'clock before Sara was satisfied. It was only a short run to the hotel, but Zeke had been starving since seven-thirty. "Meet you in the restaurant," he suggested as he pulled the equipment case from the car.

"I'm not hungry. See you in the morning."

"Breakfast?"

"Be out here at seven a.m., Sherpa."

Frustrated, he watched her pull the rolling equipment case toward the hotel entrance.

Shit! He turned on his heel and raked a hand into his hair. Shit! This was bullshit. He was so close. She was so close. He turned back to look at her. If only he could get her alone for two minutes. If only she'd give him a chance, he'd…he'd probably shove her up against a wall and get wet with her before he could get one word out of his mouth. He'd probably spill all over her before he could even get inside her.

She was so close. And so fucking far away. There might as well be a three-foot thick, concrete wall between them. Concrete wall with a lead-fucking-lining between them. He'd never seen a woman construct so many barriers before in his life. It was going to take a crane with a wrecking ball to get through to her. A wrecking ball at the end of a huge mast.

At that, Zeke couldn't help but smile.

* * * * *

But Zeke wasn't smiling the next afternoon in the parking garage. He'd missed breakfast after a restless night of frustrating Sara dreams. Waking at six forty-five, he raced from the room without showering and found Sara waiting for him in the SUV.

To make matters worse, Sara didn't stop for lunch.

"Don't you ever take a break?" he asked her.

"Take a break, if you need one," she'd replied.

"I don't need a break," he answered, "but I do need to eat."

"Go ahead," she murmured without looking at him. "I'll be here when you get back."

"You can't run tests without me."

She looked up at him. "I can review the data."

"Okay, I'm curious. When, exactly, do you eat?"

"I'll get something at the airport. Take a break, Ezekial."

Zeke grimaced. Only his grandmother called him Ezekial. "I don't need a fucking break," he muttered as he turned back to the column.

"What?"

"I'll get something at the airport," he called back at her.

* * * * *

"Push. Next position. Push."

Zeke took a break when the Job Super came up behind Sara. Leaning against the concrete column, he pulled his wrist over his eyebrows.

"How does it look, Miss Walker?"

She nodded, and looked back through her notes. "You have a few areas of concern, Tom. Uh. Column Ten, Level Two; Column Twelve, Level Two." She turned a page. "Column Ten, Level Three."

The engineer made a face of impatience. "Are you sure? We weren't expecting problems. This testing was supposed to be routine. I hate to attempt exploratory drilling if there's nothing wrong with them. There's a lot of PT cable running through these columns. I'd rather not hit PT."

Zeke felt himself bristle at the man's aggressive attitude. He didn't like the way the guy was pushing Sara, and he didn't like the way he was questioning her results.

Sara gave the engineer a careful look, "Well. Column Ten, Level Two looks the worst. Why don't you try poking a small hole into it? West side? Five feet from the floor? You ready Ezekial?"

Ezekial! Zeke swore under his breath. He glanced at his watch as he pressed the transducers against the column. "It's four-thirty, Sara."

"Right. I just want to do a few additional tests to confirm our results. I think we can make the airport in thirty minutes."

An hour later, they were throwing their equipment into the case. Zeke checked his watch again. They'd better make the airport in thirty minutes. Swinging the equipment case in one hand, Zeke started down the ramp after Sara.

A circle of hardhats surrounded Column Ten on Level Two.

"Find anything?" Sara asked.

One of the men stepped backward.

"Man!" Sara sounded surprised. The small exploratory drill hole had been widened to reveal a large void at the center of the column. "A family of raccoons would be comfortable in there!"

Zeke watched Tom frown with a slight nod.

"Get some bags mixed and we'll fill it in," Tom said curtly to the hardhat beside him.

"Are you going test the other two I suggested?"

Tom shrugged at Sara noncommittally. "We need your report as soon as possible."

"Right. I'll have the results to you day after tomorrow."

* * * * *

Sara kept busy on the flight back, analyzing data.

At first disappointed when he saw her pull out the computer, Zeke decided he could work with the situation. Using the excuse that the screen was hard to read from his angle, he put his elbow on the armrest between them and crowded her as he followed her analysis. A few well-placed questions made his close presence legitimate.

She smelled like—Sara—he decided. She smelled like hard work and clipped conversation and damp, no-nonsense sexuality. He had to assume that she would approach sex as she did everything else, with intensity, complete focus and the sort of thorough application that would leave a man used up and begging to be used again.

"Don't you ever stop working?"

"Not when I want to get these results to the client by Friday."

"What do you do when you're not working?"

She stared at the screen and didn't answer.

"Do you ever…listen to music, go to concerts?"

"Do you?"

"Yeah."

Zeke thought about the last concert he'd attended. And the woman he'd attended it with. It was a rock concert. His date had drunk too much and talked too much, and just about driven him out of his mind, going on and on about the band and their last concert, and what they were wearing and what they'd done—right down to the last, minute, frigging detail. He looked down on the quiet woman beside him.

"I like to travel," Sara told him. "And ride. I have a Quarter Horse."

"Tell me about your horse."

"She's a sorrel. Fourteen hands."

"Not too big, then."

"Not too big. She's a handful, though."

"Hard to handle?"

"A little bit."

"What do you call her?"

"Sorrel."

Zeke nodded his head.

"Not a very original name, is it?" She sounded apologetic.

"Maybe not. But it's...straightforward, accurate."

Just like Sara, he thought. Straightforward and direct as well as intense, focused and thorough. What more could a man want in a woman?

Back in the airport, up at the baggage claim, Zeke lifted the equipment case from the carousel.

Normally, Sara hired a porter to help her out of the airport with the heavy equipment. Glancing around, she tried to locate one of the navy-blue caps, but by then, Zeke had offered to help. After a short argument—wherein she pointed out he was parked at least a half mile from her jeep—she accepted his help.

He lifted the seventy-plus pounds like it was nothing. The sturdy, black equipment case looked like a briefcase in his hand.

Tossing it into the back of Sara's jeep, he reached to close the rear hatchback door.

"Thanks, kid."

He slammed the door and jammed his hands in his pockets. "I'm not a kid, Sara. And I don't like Ezekial, either."

It was dark in the parking lot. But not so dark he couldn't see she looked like she'd been stung.

"Whatever, Rutherford," she mumbled.

"What's wrong with Zeke?" he asked as she turned away.

She unlocked her door, threw herself into the driver's seat and fumbled her keys out of her pocket. *Nothing,* she thought. There was nothing wrong with Zeke. Not a damn thing.

And that was the problem. He was perfect—and driving her perfectly nuts. Working with him the whole damn day, trying to concentrate on the test results, getting the notes down, when all she really wanted to do was get his pants down, get down on him and get some real results. She jammed the key into the ignition slot and cranked it viciously.

She'd like him jammed into her slot, like him to crank into her and she didn't think ignition would be far off if he did. She felt her forehead pinch into a painful frown. It was pure, perfect agony, watching those incredible hands of his handle the test equipment, when all she really wanted was those hands handling her equipment. Working every single pink button she possessed. Possessing her female connections, working his way into her, slotting his male fittings into her socket until the connection was complete and consummate, and they both ended up soaking wet, sparking into orgasm and shorting out on each other.

She backed the car out with a shriek of rubber.

The way his T-shirt stretched across the flat muscles of his chest. His T-shirt damp and sucking up to his chest in the warm, sweaty parking garage. Shit! She didn't even want to think of how he'd smell, steamy and hot inside that damp T-shirt. She'd gotten a hint of that in the airplane when he'd pressed up against her, his face almost touching hers.

How the hell was she supposed to hold out against that kind of hot, hard, male perfection? She needed sex. Not the steady, monotonous, lawyer-type sex she'd gotten from Ericson. No. She needed something hard and heavy and electric—the kind of sex she'd bet everything she owned she'd find with Zeke. But it wasn't going to happen. She wasn't going to let it happen. He was too young, too tall and too damned close. She was old enough and smart enough to know not to date, let alone screw, someone she worked with.

Giving him a last hungry glance, she hit the gas pedal. The jeep's tires squealed as she peeled out of the parking lot.

Chapter Five

"They need more testing in Dallas."

"When?"

"They want you there early tomorrow morning," Karl said. "They found more voids and want to extend the testing to more columns. Can you get out today?"

Sara gave it no more than two seconds thought. "I guess so."

"Take Rutherford with you."

Sara smiled grimly. It had taken a week, but she had everyone calling Zeke by his last name.

She reserved a flight leaving in a few hours then stopped by the office Zeke shared with Nick. "I'm on a three o'clock flight to Dallas. Karl wants you to come along."

He blinked at her.

"It just came up."

"What are you going to do about clothes?"

"I always have a backpack with a few things. You should too," she lectured. "Fly out tomorrow morning if you like."

"No. That would put you at the job site two or three hours ahead of me. I'll...manage. Do you want to take your car or mine?"

Sara watched his gaze harden as she took a step backward, as though he knew what she was going to say. She said it anyway, damned if she was going to spend an hour trapped in a car with that mouthwatering, cunt-dampening body of his, followed by two hours on the plane, then another hour getting to the site...damn.

"You can take your car. I'll take mine. I'll see you on the plane."

"That's bullsh—we're going to the same place."

But she'd already turned and was halfway down the hall.

* * * * *

Speeding through drenching Dallas rain, the SUV pulled a long tail of water behind it. Zeke turned to check the traffic as Sara flipped on the left blinker.

"Does my driving make you nervous, Rutherford?"

"Not yet," he answered. "You drive fast, but I haven't seen you make any mistakes—*Walker*." He peered out into the rain. "You don't mind if I call you by your last name, do you?"

She smiled at him sideways. "I usually reserve that privilege for my lovers, but I guess I can make an exception in your case."

He nodded. He didn't tell her he didn't plan to remain an exception. "And do you refer to *your* lovers by last names as well?"

She didn't answer, but he caught her expression—slow, dawning realization that she'd made an error.

"Hey," he said, "Rutherford's fine with me." He nodded his head and smiled. "Man, I'm hungry. It's seven o'clock Denver. Can we pull in for fast food somewhere?"

"There's a restaurant at the hotel." She felt him watching her. Felt his resentment.

"Okay then, Walker," he said like a threat. Her eyes flicked in his direction but he looked straight ahead into the wet Dallas night.

He'd said he was starving, so she figured he'd head right for the Tex-Mex restaurant, downstairs. She took her time, showered and watched the Dallas news before she headed for the elevator. Taking a booth and ordering a beer, she hadn't been there five minutes before Zeke slid in beside her. She squinched into the corner as though he was a leper and glared at him. He gave her an easy smile. "I don't want to have to shout, Walker."

Her expression indicated his explanation was insufficient.

He made a face then stared down at the tile tabletop. "I'd like some advice, Walker. It's...personal." He appeared to struggle with the admission.

She regarded him warily.

"It's about this girl—woman—I'm dating."

Inwardly he smiled at the transformation this disclosure worked on Sara. She relaxed—instantly relaxed—visibly relaxed—as she reached for her bottle of beer.

"Yeah?" she said with interest. The waitress interrupted to take their order. Zeke ordered a massive Tex-Mex marathon meal while Sara pointed to an appetizer on the menu. "Yeah?" she prompted him.

He nodded his head at the table, looking uncomfortable. "It's been a few months." He took a breath. "Almost two months—and I'm having problems...getting anywhere. I want to fuck her." He stopped when Sara flinched.

"Well, there's your problem," she muttered.

"I'm sorry, Walker, I might have guessed you'd be old-fashioned. I want to make lo— Well, I definitely want to have sex with her. And I thought since you're older—thirty? Maybe you could give me some advice."

Thirty. That was kind, she thought.

"She's older. She's actually probably closer to your age than mine. I was a bit of a nerd in high school, college. It's not like I have a lot of experience. She's old enough to have had a few guys and...and if I ever do make headway...I want to impress her. Maybe you can tell me what I'm doing wrong. Give me a push in the right direction."

She knew exactly what direction she'd like him pushing in. And it was hard to imagine him doing anything wrong.

But.

"Well. I don't know about you, but most guys are in too much of a hurry. They'd actually get further, faster, if they held back a bit."

Turning gold-brown eyes on her, he nodded seriously.

"Anticipation. It drives a woman crazy."

He looked interested and raised one eyebrow.

The waitress delivered Zeke's beer as Sara warmed to the subject. "Like instead of trying to get your hands on—what's her name?"

"Dea."

"Instead of trying to get your hands on Dea's chest or between her legs, just slide your hand down her thigh to her knee. And leave it there."

"Leave it there."

Sara nodded.

"How long?"

"Until it drives her crazy."

He smiled slowly. "What if it drives me crazy first?"

She gave him a severe look. "You're just going to have to be tough."

He nodded. "What else?"

She tipped the beer into her mouth and searched her memory. "Well," she said with sudden enthusiasm. "You know what's really nice?" She didn't wait for his response. "Take your finger and smooth it over her lips, come back and do it again, come back and pull her lips open a bit and..."

His little finger was against her bottom lip as the knuckles of his hands rested against her cheek. "Like this?"

This had happened once before, Sara thought. She'd read about it. Read how God had once stopped the earth on its axis.

The world stopped spinning, Sara's heart stopped beating, and her lungs neglected their main purpose as Zeke's finger slid along her lower lip, came back and tugged it down, and slid along it again, just inside the wet surface of her bottom lip. With his eyes holding hers, he lifted her upper lip and gave it the same treatment.

"Yeah," he said softly, "I think I get it."

His lips were about two inches from hers. Staring at them longingly, she sucked her own in tight against her teeth. Vaguely, she noted the waitress had delivered their food.

"Thanks for the demonstration, Walker," he said. "Now, about the hand on the knee."

At that point, Sara realized the full error of being trapped on the inside seat of a booth with Zeke Rutherford. With no exit and no way out, her eyes frantically sought a means of escape. Zeke laughed. "Relax, Walker. I'm not actually going to put my hand on your knee." That said, he put his left hand high on her thigh and navigated it deep between her legs, his little finger resting about a millimeter from her sex, her sex pouting in disappointment as her lips filled out in an effort to put a kiss on the finger just out of reach.

"How am I doing?" he asked, as he picked up a taco with his right hand and crunched into it.

She picked his hand off her thigh and placed it carefully on his own. "You're… You're a natural, Rutherford."

She swallowed some beer and tried to force the tiny appetizer down her throat, at the same time trying very hard not to think of Dea and all the kisses she was going to get out of those fingers. Geez, two months! Dea had been holding him off for two months!

What was wrong with the woman!

Chapter Six

"Push."

With both hands above his head, Zeke pressed the transducers against the column.

"Push. Okay. Take a break."

Zeke watched Sara pull up the bottom of her T-shirt and wipe at the sweat on her upper lip. For two tantalizing seconds he caught a glimpse of skin. "Why do you wear a black bra with a white T-shirt?" he asked. He wanted to laugh when she raised her eyes to his, wide with disbelief. An instant later, when he saw her lower her eyes to the front of her damp, sweaty T-shirt, he did laugh. "You didn't know."

She shot a glance around the parking garage and frowned at him warningly.

"You didn't know, Walker. You don't even know that you're wearing black underwear."

She bit her lips between her teeth. For an instant, he was sorry he'd teased her. But she came back. Pulling the front of her jeans away from her body, she peered down into them. "It's only the bra that's black," she informed him with false pique. She pointed at the column. "*Next two points,* Sherpa."

He positioned the transducers.

"Push."

"So the rest of it is pink?"

"Next point."

"Red?"

"Push."

"I'll be disappointed if they're white, Walker."

"Pay attention, Rutherford. You're not pushing hard enough."

"How can you tell?"

"I'm getting a crap signal. Shit, Rutherford. Try to act professional, will you?" Stalking toward him, she slid between him and the column and clamped her small hands over his. "*Push. Hard*! Like this!" Craning her head over her shoulder to view the computer screen, she didn't see the gold sparks in his eyes.

Pay attention! Like he couldn't do this with his eyes shut. Push? Hard? Like she was pushing him? With her hot little body caught between him and the concrete column—with no place to go.

Push? Hard?

"Like this?" He leaned forward and put all his weight on her, pinning her against the column. His dick obliged him with a quick response to her curving presence beneath his body. "Hard enough for you, Walker?"

His tone was coolly professional, she noted. And his body was hot-hot-hot against hers.

"I'd like to pay you some attention," he said in a low, quiet voice. "How much do you want? Because I've got a thick wad here in my jeans that ought to be enough.

"Want me to push, Walker?" he whispered. "Just give me the word and I'll push you right to your limit. And right over the edge." Flexing his knees, he scraped his hard length into the small of her back.

When he eased off a bit, she turned to face him in the small space between his body and the column.

He smirked down on her with a look of pure, male confidence.

"I apologize, Rutherford," she told him. "It appears you *have* been paying attention, after all." Her eyes slid down to his crotch then back to his eyes. "Now if you could concentrate on your *work*?" She slid out from beneath him. "And Rutherford. *Try* to look professional. *Push*."

She shook out her hands as she returned to the computer. Oh, man—oh, man—oh, man. That was close. Too close for comfort. Her breasts pushed into the cool concrete column while Zeke pushed hot against her back. The hard ridge of his erection scraping into her crease and rising forever into the small of her back. This was her fault. She should have straightened him out last night in the booth.

She saved the data and typed in the next file.

Shit! She probably *had* straightened him out last night in the booth. She should have set him straight…wrong word again. She should have let him know their relationship was strictly professional. And that it was going to remain strictly professional.

Even if it killed her.

Zeke watched Sara, her attention fixed on the computer as she picked up the pace of the testing. He barely had time to think as she kept him moving from point to point.

Which was just as well.

He knew his behavior was out of line—way out of line. But Christ, she'd just about crawled underneath him. One minute he was leaning into the cool, hard concrete, the next thing he knew she was right there. Right where he wanted her.

And had been wanting her since dinner in the booth last night. Underneath him—warm and soft, fitting against his body like a puzzle piece long sought for and finally found. Coming together perfectly, connecting at every touch point, recognizing it with the sort of satisfaction that comes only after trying scores of others that looked like they might be right, only to discover they never quite meshed.

What sort of man could resist that sort of temptation, the temptation of Sara Walker's warm curves stretched out against cool, smooth concrete?

A dead man, he decided. A zombie. A man with a great deal more strength than he.

* * * * *

"*Take a break,*" she told him twenty minutes later.

He was surprised when he turned and found her grinning at him.

"'Thick wad'? That's crude, Rutherford." Walking up to him, she took the transducers from his hands. "Switch places. You operate the computer. I'll let you push me around for a change. How does that sound?"

He nodded as they passed each other. "You want me to answer that question, Walker. Or you want me to remain professional?"

He glanced up at her as he set up the next file.

Her smile was full of mischief. "If you're going for professional, Rutherford, you're still a long way off. But keep it up, I imagine you'll get there in the end."

"Well, which is it? You want me to keep it up or act professional? Make up your mind." He flicked her a smile then returned his attention to the computer screen. "*First position,* Walker. *Push.*"

Glancing up at her frequently, he watched her work her way up the column, stretching now, to reach the points above her head. The next time he looked up, he froze.

She'd climbed up onto the waist-high wall to reach the next two points on the column. They were testing on Level Three. On her left side was a fifty-foot drop to the road below. "Walker," he said softly, "what are you doing?

"Get off the wall," he told her, before she could answer.

She turned her face to him, frowning in her concentration.

"I don't want you up on that wall." His voice was quiet, his actions smooth. Moving out from behind the computer, he started toward her. "Get off the wall, Sara."

Reaching her before she had time to react, his hands shot up to clamp tight on her waist. With a jerk, he had her off the wall.

The transducers jumped in the air and she grappled for the cables, only just saving the equipment before it hit the ground.

"What are you doing?" she hissed between clenched teeth. "These things are worth a thousand dollars!"

He didn't answer her immediately, and he didn't look the least bit apologetic. Instead, he appeared to chew on a mouthful of words.

"There's a fifty foot drop on the other side of that wall," he said with a voice like crushing steel. "What the hell did you think you were doing? We could have had a ladder here in five minutes."

"There were only two more points, Rutherford. We could have had them done in five seconds."

"That's not the *point*. You might have fallen."

And only then did she notice his hands, still locked on her waist, iron-hard and holding on like he'd never let go. Beneath the steel grip was a slight vibration and she was suddenly sorry, recognizing the level of force it would take to make steel tremble. "Oh, shit. I'm sorry, Zeke. I wasn't thinking. I get in a hurry sometimes. I just...sometimes I don't want to spend the rest of my life just staying alive. Do you know what I mean?" She searched his eyes and knew immediately he did *not* know—had *no* idea—what she meant.

His eyes locked on hers. "Give me the transducers," he said grimly. "I'll take over here."

*****

Karl stopped by her office. "How'd the testing in Dallas go?"

"I think they have problems."

Karl grimaced. "Clients don't like problems."

"I don't like them either. But I think they have problems. Big problems. I'm going to recommend they test everything, from the basement up."

The phone rang and she reached for it. "See you in a minute, Karl.

"This is Sara," she said as she picked up the phone.

"I'm sorry," the female voice on the line apologized. "I asked for Zeke Rutherford."

"Zeke's just going into a meeting. Shall I give you his voice mail?"

"Uh…yeah," she started. There was a pause. "Do you know him?"

"Zeke Rutherford? Yeah, I work with him."

"Is he as sexy as he sounds—on the phone?"

The woman on the phone didn't see Sara's frown of annoyance. "Every bit," she gritted into the mouthpiece. "Can I take a message?"

Jotting down the message, she shot out of her office and was almost bowled over by the man coming up behind her. Quickly, she stepped to the side of the hall.

"Man, you're jumpy." Zeke slowed as he passed. "I wouldn't have run you over."

"Just being prudent, Rutherford. I get out of the way when there's an eighteen-wheeler bearing down on my backside, as well." She slapped the phone message into his hand as she fell into step beside him on their way to the conference room. "Who is she?"

"Who?"

Sara nodded at the message in his hand.

Zeke couldn't help but smile at what appeared to be a little healthy, female jealousy. "Jean? She works for a plastics company. Lightweight cases. Who did you think she was?"

"One of your girlfriends."

"What made you think that?"

"Because of what she said."

"What did she say?"

"She said, 'I might be nuts, but I think Zeke sounds incredibly sexy.'"

"Yeah? She said that? So what did you tell her?"

"I agreed…she was nuts."

Zeke's mouth flattened as he nodded. Reaching a hand out, he flicked the tip of her left breast.

Shocked, she stopped to stare down at the dark jacket of her suit then up at him.

"Lint," he smirked. "Try to look professional, Walker." Pleased with himself, he continued down the hall ahead of her.

Hurrying down the hall, she caught back up and entered the conference room just ahead of him. "Jeremy!"

A man with silvered temples turned at the sound of her voice, smiled at Sara, took her hand and shook it warmly, familiarly, then held it.

A bit too long, Zeke thought.

"Jeremy. You know everyone here." She indicated the people at the table, temporarily ignoring the man at her elbow—all six foot four of him. "Oh. Except for Zeke, here," she said airily. "Jeremy Johnson. Zeke Rutherford. Zeke's my Sherpa."

Flinching at this announcement, Zeke shot Sara a look of annoyance as he shook hands with the man.

"Zeke? The young man you told me about? The engineer that made the 3-D representations?"

"Brand new software." Sara smiled up at Zeke. "Jeremy was impressed with the color plots you generated. Maybe you'd like to tell him how the new data analysis software works."

Momentarily set back by Sara's ability to turn on the hot and cold running emotions without warning, Zeke's eyes flicked between her and Johnson several times before he collected himself enough to launch into an explanation. As he talked, his eyes followed Sara across the room to where she settled beside Jackie.

*****

At the meeting's close, Sara shook Jeremy's hand a final time and watched him leave.

"Can you go to Kentucky?" Karl asked before she could get out of the conference room. "To log a couple of shafts? They asked for you."

She grinned. They always asked for her in Kentucky. She'd made the trip at least ten times over the last two years.

"Take Zeke with you."

She stopped grinning. On the other side of the conference table, she watched Zeke's mouth widen into a slow, satisfied smile.

Chapter Seven

"Yeah. I owe all my success to you," Zeke told her.

They were on the road south of Louisville, heading for the project.

"At least—it's good for me. I don't think it's working for Dea, though." He turned and looked at Sara with a small, expectant smile.

She remained silent.

"Any suggestions?"

"Oh, geez!" Seeing a shopping mall up ahead, Sara set her turn signal. Zeke trailed her into a bookstore where she stood before a shelf of pastel-covered paperbacks. Randomly, it appeared to him, she pulled titles, flipped a few pages and returned the books to their slot. Eventually and apparently finding what she wanted, she put a book in his hand and led the way to the cash register.

"If you want to know what a woman wants," she said as she clicked her seatbelt, "why wouldn't you read a book about it, written by a woman?"

"This?" Zeke looked down at the pastel cover without hiding his disgust. "Romance? You expect me to read romance?"

"Yeah, it's romance. It's also erotica. Read it, Rutherford. There's a limit to how much I'm willing to demonstrate."

He quirked a smile at her and opened the book.

He read while she drove. She gritted her teeth when he snorted or—worse—laughed. Once he muttered, "Yeah. Right."

"What?" she said tersely.

"Like that's ever going to happen." He turned a page.

"What?"

He shot her a look, turned the page back and read, "*Pulling his hand from her breast, he slipped both hands gently between her legs, along the insides of her thighs, and flattened her folded legs against the table. Returning his lips to the top of her cleft, he kissed her hard. Responding with a throaty cry of anguished pleasure, she jumped into his mouth. Close enough, he decided. Sliding his arms under her legs, he curled them around her folded legs and pinned her open. He gave his brother a nod and her strong, young body bucked beneath his arms while his brother hammered her full throttle.*

"Like I'm going to prepare a woman for another man. I don't care if he is supposed to be my brother. After I've gone to all the trouble of getting a woman hot enough to fuck—I'm going in myself."

She smiled at the traffic.

He watched her smile. "Shall I go on?" He riffled through the pages.

"*He brushed his lips lightly below her belly then returned his lips to her warm, open sex. Wetting his tongue, he slid it up along her slot, feeling his way through the roughly delicate ruts that led to her clitoris. Tasted her simple clean warmth, heard her suck in a breath. Smiled with relief, ached with regret. Applied his lips and tongue softly, rhythmically against her clitoris.*"

He slid a sly look onto the seat beside him then threw the book at his feet. "Yeah, yeah. I get it. Her clitoris. Only, this doesn't tell me where to find it," he grumbled, feigning disgust. "The book ought to come with diagrams. I'd be all right if I had a diagram." He pretended to sulk, then looked at Sara and grinned, "You've already said you won't demonstrate…" He let his voice trail away, giving her a chance to jump in and comment, or even volunteer should she be so inclined.

"Here's our exit," she cut in quickly. She pulled off the highway and into the first hotel, which the travel agent had booked.

"So where is it?" he asked, as she put the car into park and pulled the key from the ignition. "Come on, Walker. Just give me a hint."

She glanced at his eyes, full of spark and mischief and couldn't help a grin herself.

"I'm sorry, Walker," he drawled, confidently. "Am I out of line?"

"You're always out of line," she grumbled with mock intolerance.

He cocked an eyebrow at her. "Are you going to turn me in?"

"Yeah, I am," she growled behind a small grin. "I'll report you to Karl. Just as soon as I get tired of it." She pushed the car door open.

"Well, if you're not too tired, maybe we should explore this a bit further, Walker. Together."

"What about whatsername? Dea?"

"What about Dea?"

"Hell, Rutherford. I'm glad I'm not your girlfriend."

He met her at the rear of the car and pulled the heavy kit out of the trunk. "Yeah? Well, what would it take?"

She gave him a blank look.

"What would it take to make you my girlfriend?"

They headed across the parking lot, Zeke carrying the kit in one hand.

"What would it take? I don't know. Ten years on the positive side, maybe. Ten inches on the negative side."

"So you'd be satisfied with two inches?"

She stared at him as she held the door open for him. "You're bragging."

"No, I'm not."

"Don't be cocky," she warned him with a grin. "I was talking about your height, not your length."

They checked in, and he followed her to the elevator. "So, what else?"

She was silent in the elevator. The doors opened on the second floor.

"So what else, Walker?"

"We work together," she said firmly.

He nodded as he trailed her down the hall. "We work together." For a moment, he was silent then he took a deep breath.

"Is that the problem, Walker?" his voice was low and his eyes were lowered. "Is that why you never enter a room if I'm in it? Is that the reason you're always walking out of the room I'm walking into? Is that why you never take a seat at the conference table until after I'm seated? And is that why you take a chair just as far from mine as you possibly can? Tell me, Walker, is that why you answer all my questions without ever looking at me? Hell, I've had ten-minute conversations with you when you've never once looked at my face."

She stopped outside the door to her room and turned to him.

He raised his arms from his sides, a helpless gesture. "You work with Nick, too. But you don't have any trouble looking at him. What's wrong with me, Sara?

"How can you pass my office every morning and not stop to say hello? How can you walk past me—a dozen times a day—without ever looking at me?"

Because if I looked at you, she thought, *I wouldn't be able to stop there.*

He shook his head. "Do you even know…what color my eyes are?"

She looked at his chest. "Gold," she said. "And brown."

"So why pretend you've never noticed? Why pretend you don't care? That it doesn't matter. That *I* don't matter.

"Look at me, Sara," his voice was tight and tense. "Let me in, Sara. Open up and let me in. I promise…it won't hurt."

She stood quietly, obstinately, eyes on the ground, wanting him to leave while at the same time wanting him, period. Reluctant to open the door before he left. Knowing if he got through that door, there'd be no turning back—for either of them.

"I'll take the equipment," she said dismissively, and reached for the handle of the kit. His hand met hers as he dropped the kit. Then both her hands were in his as he put them tight against her thighs and held them there. He leaned into her and her back came up hard against the polished surface of the pine door. "Okay," he said, frustration edging his words. "Forget about being my girlfriend. What would it take to fuck you?"

Chapter Eight

He watched with satisfaction as her eyes widened. It wasn't so much shock he saw in those blue eyes, as it was guilt. As though she'd been caught whispering private thoughts out loud. As though she didn't like having her mind read. And didn't like the fact that her mind was reading the same material, was on the same page, as his.

"You're too young."

"I'll grow a beard," he growled. "And dye it gray."

"You're too tall. I've never liked having to stretch for a kiss."

"And I've never liked having to stoop. I'll pick you up." As if to demonstrate, his hands went around her waist and her back slid up the door. All the way up, until the grooved space at the top of her legs locked on the long ridge at the top of his. Locked into place with an almost audible click—a fit that felt perfect.

"I work with you, Zeke."

"I'll quit my job. Shit, Walker. What does it take to—"

"I have a boyfriend," she said, getting desperate.

"I'll kill him. Come on, Walker," he said softly, as his mouth drew very near her ear and the long line of his erection ground into her rise, loosing a flood of desire that created significant moisture and measurable heat. "I want to put you on my dick and see how long it takes you to pump me dry."

She squirmed, wondering how long it would take before her warm heat penetrated his thick canvas jeans and revealed her for a fraud. "You'd hurt me!"

Dropping her, he drew away suddenly, looking hurt himself, looking like someone had punched him in the gut. He shook his head. "No, I wouldn't," he said, his voice stunned. "No, I wouldn't," he repeated.

She felt sorry for him then. "You would if you've got twelve inches."

"Shit, Walker. I was exaggerating."

"How much—are you exaggerating?"

He held his hand up, his finger and thumb separated by a space of perhaps an inch.

"That's too much."

Which way? He opened and closed his fingers and cocked an eyebrow at her quizzically, waiting for her to approve the distance between his fingers.

"You're a nice kid, Zeke," she smiled up at him, catching her breath. "Good night."

Dragging the kit into the hotel room, she started opening latches. Plugged in the computer to charge, plugged in her cell phone to charge, plugged in the pulser unit to charge, and moaned as she walked to the bathroom to stare at the hot, glazed eyes in the mirror. Everything was going to get fully charged tonight. Except her.

She stripped her T-shirt over her head and undid the bra that was too small and too tight. Let her breasts out and lifted them as she watched them in the mirror. She closed her eyes and ran her hands up over her nipples—imagining they were Zeke's hands—opened her eyes and gave her reflection a sad look. Her hands were too small.

Slouching out of the bathroom, she unbuttoned her jeans and pushed them down her legs, rummaged in her backpack for the short T-shirt she slept in and pulled it on. She pulled out her gray sweatpants and threw them on the bed, then walked to the little kitchenette counter and poured a pot of water through the coffeemaker. Tearing two teabags open, she threw them into the glass pot. As she stood waiting for the hot water, she rubbed her rise against the counter's edge. God, she was hot—and just about one nudge away from orgasm.

Sitting next to Rutherford made her horny. Sitting next to Rutherford, trapped in a car with him, while he read erotica aloud was pure torture. Backed up against a door, trapped beneath everything Zeke had to offer—and was offering—

Groaning with frustration, she gave up on the idea of tea.

Throwing herself backward onto the bed, she rubbed her hand over the rise of her plain, silk panties.

She wanted to cry. How could she have let him get away? He'd all but begged to give her—everything—everything she wanted. Everything she needed. She traced a finger up her stomach and over her belly button. Like a brand, she could still feel where his erection had seared a line across her belly. Christ, it had been hard to close that door on him. Close the door on everything he had. If he were to knock on the door right now, she'd drag him into her room and eat him alive. Start on her knees and work her way up from there. Push him on the bed and mount him, both hands behind her as she stroked his balls and forced him to orgasm inside her without even once moving.

Opening her legs, she stroked down the length of her silk-covered pussy. With her pelvis rocking up to meet the rhythm of her hand, she whimpered as her sex throbbed in response.

The friction of her open hand sliding over damp silk inflamed the soft, fat lips of her labia and every movement, every action, demanded an answering action as her sex cried out for further contact. She found herself helpless to resist the demand. Her hands slid inside her panties as she fingered her lips open and touched herself restlessly, positioning and repositioning her fingertip trying to decide on the place that would deliver maximum pleasure—knowing even at best it couldn't be perfect.

Not without a man answering that demand, his coveted touch rough and unpredictable sliding through her sex, his lips wet in her pussy, his mouth suckling her clit, his thick tongue or long finger pushing into her opening.

Her body mad with anticipation—waiting for the unexpected thrust or stroke that was one movement more than could be endured—the sucking lips or scraping tongue beyond her control. That wouldn't stop and wouldn't disappoint, that would push her beyond the limits of her restraint and propel her toward the sort of searing, spilling bliss that was only complete when shared with a man and a man's body.

With a sob, she widened her legs, closed her eyes and imagined Zeke's long, hard body, rising on her, pushing between her legs to mount her. With two fingers on either side of her clitoris, she nipped the small, fleshy bud between two fingers and played herself toward a fast finish.

*****

Pacing his room, Zeke glared at the pastel book on the little, round table. Even though it was trash—rubbish in fact—it had given him a hard-on that wouldn't quit. He knew the best course was to take his erection and pump it out in the shower, preferably immediately, before his balls started cramping. But, God, he wanted to see her. He palmed the length of his erection that threatened the placket at the front of his jeans.

And he wanted her to see him. Wanted to see her eyes on his dick when he pulled it out of his jeans. He wanted her to see things his way. Wanted her to see the way he could take care of her, what he could do to her.

God. The things he wanted to do to her. Stripping her naked to start with, then getting damp and sweaty with her as he pumped into her mouth or between her legs—with his hands locked in her hair or clamping on her ass to hold her tight against his groin, forcing her to accept the thrust of his hips and the spearing intrusion of his cock.

Sweeping the paperback off the table, he carried it out the door.

The door slammed behind him and his head tipped back as he halted in the middle of the brightly lit hall, hesitating at the sound of the closing door—almost turning back. Shit! What was he doing? She'd just closed the door in his face fifteen minutes earlier. She didn't need him. She'd made that clear. Entirely clear.

Why couldn't he take no for an answer? She was right! They worked together. How much sense did it make to start an intra-office relationship with a woman ten years older than you? What did you do when it was over? Yeah—when it was over. When she dumped him for someone with more money, more maturity or just plain more in common with Sara Walker.

What was that conversation he'd overheard between Sara and Jackie? About some guy she was dating—Ericson. The guy was a lawyer, for fuck's sake. What could he offer her that a lawyer couldn't give her? Nothing! *Nothing,* he thought, morosely.

What was it about her? That kept him coming on? She struck him as the sort of woman that wasn't scared of much…and yet…she seemed—no, she *was*—afraid to even meet his eyes. Frustrated, Zeke's eyes closed as he pictured Sara, her eyes averted, her hands twisting together as he stood in the door to her office. Wringing her hands as though she'd like to—as though she'd like to wring him out and hang him up to dry.

He rubbed the heel of his palm into his cock as he considered the sorry bulge at the front of his pants.

That was a lot to refer to as nothing, he thought.

Zeke nodded to himself. He didn't make as much money as a lawyer. And maybe he wasn't a brilliant conversationalist, sharp, witty and intellectual. But it wasn't…accurate…to say he had nothing to offer. And, as an engineer, he knew the value of accuracy.

* * * * *

She didn't hear the first knock at the door. She was so close! Panicked, she jerked onto her elbows and listened. Eyes wild and hot, she crept to the door. "Who is it?"

"Open up, Walker."

She leaned her head against the door and closed her eyes in a long, slow blink. Between her legs, her lips were thick and swollen, hot and slippery.

"Zeke?"

"I've got something for you."

"Just a minute." She stumbled back into the room and pulled her sweatpants on before returning to the door.

Her heart was pounding and her breath was thick as she opened the door a foot.

"I finished the book."

She looked at the book in his hand and blinked slowly, raised her eyes to his face.

But his eyes were on the thin, worn fabric that stretched over her raised nipples. The cotton T-shirt had gone 'round the washer so many times, he could tell they were pink—her nipples—right through the thin stuff of her shirt. And her breasts… They were so much larger in real life. So much rounder than when she had them squeezed into the tight confines of her bra. The T-shirt was short and her sweatpants hung low on her hips, displaying a lot of taut skin that stretched across her belly and hips, and below that, a narrow bit of black silk panties.

Chapter Nine

"God, Walker," he said with constricted throat. He pushed through the door and dropped the book as one of his hands slid up her rib cage, under the thin shirt, and curved to hold one of her breasts. He pressed her into the wall just inside the door and brought his second hand up over her other breast. His rough thumbs rubbed across her tight, hard nubs as the T-shirt crested her tips to reveal her thrusting nipples. Instinctively, his knee moved to push between her legs.

"Zeke," she whimpered. Her pelvis ground forward, hitting him just below the crotch.

He checked her eyes. Her pupils were dilated to the point of no return, her normally blue eyes effectively black. His pulse leapt and surged in a rush to reach his sex. His eyes returned to the pink beneath his thumbs. "Oh, yeah, Walker," he breathed. "These are sweet. What else do you have for me?"

From deep within her throat there unraveled a sound of pure, female longing.

Zeke responded with extracted male lust as blood, hot and thick, wicked up his dick like mercury in a thermometer.

Without waiting for an answer, he picked her up by the waist, sat her on the edge of the bed and ripped his T-shirt over his head. With a hand in the middle of her chest, he pushed her back on the bed and stretched out beside her, one of his hands stroking a nipple as the other plunged into her pants and between her legs.

"Zeke," she whispered.

Her sex was wet as he slid a finger down through her furred lips. And hot. Hot to the touch. God she was hot. "What have you been doing in here, Walker?" he whispered in a rasp. "Why didn't you call me?" He looked down at her legs. "Spread your legs for me," he commanded, his voice raw.

"Zeke," she moaned.

His sex responded with raging insistence. Impatiently, he pulled his hand out of her pants as he moved to the floor, pushing her knees apart. Kneeling between her legs, he tucked his long fingers under her bottom and reached up with his thumb to trace the seam of her pants stretching in a line between her legs and pointing straight to paradise. He watched her as her head went back and—straining up onto her toes—her bottom rose an inch off the bed. With his hands spreading her legs from inner thigh to knee, he put a kiss on the seam of her sweats as he forced her legs to their limit.

Sucking in a breath, she pushed up on her toes again, thrusting her pelvis upward in a curving arch.

As she delivered her sex to his mouth, he worked his full lips over the soft jersey of the sweatpants, gnawing to pull at the thick, oversexed lips beneath, scraping the fabric into his teeth. Giving in to a rough, male hunger he'd have to rein in later, when he had her bare and exposed, her legs spread wide, her vulnerable sex open, unable to refuse his hard, full aggression. The thought alone made him pant into the damp space he'd created between her legs.

Like a flash storm, his hunger mutated into aching, scathing need, and he found himself wrenching at her sweatpants, almost tearing her panties in his rush to get them off. Flinging pants and panties behind him, he returned his hands to her waist as he dragged his hands from her waist down to her thighs then pushed between her legs again.

Thrusting her legs wide, he slipped two fingers into the warm envelope of her labia and spread his fingers, opening her lips. "What else do you have for me, Walker?" He watched her face. "Show me."

He added a third finger to her pussy and, with two fingers spreading her open, ran his middle finger purposefully over her clitoris. "Where is it, Walker," he whispered roughly.

"Oh, *God*," she gritted through clenched teeth. "God, Zeke, help me."

He ran his middle finger through the long wet slit again stopping just short of giving her the contact she wanted. The contact he knew she needed. He blew on the pearly pink nub caught between his fingers and smiled ruthlessly. "Show me, Walker."

With a sound half moan and half sob, she reached for his hand, found his finger and guided it to the hot throbbing center of her sex.

He put his finger on her clit and she cried out.

"Is that it, Walker?" His breath raced to get out of his chest, and his free hand slid down to rub the length of his throbbing dick. He touched her again, barely, wanting to kiss her in the same place, to get his lips around the pink nub of flesh and prod her toward madness. When he lifted his finger, she strained to reach him, strained to follow his touch. Her feet crawled up the side of the bed in her desperation to reach him. When her feet reached the flat surface of the bed, they pushed her up further. Pushed her bottom off the bed as her back arched down to her neck where she supported her weight.

Zeke rose with her until he was standing between her legs, his finger giving her only the merest of contact. He looked at her rutted sex exposed between his spread fingers—her clitoris inches from his face, and fought the urge to suck it hard into his mouth. She'd probably scream. Scream with sweet, aching pleasure. His eyes went to her face on the bed. He couldn't reach her to cover her mouth.

Ah, Shit. Dragging his teeth over his tongue, he leaned over and flattened his dry tongue against her clit. And was gratified to see her clamp both of her hands over her own mouth.

"Zeke!" His name was a muffled scream from behind ten fingers.

With the fingers of one hand beneath her bottom, helping to support her weight, his finger played her clit while his thumb rested just beneath her opening, toying with the flesh that rimmed her shining vulva. Fascinated, he watched her narrow slit shudder and quake several times, then quiet again.

Oh, man, she was so ready. Her little pink cunt was so wet and open, and just begging for a man and all the damage a man could inflict.

And he was just as ready to deliver, his cock a granite mass of crazed flesh, mad to fight inside her hot channel, feel her hot sheath wrapped tight around his dick as he delivered all the racking punishment she could handle.

Reaching around to his back pocket, he experienced an instant of desperate, dread panic. Both wallet and condoms were back in his room.

With a groan of agonized restraint, he fought the instinct to pull his dick and cram into her. He needed this fuck—needed her on the end of his cock. He groaned again, knowing that her need was just as urgent as his own.

"Zeke! *Please.*" *Please, Zeke,* she prayed. *Just stroke me once and I promise I'll come right into your hand.*

He did better than that. Improvising, he slid his finger down to her opening and, with his thumb nudging her clitoris, thrust his long middle finger deep into her socket.

Immediately, she came on his finger. Wet and clutching, her body swallowed along the length of his finger, reopened and swallowed again. Her watched her body, her face—fascinated—while her vagina clenched on his finger in spasming shockwaves. *God. Could a woman really orgasm that long?*

"Oh, Zeke—oh, Zeke—oh, Zeke," she was still whispering when he lowered her back onto to the bed. Her eyes opened and fixed on him with a look of pure, moaning worship. "Thank you."

His muscles jumped in a clenched jaw, and he felt a frown etch itself into the space between his eyebrows. With a surly look at her warm, wet pussy, he cursed himself. "You want to thank me? I'll let you thank me." God, he wanted her—wanted inside her. Inside where he knew she was soft, swollen and wet. Wanted to fuck her with bruising intrusion she'd still be feeling three days from now.

"How thankful are you?" he asked roughly as he got on the bed and straddled her between his knees. He wrenched his fly open and pulled out his dick.

In answer, she ran her hands up his hard thighs. Her eyes never left his straining cock, dark and angry in his hand. She stared at the veins that wrapped his shaft like twisting dark wire. "Very thankful," she answered with sincerity.

"Yeah. Well, you can be thankful with my cock in your mouth."

Chapter Ten

With a large hand wrapped behind her head, he angled her mouth up to meet his cock. With his other hand around his shaft, he pressed his hooded tip against her lips. Pulling her elbows back to support her weight, she kissed the wide, blunt head rearing at her mouth. A silvery thread of semen welled at the neat slit in his cock head and she touched her tongue to the small opening, licking away his shimmering output.

"Open your mouth," he rasped, just before he forced himself between her lips. His hips rocked as he insinuated himself more deeply into her mouth. Reaching for her hand, he almost unbalanced her as he brought her hand to wrap around his shaft then covered her hand with his own. Together they pumped him toward his finish.

But at thirty-four, a woman isn't completely ignorant. She knew what a man liked and where he liked it. Sucking hard, she dug her tongue into the bottom front edge of his mushrooming hood. His hand tightened around hers and he stilled—grew impossibly large between her teeth—just before he exploded into her mouth. She sucked him hard as he let loose into her mouth, and continued sucking at the thick flesh until he was lank between her lips.

He collapsed on the bed beside her.

"That thankful enough for you, Rutherford?"

He groaned in answer and, with his long fingers still caging her skull, pressed her face into his groin.

She woke with her cheek against his hard belly, his big hand still cradling her skull. Carefully, she disengaged herself, opened the curtains a crack and padded across the room to make coffee. When she turned around, he was sitting up and watching her. The meager morning light filtered through the crack in the curtain and shadowed his expression. "What're you looking at?"

His eyes rose from the perfect triangle at the top of her legs. "Sorry if I was rough last night," he said tentatively.

She sipped the black liquid and made a bitter face.

"When you get me going…I feel like…I'd kill for what's between your legs." Blood started pounding its way into his penis and his morning erection took on serious aspect. Pushing himself to the edge of the bed, he tucked his length inside the pants he still wore and zipped the jeans up far enough to keep them from sliding off his hips.

She watched his back and the Celtic knot tattooed at the base of his spine. "You didn't hear me complaining," she affirmed quietly.

"It will probably happen again," he suggested, not looking at her, but across the room.

"You think so?" There was a hint of laugher in her question.

She watched his shoulders ease. "I'm sure of it."

"I love an optimist." She slid a sneaky smile in his direction. Rested her eyes on the Celtic knot, where she very much wanted to kiss him. "God, you're beautiful," she told him.

She wanted to cry, he was so beautiful. And so young. And could only ever be temporary. Shit. She couldn't hold onto men her own age. How was she going to hold on to something as perfect as this? With every sexy young thing out there angling for him, not to mention Dea who evidently, already had an angle on him.

He stood and nodded her way. Finally smiled.

"What're you smiling about?"

He picked his T-shirt off the floor. "I'm no longer the exception," he said, pulling the T-shirt over his head. "Now you have a reason...to call me by my last name. Assuming it happens again, do I need a condom?"

Which just increased her desire to kiss him. Most men weren't mature enough to initiate this conversation. "I'm safe. And protected."

He nodded. "I'm good." His voice was warm, as was his gaze, and he looked like he was ready to initiate more than conversation.

She grinned. "Come on Sherpa. It's seven o'clock. I want to be onsite in half an hour. Where'd I leave my bra?"

"If it's black, it's behind the chair." Crossing the room, he scooped it up and started laughing. "What? What's this?" He dangled the bra from one finger. "Shit, Walker!" he said, suddenly struck with a new idea. "You're a nerd."

She frowned at the twist of shiny electrical tape in between the cups of her bra, holding the bra together like a broken pair of eyeglasses.

"I've been meaning to get a new one," she explained. "It broke...recently...while I was in the field."

"How recently?"

"I've been busy!"

"I'd say it's time for a new bra, Walker. This one doesn't fit you anyhow." Rolling it into a loose ball, he tossed it basketball-style across the room. It landed in the small, round trash container. With a pleased smile, he sauntered the few steps toward her, pushed her T-shirt up out of his way and lifted her breasts in his hands. Crowding her back against the counter, he forced her spine to arch and her breasts to curve up into his cupped palms. He put his full, warm lips against her temple. "Get a new bra, Walker. It's a crime to bully these beauties into that torture chamber you think is underwear."

"What do you mean, it doesn't fit?" she argued as she pushed at him. "It's all I've got and I'll have to wear it. I'm not showing up at the job site in...nothing but nipples!"

She laughed but she was embarrassed, too. And wishing she'd put a little more effort into projecting a smooth, sexy image of herself. She smiled wryly to herself. What difference did it make? It's not like she expected much more out of Zeke Rutherford, regardless of his optimism.

His mouth dipped toward hers and his hands fastened around her waist to lift her. "On the counter, Walker." It was the only warning she got, the words a warm murmur in her ear.

"Zeke," she protested with another push. "I want to be at the job site in—"

"Half an hour. I'm not deaf, Sara. This will only take a minute. Open your legs and scoot up here to the edge." He pulled her toward him as his dry lips brushed her cheek on their way to her lips.

In an attempt to evade his kiss, she tossed her head. She heard the soft burr of his zipper and felt the thick, warm head of his cock nudging into her folds with a soft, insistent pressure.

"Hold still," he growled. "Stop fidgeting, woman." Abruptly, he stopped, his eyes full of sparking threat. "Okay, Walker, you asked for it." Slowly, with his eyes latched on hers, he reached for her coffee cup and filled his mouth with the hot brew. His eyes flashed gold. Then, just like that, his head was between her legs as he dropped to his knees. With both hands firmly grasping her ankles, he put one of her feet on his shoulder and the other on the counter, exposing and opening her sex to the long, hot sweep of his warm, wet tongue. She gasped at the sudden raw contact, the smell of coffee mingling with the scent of last night's lust.

Morning coffee had never smelled or tasted, or felt, so good. Her hands fisted in his hair, but all she could do was hold on while he dragged a long, hot, even stroke right from her deep, soft notch to the nick of her cleft. Her head went back, her eyes closed, and her legs relaxed to open and invite the invasion of his tongue at its deepest level. He rumbled a growl of approval, and the vibration set off a series of shivers through her vagina where he now concentrated his tongue, the rough tip pulling and tugging the soft, giving flesh of her vulva, her vagina approaching orgasm and ready to spill into his mouth with only a little more provocation.

His grip on her ankles tightened as his tongue's action became more aggressive and he pulled her bottom closer to the counter's edge at the same time he pushed her closer to the edge of climax. A final pull up through her folds started her into the final stretch, and she throttled back the anguished pleasure that tried to fight its way out of her throat in the form of a tattered, choking scream.

His big hands moved to her hips and held her sex against his mouth, allowing him to dominate and control her orgasm. His tongue slid up and down between clit and vulva playing her fevered sex for every last shred of pleasure it could pull out of her shuddering cunt.

When she finally opened her eyes, he was standing between her legs, his hand wrapped around her cup, sipping at her coffee. His smile was supercilious.

Almost immediately, she forgave him. He had a right to be pleased with himself.

"What about you?" She eyed the dark head of his cock pushing through the V of his partially zipped jeans.

He glanced down and shrugged with an air of supreme, male superiority. "I'll pump it out in the shower."

Her eyes followed him across the room as he stretched lazily on his way to the bathroom. Oh, man. Everything about him was so…long. Long arms stretched over his head. Long fingers—long legs—long, sexy, naked torso. And the longest package she'd ever seen inside a man's pants. Oh, yeah. The guy was hot and desirable, and every woman's one-night-stand dream date.

He closed the bathroom door behind him and for a long while she stared at that closed door. No. She didn't expect much more out of Zeke Rutherford. But she wanted more. She wanted more Zeke Rutherford and more sex, as much as she could possibly fit into her…schedule.

She heard the shower start followed by the sound of his voice. "You going to give me a hand with this, Walker?"

Chapter Eleven

"Oh, shit. OSHA police."

"What?"

"Occupational Safety and Health." Sara glanced at her life vest hanging from one of the access tubes.

"Aren't you supposed to be wearing that?" Zeke asked.

She shrugged, "I wear it in the winter. It's too hot in the summer."

An aluminum boat bumped up against the twelve-foot diameter shaft standing in the middle of the lake amongst a crop of other shafts. Small waves generated by the dying motor slapped at the concrete pier. Zeke caught at the boat's tie line while Sara waved at the man in the boat and greeted him cheerfully, "Hi, Darren. How's Ishtar? She drop that foal yet?"

"Any day now."

"This is Zeke Rutherford." Sara introduced Zeke as Darren stepped out of the boat onto the small concrete island. "Zeke Rutherford, Darren Black. Zeke's my—"

"Co-worker," Zeke cut in. "I work with Sara," he said, as he finished tying off the boat and extended a hand.

Darren wasn't more than six feet, but it was a burly six feet. He shook hands with Zeke then ignored him. While Zeke pulled cables on Sara's cue, Darren and Sara swapped horse stories.

Watching the pair crouched close together, huddled over the computer at their feet, Zeke decided the time was right to continue his training.

"Hey, Sara. Isn't it about time for us to change positions?"

Distracted, she looked up then glanced at her watch. "I was going to change at noon but if you want—"

"I'm ready to collect data now," he said firmly, as he caught and held the inspector's eye.

Five minutes later, Zeke was throwing Darren the tie line as the OSHA inspector pulled the motor back to life.

"And Sara," Darren called out, "put your life vest on. I wouldn't want to have to write you up."

Sara blew out a breath through pursed lips as the boat chugged away. "Close one," she pointed out.

Zeke laughed. "That man's never going to write you up."

She questioned him with a look.

"He could have asked you to put your life vest on when he first got here. *Pull.*"

She looked down at her damp T-shirt, clinging to her breasts.

"He's interested in you."

"What makes you say that?"

"The way he looks at you. The way he tried to crush my fingers when we shook hands."

She looked at him, surprised. "Why would he do that? You're just my Sherpa. At least, as far as he knows."

Zeke shrugged with a deep chuckle. "Maybe because I was trying to break his wrist at the same time."

Sara snorted. "How smart is that, Rutherford? The guy shoes horses in his spare time. *We're up.*"

"Now you tell me! The guy's got a steel grip strong enough to bust— He doesn't have any reason to be interested in you, does he?"

She quirked a smile down at her chest as she let the cables slide through her fingers and down the next tube pair. "I don't know. You tell me."

"That's not what I mean."

"*Ready*," she reminded him.

"You know what I mean, Sara. How many times have you been out here?"

"Ten times, at least." She paused long enough to tease him. "I'm not interested in OSHA inspectors," she told him.

"Yeah. Well, what are you interested in?"

"Finishing this shaft. *I'm ready*, Rutherford."

"*Pull*," he told her.

* * * * *

"Let's do that again," Sara said, as she frowned at the computer screen.

With a glance over his shoulder, Zeke dropped the transducers back down the tubes. He was back to pulling cables while Sara collected the data. Dark, threatening weather raced toward the shaft they tested, a small concrete oasis in the middle of the troubled, tossing lake. The walkie-talkie crackled, and Zeke let the cables slide through the fingers of one hand while he reached with his other for the phone clipped to his life vest. The super's voice was choppy on the transmitter. "I gotta get you guys off that pier before the storm hits. I'm sending the cage over."

Sara ducked under the cables and pushed Zeke's thumb along with the button to activate her response. "Hey, Mike. We only have two more tests. If we leave now, we'll have to come back tomorrow. We'll have to charge you for another day." She released Zeke's thumb, ducked back under the cables, pushed a sequence of buttons on the computer and signaled Zeke to raise the cables.

Zeke had the transducers halfway up before Mike came back, "Okay, Sara. Ten minutes."

Even with Zeke pulling at top speed, the two final tests took the full ten minutes. They were tossing their equipment into the case as the crane turned on the nearby barge and the man cage swung across the lake. By that time, the storm was ugly and full upon them. Lightning flashed in the not-too-distant distance. Bullying thunder grumbled a threat and big, hot drops walloped out of the sky with angry intent. With the kit on the floor of the man cage, there was only just room for two people to stand. Zeke locked his harness to the cage and Sara hugged the field computer to her chest as the cage glided smoothly into the sky.

Lightning scored a close hit and Zeke flinched. He checked Sara's face as she leaned against him, looking out into the storm with keen interest. His T-shirt was soaked and clung to every one of the several lean curves on his chest. Sara's T-shirt clung to two curves in particular. There was a blinding flash of light and noise and the cage lurched to a swinging halt. Automatically, both riders turned to look at the crane from which the cage was suspended.

Mike's voice scratched into the air, "That last strike seems to have affected the crane's electrical supply. Don't panic guys. It'll take a minute to get the backup generator running."

Zeke's eyes dropped to check Sara's face. Her eyes glowed in the pre-storm electrical light. The fact that she wasn't afraid should have been reassuring. But. Zeke's eyes followed the crane's mast up into the air, high above the big, bare lake. "Hey, Walker. Tell me I'm wrong, but hanging from a crane in the middle of an electrical storm doesn't seem like a safe situation."

"That's why they want to get us out of here."

"Do cranes ever get hit by lightning?"

"All the time," she murmured. "The cab is insulated and the crane is grounded. So the crane can take a hit without the operator getting hurt."

He looked at the metal body of the cage. *Christ.* "So the operator would be okay..."

"But we'd fry."

Christ.

"Don't worry." She turned to smile up at him, eyes lit. "You can feel the lightning just before it hits."

"Great. So I'll have some warning just before I fry."

She nodded. "If your hair starts to lift, I suggest you jump. That's what I plan to do," she laughed.

She laughed! He looked down at the surface of the lake, maybe thirty feet below. "Then lightning strikes the lake and we die anyway."

She shrugged, and indicated the barge on which the crane floated. "We'd only have to swim twenty feet or so. Think you could swim in steel toes?"

"I could if I had to." He looked at the computer clutched in her arms and she followed his gaze.

"It's waterproof," she said. "And I think it will float…a bit."

He gave her a look that said women and children first.

"There's no way I'm coming back out here to repeat ninety-eight tests!"

The walkie-talkie burped and scratched again, "Uh. Sara. There's a problem."

Mike's problem was obliterated in a flash and blast that occurred simultaneously—a very, very near hit.

Zeke's legs were over the side of the cage as he grabbed for Sara and yanked her from her feet.

She struggled in his arms. "Rutherford!" she screamed.

He was inclined to ignore her.

"Your harness lock!" With one arm around the computer, she reached to unhook him from the cage.

As for her harness? She'd never locked herself in.

They went over the edge and plunged a long way down into the water. When Zeke surfaced, he twirled in the water, looking for her. Two orange hardhats floated nearby. Amazingly, he felt the computer bumping up his length just before she broke the surface, sucking for air. With his hands gripping her waist, he treaded water for all he was worth. "Shit, Walker. You *can* swim can't you?"

"Of course I can swim," she said, parting the screen of wet hair before her eyes. "Just not very well." She was laughing as her mouth disappeared below the water line.

Wresting the computer from her grasp, he struck out for the barge while she dog-paddled along behind him. With one hand on the edge of the barge, he reeled her the rest of the way in and pushed her toward a set of hands that reached down for her. With his feet only just on firm concrete, a blast cracked the air behind him. He might have turned but his eyes were riveted on Sara's as she gazed up at the cage with rapt fascination. And he knew. The mast had been hit.

Chapter Twelve

He still hadn't said a word.

They'd dried off a bit in the client's trailer while Sara insisted there was no need to fill out an accident report. "What am I going to report?" she protested. "I'm wet? The injured parties sustained—wet clothes?"

With a hurried goodbye, she made her escape and Zeke followed her. Once out the door of the trailer, she headed for the rental car but he got in front of her, opened the driver's side door and slammed into the driver's seat. The keys were in the ignition where she'd left them. He ratcheted the seat back with abrupt violence, making room for his long legs, and turned the key. Slowly, intently, he guided the car off the site and down the paved country road, pulling his seatbelt across his body at the same time.

She watched his clenched jaw. "Anyone might have made the same mistake," she soothed. "You're still young, inexperienced."

He put his foot on the brake, turned onto a dirt road and stopped the car. He didn't look at her. "*What* are you talking about?"

"Your harness lock," she said slowly, feeling her way. "You forgot to unhook it before you jumped. You'd have been hanging helpless from the cage when the lightning hit."

He turned toward her slowly, staring his disbelief. "Oh! Thank you. Thank you very much. For saving my life. The life that *you* put in danger in the first place! We should have been off that lake long before the storm hit."

"I'm—"

"You want to behave irresponsibly, Walker, that's your business. You had no right to risk my life."

"I'm sorry," she delivered emphatically. "All that equipment—" she waved her arm behind her "—sitting idle, costs the client millions. I'm used to getting the job done. At any cost."

"Not at the cost of human life. My life. You're not a fucking Navy Seal."

She returned his angry stare, grinding her teeth. "You're right!"

"You're damn right, I'm right."

"And that's why I normally work alone. I told Karl I didn't want a Sherpa."

His eyes snapped to hers, full of warning fire.

"I'll tell Karl we can't work together." She stared out the window. There were several moments of silence as Zeke digested this unanticipated piece of information. "You gonna drive, Rutherford?" she said impatiently, "Or do you want me to?"

He started the car and slipped it into gear. They drove at least thirty miles without speaking. "Walker. I didn't mean… Walker, I want to work with you."

Suddenly angry, she spun on him. "No, you don't. Be honest—with yourself at least, if not with me. You want to work with someone that looks like me but behaves responsibly. You want to work with a nice, safe, conservative engineer that—just conveniently—has a nice ass and a sweet set of tits. Newsflash, Rutherford! That's not me."

Twenty more miles passed in silence as Sara stared angrily out the side window. "You're right," he said finally. "You want the truth? I don't want to work with you. I want to fuck you. I always have."

She continued to stare out the window. Shrugged angrily. "Now there's a revelation. I've seen *When Harry met Sally*."

"What does that mean?"

"It's an old movie. Before your time, evidently. Billy Crystal kindly pointed out to the whole female population that men just want to fuck women—all of them, if possible. Otherwise, as many as possible—and in no particular order. Preferably with no strings attached."

He chewed on the inside of his mouth. "No. It's not like that. I want to fuck you with—"

With what? And why was it difficult to think about? Why was it even harder to express?

"I want to fuck you with love."

"Is that possible?" she asked tightly.

"*Damn it,*" he exploded. "I'm trying to be...honest, Walker."

"Yeah, I imagine that's hard."

"Don't give me that shit, Walker! Is it hard for you to imagine I want to live? That I don't want to die at twenty-*fucking*-three?"

"Yeah, well, you might feel differently if *you'd—*" She turned her head quickly and her voice disintegrated, catching in her throat.

The car fishtailed on the highway as Zeke braked and got the car on the shoulder. "*What—*"

But she was out the door.

Zeke fought his way out of the seatbelt and shoved himself onto the road, slamming the door behind him. Sara was on the edge of the asphalt, walking backward, her thumb out. Cars whipped past at seventy, dragging her hair to whip around her face. "Shit, Walker. What the *fuck* is wrong with you?" His words were lost as a long semi screamed past.

Then he saw the tears. The fragile drops looked out of place on Sara's face—Sara who laughed at lightning.

"Leave me *alone,* Rutherford!"

But he was against her by that time, his fingers in her hair, his palms holding her temples.

Her hands clamped around his thick wrists then stopped just short of yanking them away. She clung to his wrists as he stooped for the kiss and she stretched to reach it—as though her life depended on it.

How he got her back to the car, he couldn't be certain but it must have involved some lifting. The next thing he knew he had her off her feet, pressing her into the passenger side door, raising her face where he could properly reach it.

He hesitated an instant, torn between the gentling she probably needed and the all-out rape his body demanded. He forced a compromise from his body—promising himself a full, hard consummation at the earliest possible opportunity—and held her face carefully while his lips nudged into hers. Played with her lips and kept playing until she was moaning into his mouth, arching her breasts into his chest. Kept at her until her legs opened to creep up his flanks and fasten behind his back.

Getting his hands on her shins below her knees, he unfastened her legs as he pulled them up and pressed them toward her. With the ridge of his cock aligned with the seam of her jeans, he rocked into her.

On the other side of the car, traffic hurtled along the highway, sucking at the air, rocking the car as Zeke rocked into Sara, rubbed into Sara, flexed his knees and scraped his dick up the seam of her jeans. Damn! In a minute, he was going to have to tear her jeans open and properly fuck her.

Her fingers dug into his forearms and he watched her face as her head went back on the car's roof, her eyes closed. Her head whipped side-to-side on the roof of the car and she canted her hips to put her jean-clad pussy fully against the placket of his jeans. "Oh, no, Walker. Oh, no. Don't tell me you're going to come. Don't tell me you're going to come on me right here."

Her clawing wail was lost as a truck dragged it down the highway. It was too much. Watching her head jerk backward, knowing she was creaming for him at that instant, knowing her cunt was clenching, wet and empty where his cock should be filling her. Zeke shoved up against her and started to release inside his jeans. He put his body hard against hers and smothered her scream in his mouth as he continued to pump out between her spread legs.

Chapter Thirteen

"I don't want to talk about it," she said, when they were back in the car. She reached for the radio, turned up the music, and slid the dial to put the music in the front of the car. There were a few more moments of silence while Zeke waited, giving her a chance to change her mind. Eventually, he started the car and eased it out onto the highway.

They were on the outskirts of Louisville before she spoke again. "You still mad, Rutherford?"

"Hell, yes. I'm still mad." But his voice was thoughtful, distracted.

"Too mad to have sex with me?"

His eyes cut to her—back to the road—cut to her again. "Too mad to have sex? Hell, Walker. I've never been *that* mad in my entire life."

She nodded to no one in particular as she grinned out the window.

"What about you?"

"What do I have to be mad about?" She peered out the window contemplatively. "What we need, Rutherford, is a quiet, out-of-the-way, deserted road."

"Didn't get enough of me last time?" he said, with the beginnings of a grin.

"Didn't get any of you last time," she pointed out.

His eyebrows drew together in a painful expression as he swallowed hard. "I'll find someplace," he promised.

She laughed at his determined expression as he pulled off the highway.

When he pulled over, he looked over his shoulder then checked his watch. "We've got about fifteen minutes."

She pulled his wrist under her nose and scowled at the watch's face. "Forty-five," she told him.

"Fourteen minutes," he insisted, and when she opened her mouth, "You're wasting time arguing."

For about two seconds she stared at him. Unzipping her pants, she wriggled them down her legs, complaining the whole time. "Man. You're...conservative, Rutherford. Predictable. Don't you ever take risks?"

"I'm in a car on the side of the road getting ready to have sex with a naked—"

"—half-naked."

"—half-naked woman in broad daylight."

"You say that like it's a bad thing. None of it's illegal," she muttered.

When she looked at him, he wasn't smiling.

"Yeah. I take risks, Walker," he said quietly. "Every time I look into your eyes." He held her gaze until she looked away. "What about you, Walker? You take a lot of risks. Why is that?"

"I could tell you, Rutherford. But it would take more than fourteen minutes."

"Thirteen minutes," he told her as he levered his seat back and unzipped his fly.

"Thirteen minutes," she said breathlessly as she watched his hand open his fly and push his shorts down to clear his cock.

With a hand around his cock, he grimaced at the rigid, veined flesh in his hands. "Still sticky," he told her.

"That's okay. I'm still wet." She crawled over the console and straddled him just below his cock. Aggressively, she pulled his cock forward and held it against her cleft as she rubbed her wet labia onto his dick.

"Twelve minutes, Walker. Better get on."

"Don't rush me." She glared at him.

With his big hands around her waist, he lifted her, moved her forward and dropped her onto his cock.

She gasped at the full, thick intrusion of his entry. But he wasn't done with her. Slowly he raised her a few inches, watching her on his cock, where he stretched into her vulva, then pushed her down to meet his thrusting hips. He watched her vagina—the delicate pink flesh of her opening forced wide—take the unrelenting barrage for several minutes before he glanced at her face. His hips stopped.

"I'm sorry, Sara. Are you all right?"

"Zeke. I don't think I'm going to make it in twelve min—"

"Ten minutes."

"I don't think I'm going to make it in ten minutes," she almost sobbed. "You're just too big."

He groaned. "You're just making it worse, Sara."

She gave him a sad little smile. "Feeding the flames?"

"Feeding my ego," he told her. "Come down here and kiss me, Sara."

Sara lowered her chest onto his and for a long time he did nothing more than kiss her. They both moaned when he finally broke the connection. "You set the pace, Sara."

She began to rub herself against his body.

"No. Don't rush it, Sara. Take your time."

Moments later, she was pushing herself up on rigid arms while she forced her slippery sheath onto his cock with a steady reciprocal motion. Her full, heavy breasts hung before his eyes and he reached for the back of her bra. Popping the snaps, he pushed bra and shirt up above her nipples and craned forward to take her in his mouth as he sucked areola and nipple deep between his teeth. When she started to whip into orgasm, her reddened nipple was torn from his rasping teeth, and he watched her go wild on his dick.

Her hair was a wild spray slashing at her face as she warped into orgasm at hyper-speed and time was hard-pressed to keep up with her. As her face blurred before his eyes, he watched, overwhelmed with the keen, cock-busting satisfaction of knowing—he'd done this to her. Her cunt throttled his dick mercilessly and it required every ounce of will he possessed—along with a great deal of sweat—to choke back his own release. As the sweet, clenching pulses ebbed into remission—she sank back onto his chest.

He smiled down on her head. "Get everything you wanted?"

She nodded into his chest.

"Good. Now are you ready to be fucked?"

She nodded again.

"Hard?"

She pushed herself back up to sit on his cock, and his hands clamped onto her hips as he drove himself up into her at the same time he forced her hips down to take all of him. He watched her face as she sank her teeth in her bottom lip, wincing at the power of his attack. He kept pounding into her, pounding toward his release. Damn. She was dripping, sopping, splashing wet from her two earlier orgasms and he moved her on him easily. Her breasts lifted, fabulous and generously beautiful as her hands went behind her. He felt her hands slipping on his tight, wet balls. With a roar, his hips shot upward and surged into her violently. Slammed up into her cunt. His eyes widened to see her writhing on him, sharing his orgasm in jerking, shivering, wild-eyed wonder.

Her eyes were dreamy as she came out of coitus and smiled at him. Stringers of light threaded in through the windows and fingered her face as she basked in post-coital euphoria.

He'd been right about her—intent, focused and thorough.

"What?" she asked him with a soft, curious smile, and he realized he probably looked a little stunned.

"That was..."

"Mind-shattering?" she suggested.

"More like mind-altering. That was intense." He closed his eyes, afraid Sara might see right into him, right through to everything churning in his mind. "Give me a minute."

"Hey. You're the one who's on a schedule."

She shifted on him as though to move away, and his hands tightened on her hips. For some reason, getting to the airport and catching the plane weren't as important as they had been fifteen minutes ago. All that was important was the last fifteen minutes with Sara. He wanted to somehow keep those minutes, and every memory that came with them. The memory of Sara, shoulders back, breasts thrust forward, as he pumped his hips up into the gap between her spread legs—

"Rutherford!"

"What?"

Sara laughed. "Didn't you hear me?"

"Yeah, I heard you—but say it again anyway."

"What was that you were shouting? There toward the end?"

He shook his head. "I'm not sure I remember."

"Something about my being *such* a good fuck?"

He stretched his arms behind his head. "That sounds about right."

"Thanks," she told him. "The feeling's mutual." She slid off him with a sigh and fumbled around for her clothes.

Slowly, he lifted his watch in front of his eyes. "Perfect timing," he announced.

She grinned at him, "Yeah, it was. Perfect both times. You're good, Rutherford."

"Thanks," he said, as though he deserved nothing less.

"Sara," he started, as he rearranged his clothing. "I still want to know…about everything else. Sometime when we have more than fourteen minutes."

"Do yourself a favor, Rutherford, and don't ask," she said as she poked her feet into her panties.

"Why not?"

"Because it's my observation that men don't like to watch women cry. In addition, I find it personally embarrassing." She turned on him. "Do me a favor, Zeke," she said softly, "and don't ask."

Chapter Fourteen

She looked into the small package with a stunned expression. Reaching inside, she fingered the aqua lace that edged the feminine bra then turned over the size tag. "How did you know my size?"

"I knew what size your old one was. Knew it didn't fit. Made some assumptions based on…volume." His eyes sparked and he laughed. "I *am* an engineer," he reminded her.

She looked up, lips parted. "Hell of an engineer," she breathed.

"Put it on."

"What? Here?"

"Hurry up. I want to take it off."

She nodded down at the box then looked up at him. "You're a nice kid, Rutherford."

Kid! He shook his head. "Oh, no. No, Walker. You said we could…"

She kept her eyes on the pink tissue, unwilling to meet his eyes. "I don't mind when we're out in the field, Rutherford—but not officially. Not here in the office. Not here in Denver! You could lose your job. *I* could lose my job."

His eyes filled with something very much like panic. "It's six-thirty. We're alone." He shook his head. "Once or twice a month isn't going to be enough, Walker."

"What about Dea?"

He looked a bit blank for an instant. "I've been thinking about dropping Dea," he recovered quickly. He followed her eyes to the office door. Reaching for the door's edge, he closed it behind him and leaned against it with a take-no-prisoners, give-no-quarter look.

She grinned up at him. "*He Shot the Bolt.*"

"What?"

"My favorite painting in the National Gallery, London. It's called *The Bolt*. An 18th century nobleman is bolting the door to his bedroom while he holds in one arm a woman that implores him to...unlock the door? Unlock her heart? Unlock her passion?"

"You've been to England?"

"I go every spring when the rates are low."

"I want to go with you next time."

With a sigh, she removed her eyes from his and returned them to the lacy underwear in her lap.

Leaving his post at the door, he moved behind her chair, slid his hands over her shoulders then down to cover her breasts. Leaning over her, he put his lips on her temple, cupped her breasts with his long fingers while his thumb and forefinger searched for her nipples flattened inside her bra, underneath her sweater. "I can't find them, Walker. Bring them up here to me." Slight pressure beneath her breasts directed her upward. "Get up here, Walker."

"Zeke." There was a flat note in her voice that would brook no nonsense.

And he was inclined to brook no refusal. "Don't make me beg, Walker," he said—his lips against her cheek. "Don't make me stoop for a kiss. Come on, Walker. Get off your ass. You're sitting on what I want next." His hands slid to her waist and he encouraged her out of her seat as he pulled her up the back of the chair. Once he had her perched on the back of the chair, he put a kiss on the corner of her mouth while he slid his fingers under her sweater, unsnapped her bra and pushed his hands into the cups. "Oh, God, yes. There they are." He pulled her back into his chest while he thumbed her nipples. "I want to come with you, Walker."

Her head fell back on his shoulder as she pushed her breasts into his hands and covered them with her own. Twisting his hands to capture hers, he took her hands and put them behind his neck, then scraped his palms down her sides and pulled her closer to him. His hands explored the curves of her behind as he checked to determine if he'd pulled her back enough for a rear entry. Dissatisfied, he tugged her toward him a few more inches. His finger slid behind her and into her crease but the skirt wrapped tight across her bottom wasn't thin enough for him to gauge his success. Impatiently, he yanked it out from under her and ran his finger again into the saddle between her cheeks, over the silky underwear, probing for her opening, knew he'd found it when his finger intruded into warm, damp territory.

Step One.

Letting his eyes slide down her body, he paused to appreciate the vision of puffy, pink nipples straining erect, exposed below the tangle of sweater and bra he'd pulled above her breasts. He watched as her breasts rose with deep, rapid motion.

Her weight was now supported where her thighs hit the chair back, where she leaned her back against his chest, and where her arms stretched behind his neck. Reaching around to her sides, he got his hands under her thighs and pulled her legs apart. "Take your feet off the seat and put them on the arms of the chair."

"I'll—" she panted. "I'll fall."

"No," he whispered. "I've got you. I've got you, Walker." Pulling the front of her skirt high on her thighs and out of his way, he slipped his hand into her panties and along the warm lips of her sex. She caught at a sobbing breath and he smiled. "Your feet," he reminded her. Obediently, she lifted her feet to the chair arms. Again, he appraised her body, her legs spread wide to reach the chair's arms—her skirt rucked all the way up to the top of her thighs. He watched his hand stretching into her panties. He cocked his head and pulled his wrist away from her body, and gazed down her flat stomach into her panties. Soft curling hair lay damp against the full lips of her sex, where his fingers now nudged her open.

With the fingers of his left hand inside her panties spreading her lips, he brought his right hand to her and slid it along the silk that stretched tight over her open pussy. She made some incomprehensible sounds of simultaneous pleasure and distress while he moved his finger, marking out an ellipse on the smooth silk, stroking her clitoris through the flimsy stuff of her panties.

Step Two.

Zeke watched her face while his finger teased a moaning response from her throat. Leaving his left fingers in her panties to keep her lips open, he removed his right hand.

"No," she keened in a small whine. "No. Zeke."

Ignoring her, he got his pants undone and pushed his shorts down enough to release his cock. His breath was tight in his chest as he wrenched the back of her panties down far enough to give him access to her opening. With one hand, he pulled her cheeks apart the best he could then ran his fingertip into her pussy to make sure she was ready.

"Damn, Walker. Is it just me? But, damn, you're wet. Do you usually cream this much for a man?" He put a sucking kiss on her neck. "Or *is* it just me?"

A muffled cry was her only response as she sank her teeth in her bottom lip.

He glanced down at his dick with hard satisfaction. His cock stretched out thick, the skin taut. He had the girl perfectly positioned for maximum penetration. Standing behind her chair while she perched on the edge of the chair back, her cunt waited for him at the optimum elevation. Flexing his knees, he fed his cock into the wet mouth of her opening—slowly—stopping halfway into her.

Step Three.

"Let me come with you," he murmured into her ear. "Let me come with you, and I'll let you come with me."

She released an anguished sob. "What do you mean?"

He straightened his legs and he felt his blunt head come up against her limit. "If you're going to be obstinate, I'll pull out the minute you start to orgasm."

"What makes you think I'm going to come? I told you I've never had it like this."

"Did you?" he murmured as he jerked into her, hard. "I thought we were talking about the radio."

She whimpered.

Inside he stretched her out to her absolute limit. Although she was hot for him and although his thick presence was exciting, she wasn't sure she'd be able to orgasm on him. The rear entry was new and strange to her. She wasn't sure she'd get everything she needed. "I'm not sure I'm going to—"

"You'll come," he said with decisive assurance. Returning his right hand between her legs, he dragged the length of his finger up over the wet silk covering her clit. "You'll come, if only under my hand. The question is—do you want my cock up hard against your cervix when you come?"

"You wouldn't," she gasped.

"Yeah, I would," he said ruthlessly. "Let me come with you if you want the full fuck." He drew out of her two inches then drove back in to give her a taste. She shuddered.

"Make up your mind, Walker," he said as he positioned his right hand again, over her clitoris. He nudged her through the silk covering of her panties.

"Last chance, Walker." He retracted his dick all the way down to her opening.

"No, Zeke," her voice was a keening wail of desperation. "Don't...don't."

He thrust into her and at the same time stroked his finger over the wet surface of her silk panties.

"Don't stop. Don't stop," she moaned as she canted her sex forward into his hand, putting a surprising amount of torque on his dick when he least expected it.

Zeke's eyes widened at the same instant he knew it was all over. At the point of maximum penetration and torqued out to his limit, he surged thick and hard inside her. His fingers stiffened at the top of her cleft, and he had just the presence of mind to pull his hand over her sex one more time. She started to orgasm at the same time his release scorched through his erection in a slow rush of prolonged pleasure.

So much for Step Four, he thought afterward.

Appreciatively, he palmed his hands under her cheeks. His penis slid out of her, content in its defeat, and he took an instant to tuck it away before he returned his hands to worship her curving backside. She relaxed against his chest, arms still around his neck in a languid stretch.

"You give up, Walker?"

"Mm-hmm," she hummed.

"Does this mean I get to come with you?"

He held his breath until he felt her tiny nod against his chest. *The spring—months from now.* "Looks like we have a long-term relationship going here, Walker."

And a long-term relationship would give him plenty of time to work on Step Five—why Sara Walker had an apparent death wish.

Chapter Fifteen

"Yeah. As if anyone's going to volunteer."

Sara watched her reflection in the microwave door. With his deep voice and easy confidence, at only twenty-three, Zeke was already a commanding presence.

He stood with Nick just inside the conference room. Sara warmed her tea in the microwave and loitered at the sink until Zeke took a seat for the weekly staff meeting. Once he was seated, she took a chair diagonally across the table from him. She elbowed Jackie as she slid into a chair. "What's up?"

"Karl is looking for someone to go to Iraq."

"When?"

Jackie shrugged. "Two weeks. One of the bridges that was bombed. They're trying to decide if it's salvageable."

"Why aren't you going, Karl?"

Karl Schueller nodded at Sara as he entered the conference room and took a chair beside her. "I'm in India, otherwise I would. I'm not too keen on sending any of my engineers into a war zone. But I'm looking for volunteers. The army will fly us in, escort us—guard us, actually—during the project."

"Didn't an army helicopter get shot down last week?" Jackie muttered.

"What about accommodations?" Sara asked. "Would it be hotel or army tents?"

"You could take your choice."

"Yeah, take your choice," Nick pointed out. "Either way you're a target. Personally, I recommend the Palestine Hotel. How many times has it been hit?"

"Is the army offering any form of hazard pay?"

Karl shook his head.

"You're going to do the job at standard rates and expenses! Come on, Karl."

"Anyone?" Karl looked around the table, ignoring Sara.

"And I don't suppose our life insurance policies would pay up either—if we're killed—because it would be an act of war?"

"I don't know, Sara," he said with impatience. "But we can check into it. Probably not."

"Oh, well. I'm in then."

"Wha—" Everyone turned to watch Zeke spew cola from his nose in a stunning reverse discharge. "What—" he recovered quickly, pressing his sleeve to his nose "—kind of testing are we doing?"

"Slab integrity," Karl told him, distracted. "Sara. To tell you the truth, I was thinking of someone more...threatening. More substantial. Someone bigger."

She laughed. "Someone bigger will just make a bigger target, Karl."

"I don't know...how safe the streets will be."

"I'm not going to be on the streets. I'll be with the army the whole time, traveling back and forth from their—camp, I guess."

"Still. I'd feel better if you had a Sherpa with you." His eyes wandered across the table to Zeke. Everyone's eyes followed Karl's.

Eyes full of recrimination, Zeke's gaze locked on Sara's.

She smiled him a challenge across the conference table.

Zeke smiled tightly and said nothing.

*****

Zeke's heart did a twisting vault followed by a backflip. His chest heaved as he ratcheted into a sitting position. Blinking, he tried to focus on the gray light of his world and put the nightmare world behind him. With a deep breath, he stared at the empty space in his king-size bed.

She had been falling.

There was a sound like an explosion then there was concrete falling. In his dream, he watched her hardhat blown from her head, watched the yellow plastic skitter off an abrupt edge and plummet to the earth. She followed.

He hadn't been there. He'd been too far away—too far away to stop it.

Like a disembodied observer, he floated above her, looking down on her crumpled body. A crane hovered at her side, regretfully, sorrowfully, with hangdog attitude. "Why didn't you catch her?" he raged at the crane as though it were the machine's fault. But he knew it was his fault, too. Together, they could have saved her.

Chapter Sixteen

With a cluck of her tongue, Sara spurred Sorrel up the driveway at a trot, all the time frowning at the black truck in her driveway. The mare headed behind the house toward her gate and Zeke un-leaned himself from the side of his truck to follow. She had the girth strap loose by the time he joined her.

"I've never seen anyone post in a western saddle," he said, tucking the saddle under one arm and getting the saddle blanket with his other hand.

"What are you doing here, Zeke?" She pulled Sorrel's halter down her face, opened the gate and gave the Quarter Horse a pat to start her through.

"You haven't invited me up," he said, "so I invited myself. You have a nice place."

"Yeah. And it's *my* place. How'd you find it?"

"Mapquest."

She headed for the house, shaking her head. "I've been to Mapquest. They've got my house in the wrong place."

"So I drove around for a while."

She opened a door to a walkout basement, reached inside to hang up the halter then reached to take the saddle from him.

"I'll get it."

But she yanked it out of his hands, and shoved through the door where she threw the saddle over a sawhorse just inside. Quickly, she turned and got herself back out the door.

But, by now, Zeke had gotten the message. "You're not going to ask me in," he stated.

"Zeke. You're a nice guy. And I like you. Like making…having sex with you. But I don't want you all the time, and everywhere. You can't just turn up, uninvited. What if I'd had someone else here?"

"You don't have a boyfriend," he said quickly.

"How do you know that!" she said with exasperation.

He looked at the ground. Because he found the idea unacceptable. But he couldn't tell her that. She didn't have a boyfriend. He wouldn't let her have a boyfriend.

Man. Were all older women like this? Like they didn't give a damn whether you came or went, stayed or left? Like they didn't care if you loved them, or fucked them or not? Like they didn't care if you fucked *other* women.

Dea, he thought with bitter revelation—a mixture of frustration and regret. He looked her in the eye. "You don't have a boyfriend," he repeated.

"No," she said. "I don't have a boyfriend. I don't want a boyfriend. And I don't want you in my life, all day, everyday. I don't want to share my every intimate detail with you. I don't want a permanent male fixture in my home. I don't want you in my house and I don't want you in my bedroom."

That last bit seemed to strike home.

He stared at her a long moment. Then turned abruptly and headed for his truck, tripped on a loose shoelace and cursed. On one knee, he yanked angrily at the uncooperative string and knotted it as he glared up at her. Almost immediately, his scowl softened. The afternoon sun was behind her and she was, simply, the most desirable woman he'd ever known.

"You're right again, Walker," he confessed with a grin. "I just wanted to get into your bedroom." Standing, he dusted off his knees. "You know that night we spent together in Kentucky? You know what the best part was, Walker?" He squinted into the sun. "Falling asleep and knowing you'd be there when I woke up." He nodded into the sun. "See you at work, Walker." Rounding the front of his truck, he opened the door.

She watched as he rolled his truck backward down the driveway and twisted it out onto the dirt road. Her shoulders sagged a little as he put the truck into gear and accelerated up the street. Scuffing into the house, sulking, she closed the door behind her and headed through the dark hall to the stairs that led up to the main living area.

With one foot on the first step, she stopped to stare at it. Raised her second foot to stand on the step for a moment, and then hopped back down as she performed some quick mental calculations. Stepped back away from the stairs and tried to picture in her mind—then made up her mind—and reached for her purse, for the cell phone she never used. Dialed Zeke's cell phone which was clipped to his belt and was always on.

Zeke picked up the phone after the first few notes, saw the number that had dialed him and swerved across the road to start a turn.

"Rutherford," she said after his first "hello". "Can you get back here?"

"I'm turning around now."

Chapter Seventeen

"I think I've found the solution to our problem. Our height problem." Sara led him through the lower level of her house to a set of stairs, got up on the bottom step and turned to face him. The steps had an eight-inch rise and that put her…that put her within comfortable kissing distance, he realized.

"Walker, you're a fucking genius," he whispered as his hands slid into the hair behind her ears and his thumbs rode over her cheekbones. With his eyes lowered, he brought his full lips to hers. And those full lips attacked her aggressively, possessively without reservation. As though they'd been made for this purpose alone, to make love to Sara Walker.

The hard hands caging her skull manipulated her head to suit his purpose, his strong, hot lips manipulated hers to suit his purpose, while his purpose evidenced itself between their bodies, rising hard and thick against her groin.

When he stopped—sucking in air—to stare at her face, she used the opportunity to lower her eyes down their bodies. The placket of his jeans was positioned almost perfectly, she noted with satisfaction. He was still a bit over the top but the situation was workable. Definitely workable.

He returned his lips to hers while she unbuttoned his fly and slid the zipper down. While crushing her lips closer, he leaned his lower body away to give her room to work. Spreading his pants open, she pushed her hands into his shorts and stroked his length out with warm fingers. He stopped kissing her to look down his body and watch her hands in his shorts, palming his cock. Her fingers fought their way lower and he shifted to allow her access to his testes. When her fingers curled around his balls, he let out a small, sighing groan and raised his eyes to the ceiling, his expression one of worshipful thanks.

When she removed her hands, he helped her off with her shirt and bra, quickly got rid of his own shirt, and moved to pull her chest against his. But she grasped his hips and turned him to switch places, putting herself at the bottom of the stairs as she pushed him up onto the step she had just left. Pushing his loose jeans down past his hips, she cupped her breasts and rubbed her nipples along the soft skin covering his thrusting dick.

"Oh, man," he croaked. "You like that, too?" His hands reached down to stroke her hair as she stroked his sex with erect nipples at the same time she fingered his soft parts. His hips began to move and his knees flexed as he thrust his length to rub a rhythm of want against the nipples of the sweetest tits he'd ever come up against.

All at once he stopped. Grasping the root of his cock, he looked down at her in alarm while she raised her eyes to smile at him. "Shit, Walker, I'm going to come right onto your tits."

Her eyes widened as her alarm matched his. "No you're not. Switch places," she demanded. "I want you inside me when you come."

She resumed her position on the step above him and together they fumbled to undo her pants while Zeke stooped to kiss her nipples. With eager aggression, he tried to enter her while she struggled to get her pants down her legs and all the way off. The instant her pants no longer confined her legs, he pushed his dick down and between her legs, knees bent, probing hungrily for her opening.

But she turned on him.

Spread her legs wide for him.

And angled her body downward to rest her elbows on the carpeted step two above where she stood.

He looked down on her sex, inches from the jutting steel of his cock. "Beautiful presentation, Walker." His voice was strained. "You're...you're really asking for it."

"I'm asking for it, Zeke."

The sight of Sara's thick, puffy lips framing the pink heart of her sex was almost enough to make him spill. Tightening his fist around the root of his cock, he reached out with his other hand, stroking the thick, pouting lips of her labia. When she pushed the thick curve of her sex into the cup of his palm, he felt the pressure of pleasure build inside his other hand, as his dick threatened to explode in a hot spray of ejaculate.

Setting his legs apart, he braced his feet and touched his hood to her opening for an instant—before mounting her—then thrust hard all the way in, heard her gasping cry.

"I'm not going to last," he warned her as his hips accelerated against her backside with pile-driver ferocity, and his hands clamped her thighs like she'd better not complain.

"This...one's...for you," she grunted as, elbows firmly placed, she levered her body back hard against his.

His admission received and her permission granted, he drove into her with more fucking power than he'd ever put into a woman. She took several more violent thrusts without complaint before he rammed his dick, fully armed, right up against her cervix and held tight. Heard her warm cry of surprise and released into her with a single word of worship, "Sara."

Chapter Eighteen

"Every now and again, it's nice," he said cautiously, "not having to wait."

She nodded.

Dissatisfied with her response, he continued, "I wasn't too rough, was I?"

She smiled. "Every now and again…I like it a bit rough. *Pay attention, Rutherford.*"

He seemed relieved. "Even when you don't make it?"

She frowned at the computer monitor. "Well. I wouldn't want you to make a habit of it. But yeah, even when I don't make it. *Next position, Rutherford*. Sometimes…it's nice to feel a man's…presence, his passion filling you…hard and strong, deep inside. Knowing he could hurt you but he wouldn't. Knowing he could protect you if he had to."

They were in her garage, crouched together on the floor, using the concrete slab to run a new piece of equipment through its paces. "It's nice to think a man finds you so desirable—he wants you bad enough—to take you without restraint, and yet cares enough about you to do it without hurting you."

He watched her face, beautiful and thoughtful as she listened for the clicking signal. "God, Walker, you're making me hard just listening to you."

"Hand me the hammer, Rutherford," she told him. "No. The little one." She tapped the slab and watched the readout.

"Call me Zeke, Sara."

"Don't want to be the exception anymore?"

"No. And yes. I want to be the exception to the exception."

"Zeke makes me stutter," she lied, and her lips curled up at one edge. "Z-Z-Zeke," she fumbled the name in her mouth to demonstrate.

He watched her lips form his name, watched her tongue in her mouth. "You're driving me crazy, Walker." Leaning into her, he opened his mouth and stroked into her mouth with the tip of his tongue, directed his tongue over hers, thrust softly against her upper lip. Pushing her bottom lip down, he sucked it between his teeth. "I want to taste you, Walker," he rasped into her mouth.

Automatically, her lips parted to readmit his tongue.

He shook his head and whispered against her lips, "I want to taste all of you, Sara. I want to spread your legs and suck on you until you beg me to fuck you. Let me spend the night, Sara." He felt her shiver and taking that as a good sign, he put his hand behind her head and lowered her onto the cold, concrete slab, pinning her beneath his long body. He played with the hair that slanted over her forehead and smiled into her eyes as she stretched her arms over her head.

"Next position, Rutherford," she teased, "and push."

"Push hard?"

"Not as hard as last time. I'm not sure how much of you I can take."

"You can take all of me," he advised her with a growl. "You did last time."

"I did, didn't I?"

He nodded. His eyes turned serious again. "Why do you call your lovers by their last names? Why do you call me Rutherford?"

She shrugged. "To keep things in perspective, I guess."

"To keep me at a distance, you mean."

"Guys…don't hang around forever," she said matter-of-factly, and returned his gaze unapologetically. "Men are such…conformists. You're a conformist," she accused him.

"And you like to break the rules." He held her still beneath him. "Why?"

She returned his questioning gaze with stubborn silence. "You like to follow the rules."

"I like to break your rules. So what do you say, Walker. You going to let me spend the night?" He kept his tone deliberately light, hoping his voice wouldn't betray the creeping desperation that tangled up his emotions.

She shook her head. "Pay attention, Rutherford," she said softly.

"I'd like to pay you some attention. Let me spend the night. Because, don't tell your mother, Walker, but I want to sleep with you." Hesitating a moment, he struggled a bit with the next words. "I want to wake up and know you're…safe."

She looked at him like his sanity was in question.

"I'm worried about Iraq."

She shook her head sympathetically. "Don't feel like you have to go with me. I'll get a soldier at the job site. My Spanish is improving. *Dame la mierta.*"

He only smiled a little bit. "I don't want you to go. You take chances, Sara. Too many chances."

She sighed. "And that's why I don't want you involved in every aspect of my life, Zeke. I'm thirty-four. I've been around awhile. I don't want to be improved." She looked out the darkened doorway. "It's getting late."

He took the hint. "I'd better get going," he said as he levered himself to his knees. His hands locked around her hips and turned her quickly, pulling her to her knees at the same time.

"Zeke, what are you doing?" she laughed.

"Goodnight kiss," he explained briefly.

"For me or for you?"

"For both of us," he said with quiet authority.

Swiftly, his hands reached around to undo her jeans—he pulled them down over her bottom along with her panties, pushing her legs as far apart as the jeans would allow. "Get down on your elbows," he told her, and the demand sent a thrum of wanton expectation to press deep in her womb. With her bottom in the air and Zeke behind her, she waited for the thick thrust of his cock. He kept her waiting as he slowly plucked at the buttons on his jeans.

When he finally came to her, he didn't enter immediately but instead slid the wedge of his cock head through her folds. She settled onto her forearms and relaxed to enjoy the give and take of Zeke's shaft, as he played his dick through her folds with quiet, all-the-time-in-the-world patience. Brick-by-brick, he built her need to the point where she thought it would topple before he could get inside her. Just when she thought she couldn't take one more sliding, teasing thrust, he wedged his head just inside her opening. She felt his hard hands on her hips as he inched into her with maddening delay. As she pushed back to invite him in more deeply, he thrust forward at the same time. She sucked in a breath as he penetrated her deep and hard. Pulling his cock an inch, he delivered a few small nudges to the back of her cunt. She moaned, ready for more of him.

He spoke then, and she was surprised to hear his voice so strung and tight. "Put your hand through your legs and touch me, Sara."

With her weight on one forearm, she heard his sudden intake of breath when she complied.

"That's right. Just like that." His raw, rasp of breath was amplified in the large, empty garage. "God," he guttered out in response to her hand's caress. "I'm going to seat myself deep inside you and fill you with cock until you come on me, Sara. I'm not going to move. I want you to stroke my balls and the root of my shaft. Stroke yourself at the same time. Stroke yourself until you come. I'll concentrate on shafting you, filling your pussy to capacity."

With her weight on one forearm, her back arched in a curve, and her bottom pressed into Zeke's groin, Sara stroked her hand over his balls, over the wet root of his cock buried into the slit of her cunt, then up through the folds of her own throbbing sex. Since he didn't move, she found herself rocking on his erection, as her fingers propelled them both toward climax.

She heard him curse, a wrenching sound, and she felt his shaft seat itself more deeply as it thickened to stretch her wide. Realizing he was close, she pulled her hand from his balls and hurried them through her folds in a rush to get to her clit and meet him in climax. His steel fingers bit into her hips as she rocketed out of control beneath him, both hands returned to jam against the floor, forcing her bottom into his lap. With a steel grip, he held her firm on his erection through every nuance and every shivering aftershock of her orgasm.

When she was done with him, he leaned over her and put his lips against her ear. "Let me spend the night, Sara." The words were a quiet command.

A suggestive thrust of his hips promised a great deal more of the same. He was still mostly hard.

When she moved to disengage herself, he straightened and clamped her hips to hold her on his dick, the action a clear demonstration of his ability to dominate her, if and when he chose to do so.

With a purr she pushed back to receive him. All of him. Slowly, firmly, he rode into her. The lazy give and take of his cock was tempting. The strong, possessive grip of his hands was enough to wilt a strong woman's resolve. With a sigh of contentment, she smiled as she wondered how far he would push her, how much he was willing to force on her.

"You wouldn't force me, would you?" Her question was a comfortable murmur.

His harsh grasp tightened just before it turned into a caress. There was a few second's silence as he pushed his cock head into the tight throat of her sex then withdrew from her completely. "Of course not."

Turning her over, he smiled and kissed her gently. "Let me spend the night," he whispered.

She gave him a smile that was an apology. "Thanks for the goodnight kiss."

For several seconds, his eyes argued with her. Finally, he blinked and looked away. With a sigh, he levered himself off the floor and pulled her up with him. "See you at work tomorrow?"

She shook her head. "Dallas approved that additional testing at the parking garage. I have an early flight tomorrow morning."

He looked hurt.

"You're fully trained in column integrity. You don't need to make another trip and the company can't afford to send you just to help me. I'll be back Wednesday morning."

Outside the garage door, Zeke put a kiss on her lips before he made for his truck. "Okay, Walker. But you need to work on your Spanish," he threw over his shoulder. "Because *dame la mierta* sounds like 'give me shit'."

He pulled down the driveway and out onto the road, hitting his headlights at the same time. It was dark in the cab of his truck and he pulled his cell off his belt, flipped it open and made sure the face was lit as he laid it on the empty seat beside him. Half a mile down the road, he smacked the steering wheel with the palm of his hand. Zeke glared at the cell phone.

Fine! He was slow, maybe. But he wasn't a complete idiot. She didn't need him. He might as well get used to the idea. The paradox was--this was at least half the reason he was attracted to her. He'd never screwed a woman that didn't want to sew him up the next morning, hang him in her closet and keep him for the rest of her life. It was something that always bothered him about women. He ought to be happy. He'd found the perfect woman—the woman who could live without Zeke Rutherford.

Now how the hell was he going to live without the perfect woman?

As Zeke steered through the canyon, Sara slouched at the empty table in her empty house. She didn't even want to think about the empty bed in her bedroom. She closed her eyes. But she'd done the right thing. She wasn't one to agonize over decisions already made. It hadn't been made lightly, that decision. She'd analyzed the situation carefully, and had concluded there was no reason to let this man work his way any further into her life than he already had. Zeke was a wonderful, fabulous, beautiful young man. But there was no sense getting used to him—men didn't hang around. She was a practical woman and used to being alone. She nodded to herself. Liked being alone.

For the most part.

In fact, the only part that didn't like being alone was the part that was in love with Zeke Rutherford.

Chapter Nineteen

"Something wrong, Zeke?"

Karl Schueller stood in the door to Zeke's office.

Zeke swiveled slowly in his chair. "No," he said. Then, "Karl. What's wrong with Sara?"

Karl stared at him a moment before closing the door to Zeke's office. He crossed the room and settled himself on the edge of Nick's desk.

"She was working for Dawson, out of L.A., one of our competitors. She had just graduated. She did a series of shaft integrity tests on a pedestrian bridge—reported the piers as sound. The bridge failed a month later—before it was completed. A construction worker was killed."

Zeke shook his head slowly as he watched Karl's face.

"She'd worked with us the summer of her senior year. I found her in a grocery store, stacking shelves at midnight." Zeke stared and Karl nodded grimly. "She'd quit her job and moved back here. I told her I was desperate for help. She's worked for me ever since."

"And the bridge?"

Karl shook his head. "You know how lawyers are. The whole thing was tied up in the courts for years. I think the design engineer ended up settling out of court."

"The design engineer. Not the contractor."

Karl nodded.

"There was nothing wrong with the shafts."

"Probably not. The shafts were probably sound. Sound but under-designed."

"And that was—"

"Nine, ten years ago."

"Ten years." Zeke's voice was low. "Who was the contractor?"

Karl looked at the ceiling for the answer. "Sandoval. Henderson was the design engineer."

"Karl, are you going to let Sara go to Iraq? On her own?"

Karl took a breath and blew it out. "I was hoping someone else would volunteer to go with her. There's still a chance my plans will change and I could join her." Karl looked thoughtful. "Carol's holding a flight for her.

"But no," Karl said. "No. I wouldn't let her go alone."

Zeke stared at the phone awhile after his conversation with Karl then picked it up and dialed the travel agent. At the same time, he opened his desk and shuffled through a stack of business cards.

*****

Zeke frowned as he pulled onto Blair Street. He'd called Carol and gotten a seat on the next Denver to Dallas flight. He couldn't justify his absence from the office or the expense of a last minute flight. Couldn't explain—even to himself—his need to see her, talk to her. But he couldn't stand to think of Sara blaming herself…a moment longer. Again, he frowned up at the concrete structure.

For a minute, he thought he was at the wrong parking garage. But there were Sara's three cranes presiding over the site with stately dignity. He parked the car across the street and stepped out. *Christ,* it was going up fast. Wasn't there…wasn't there a limit on how quickly new concrete could be loaded?

Three things occurred to him at once. First. There was indeed a limit to how soon concrete could be loaded. It had to be allowed to mature before weight could be added to it, before more floors could be stacked atop the lower levels. Second. The testing they'd performed indicated the columns supporting the parking garage floors were of questionable integrity. Third. Although any construction site generated a fair amount of noise, at this site—today—there was an underlying, low-pitched groan, riding below the usual construction clamor. It was a noise he was actually familiar with, having lived in California most of his life.

He accelerated across the road and bolted up the Level One ramp.

Not that he was expecting an earthquake in Dallas, but he figured anything that could make the same sound as an earthquake had to represent something very large and very heavy under a great deal of stress. "Sara!" His voice constricted as he tried to scream her name. "Sara!" He rounded onto Level Two, pelted across its length then up the ramp.

A high-pitched rending squeal preceded the first crushing boom of failure. At that point, he knew all he had was seconds. The fact that he wasn't already falling probably meant the structure was failing from the top down. Sara was in front of him—frozen—her wide eyes on the ceiling. Her expression, he noted with agonized frustration, very similar to the fascination she displayed when the crane had been hit by lightning. Four long, racing steps and he had her, sweeping her with him to the open edge of the garage where a tower of scaffolding stood next to the structure.

"Pick up your feet. Pick up your feet," he roared as he swung her off the ground. They made the scaffolding tower at the same instant the floor pancaked down from above. The blast of air that accompanied this event tore Sara from his hands and propelled them both forward like a pair of dice and they skittered across the plywood floor of the scaffolding. Zeke saw Sara's yellow hardhat fly off the edge of the scaffolding, and watched Sara slide across the tilting floor as, helpless to do otherwise, he raced to join her. The rickety tower of scaffolding leaned slowly but inexorably toward the ground. Sara disappeared over the edge and he reached for her, knowing it was too late. Knowing that even if he caught her, even if he didn't slide off behind her, the tower of scaffolding had reached the angle of no return. It was going down.

Chapter Twenty

According to everything he'd ever learned about physics, what happened next was not possible. And Zeke had to conclude that, despite all his sins and inadequacies, he had not been entirely overlooked by God, angels, fate or whatever form of fortune chose to smile on him at that instant.

Listing at an impossible angle, the scaffolding stopped its downward descent. Scrabbling at Sara's back, Zeke came up with a handful of T-shirt and bra. Wildly, he looked around for a reason for the impossible halt in their death fall—certain their salvation was only a temporary reprieve that would be measured in seconds—saw the thick steel cable the scaffolding angled against.

The scaffolding leaned into the cable of one of Sara's beloved cranes. The determined lifeline of steel that had stopped their fall was anchored on the ground to a load it had been ready to lift.

She laughed. Dangling over the edge of a fifty-foot drop in one of Zeke's fists, she laughed, not having lost an ounce of self-possession. She craned her head around to look up at him. "I hope the electrical tape holds."

He nodded, breathless. "They ought to make an industrial-strength bra," he said, reaching a second hand out for hers, "for women like you."

She slapped her hand into his and held on. "Good timing."

He gave her a careless laugh, or tried to. "This? This is nothing. You should see me in bed."

"I'd like to see you in bed, Rutherford. My bed—and as soon as possible. Did you get the computer?"

What! Unbelieving, he stared down at her.

She appeared to be serious.

"No." He started to grin. "But I think it's safe to say the columns were faulty."

She laughed again. "What are you doing here, Zeke?"

It took him a moment to collect his wits. "I came to tell you, you're not going to Iraq…"

She twisted her head up to him while doing a slow counterclockwise spin.

"…without me." With a strong jerk, he yanked her up and into his arms where she curled quietly, safely sheltered in Zeke's hands. "Can we stopover in London?"

"What about Dea?"

"Dea…? There is no Dea, Walker." He sighed, disappointed in her. "She doesn't exist, actually."

"What?"

"Doesn't Exist, Actually. D.E.A. Dea. It's an acronym. And I'm not that much of a nerd, either, in case you hadn't noticed."

She looked surprised.

"Geez, Walker. You're slow. Don't you get it, Walker? I've never been much of a geek and…you have the sweetest little clit I've ever tasted." As she caught on to his meaning, he stared down at the long drop. "Where's a set of stairs when you need them," he complained.

She nodded up at him, her eyes warm blue. "Stairs would be nice," she agreed. "Although, I'd settle for a bed at this point."

He held her tight while the world around the site began to slowly react. It would be a while before their rescue. "Sara," he started. "I have a friend…at Henderson." He felt her stiffen in his arms. "A good friend. I've seen the drawings for that pedestrian bridge. He faxed them over this morning."

"Zeke."

But he laid a finger over her lips. "The piers were under-designed, Sara. That's why they failed."

She shook her head.

"I graduated in structural, Sara. They were under-designed. Way under-designed. I can show you the drawings. It wasn't your fault."

He held her when she cried.

* * * * *

"Zeke!"

"Wha—" He woke with a start.

"Zeke."

"What," he said, yawning.

"I should have told you," she said wringingly. "Walker. It's a Scots name."

There was a long moment of silence in Sara's dark bedroom. Then he rolled toward her. "Hell, Walker. Do you think I'm ignorant?"

"But."

"So I'll wear a kilt if I have to. Walker, what does it take to—geez, you're slow. Don't you get it, Walker?"

As he ripped the sheet aside to expose her naked curves, she looked up into his backlit eyes. Zeke's hands were on her by then, smoothing over her breasts, down her sides, around her back as she arched into his arms. She felt his big hands pull her tightly into the heat of his long, hard body.

"Don't you get it?" he repeated more softly. "I love you, Walker. That's why I'm marrying you."

About the Author

I slung the heavy battery pack around my hips and cinched it tight—or tried to.

"Damn." Brian grabbed an awl. Leaning over me, he forged a new hole in the too-big belt.

"Any advice?" I asked him as I pulled the belt tight.

"Yeah. Don't reach for the ore cart until it starts moving, then jump on the back and immediately duck your head. The voltage in the overhead cable won't just kill you. It'll blow you apart."

That was my first day on my first job. Employed as an engineer, I've worked in an underground mine that went up—inside a mountain. I've swung over the Ohio River in a tiny cage suspended from a crane in the middle of an electrical storm. I've hung over the Hudson River at midnight in an aluminum boat—30 foot in the air—suspended from a floating barge at the height of a blizzard, while snowplows on the bridge overhead rained slush and salt down on my shoulders. You can't do this sort of work without developing a sense of humor, and a sense of adventure.

New to publishing, I read my first romance two years ago and started writing. Both my reading and writing habits are subject to mood and I usually have several stories going at once. When I need a really good idea for a story, I clean toilets. Now there's an activity that engenders escapism.

I was surveying when I met my husband. He was my 'rod man'. While I was trying to get my crosshairs on his stadia rod, he dropped his pants and mooned me. Next thing I know, I've got the backside of paradise in my viewfinder. So I grabbed the walkie-talkie. "That's real nice," I told him, "but would you please turn around? I'd rather see the other side."…it was love at first sight.

Madison welcomes comments from readers. You can find her website and email address on her author bio page at www.ellorascave.com.

Also by Madison Hayes

ꟷ

Dye's Kingdom: Wanting it Forever

Enter the Dragon (*Anthology*)

Gryffin Strain: His Female

Kingdom of Khal: Redeeming Davik

Kingdom of Yute: Tor's Betrayal

Miss April

Miss February

Miss December

Why an electronic book?

We live in the Information Age—an exciting time in the history of human civilization, in which technology rules supreme and continues to progress in leaps and bounds every minute of every day. For a multitude of reasons, more and more avid literary fans are opting to purchase e-books instead of paper books. The question from those not yet initiated into the world of electronic reading is simply: *Why?*

1. ***Price.*** An electronic title at Ellora's Cave Publishing and Cerridwen Press runs anywhere from 40% to 75% less than the cover price of the exact same title in paperback format. Why? Basic mathematics and cost. It is less expensive to publish an e-book (no paper and printing, no warehousing and shipping) than it is to publish a paperback, so the savings are passed along to the consumer.
2. ***Space.*** Running out of room in your house for your books? That is one worry you will never have with electronic books. For a low one-time cost, you can purchase a handheld device specifically designed for e-reading. Many e-readers have large, convenient screens for viewing. Better yet, hundreds of titles can be stored within your new library—on a single microchip. There are a variety of e-readers from different manufacturers. You can also read e-books on your PC or laptop computer. (Please note that Ellora's

Cave does not endorse any specific brands. You can check our websites at www.ellorascave.com or www.cerridwenpress.com for information we make available to new consumers.)

3. ***Mobility***. Because your new e-library consists of only a microchip within a small, easily transportable e-reader, your entire cache of books can be taken with you wherever you go.
4. ***Personal Viewing Preferences.*** Are the words you are currently reading too small? Too large? Too... ANNOYING? Paperback books cannot be modified according to personal preferences, but e-books can.
5. ***Instant Gratification.*** Is it the middle of the night and all the bookstores near you are closed? Are you tired of waiting days, sometimes weeks, for bookstores to ship the novels you bought? Ellora's Cave Publishing sells instantaneous downloads twenty-four hours a day, seven days a week, every day of the year. Our webstore is never closed. Our e-book delivery system is 100% automated, meaning your order is filled as soon as you pay for it.

Those are a few of the top reasons why electronic books are replacing paperbacks for many avid readers.

As always, Ellora's Cave and Cerridwen Press welcome your questions and comments. We invite you to email us at Comments@ellorascave.com or write to us directly at Ellora's Cave Publishing Inc., 1056 Home Avenue, Akron, OH 44310-3502.

Kit Tunstall
Cheyenne McCray
Kate Hill
Jaid Black
Elisa Adams
Lora Leigh

Cerridwen, the Celtic Goddess of wisdom, was the muse who brought inspiration to storytellers and those in the creative arts. Cerridwen Press encompasses the best and most innovative stories in all genres of today's fiction. Visit our site and discover the newest titles by talented authors who still get inspired - much like the ancient storytellers did, once upon a time.

ELLORA'S CAVE
ROMANTICA PUBLISHING